CW00517885

THE
RULE
OF
THREE

By Sophie Snow

TOUCH AND GO SERIES

The Rule of Three

SPICY IN SEATTLE SERIES

Legally Binding

False Confidence

THE RULE OF THREE

ALTERNATE COVER EDITION

SOPHIE SNOW

SOPHIE SNOW

For Taylor,
who made me fall in love with love stories,
and taught me to tell them fearlessly.

CORNELIA STREET

Content Warnings

The Rule of Three is adult novel that features a significant amount of explicit content and touches on some heavier topics. On page, you will find:

Alcohol and drug use, anxiety, body modification (including face/genital tattoos and genital piercings,) crowding, depression, discussions of babies/pregnancy, explicit language, explicit sexual content (including anal sex, biting, bondage, choking, double penetration, fingering, masturbation, spanking, and use of sex toys,) fatphobia, nightmares, and revenge porn.

The following things do not happen on page, but are discussed as they have happened in the past:

Abortion, abuse (physical/emotional, implied sexual abuse of a minor, child abuse,) addiction (alcoholism, drug addiction, gambling addiction,) cheating, homophobia, imprisonment, injury, overdose and detoxing, racism, and suicidal thoughts.

You can read about these content warnings in more detail at www.sophiesnowbooks.com.

Author's Note

The Rule of Three is a work of fiction and is not intended to be used as an educational tool.

Though I've done my best to show a healthy depiction of polyamory, Cass, River and Tessa's relationship should not be used a guide if you're looking to explore polyamory. Please ensure you that you do thorough research before jumping in.

Similarly, the sexual acts described in The Rule of Three are not intended to be used a guide. Please always do plenty of research and have clear discussions of consent before trying anything new.

JAY HUTCHISON AND TESSA REID SPLIT AFTER 7 YEARS

The rumors are true: it's over for Grammy-winning rock sensation, Jay Hutchison, and his fiancée, Tessa Reid, Jay's publicist has confirmed to Brightside, after two months of speculation.

It looks like true love has prevailed, and it's a happy ending for Jay, as he reportedly called it quits with Tessa two months ago and returned to Australia to rekindle things with his high school sweetheart.

Tessa, a songwriter and Grammy-winner in her own right, was a source of many rumors and controversies over the course of their seven-year relationship. Allegedly, she stole Jay, twenty-four years her senior, from right under his ex-wife, Steph Hutchison's, nose.

Tessa, it seems, has fled from London to New York with her tail between her legs. Perhaps that'll teach her to think twice before stealing other people's husbands…

Representatives for Jay and Tessa declined to comment.

CHAPTER ONE

Tessa

S he should've known better than to fall for a fucking rockstar.

Tessa turned away from the newspaper stand, her heart thundering in her chest, as the eye of the seller danced between the unflattering paparazzi shot on the cover of the tabloid and the woman herself.

She hurried across the road, shivering against the unseasonable summer chill and breathed a sigh of relief as she stepped into the bookstore, the jingle of the doorbell and smell of paper settling her nerves.

Most songwriters drew on their own experiences for their craft, but Tessa found inspiration elsewhere. Time after time, she stepped into the shoes of royals and assassins, lovers and liars. She tugged on threads of fantasy, heartbreak, *once upon a time*s, and happy endings, and wove them into four-minute elegies.

Though she wrote her own stories too, she swathed them

in metaphors, never giving more than a taste of her personal life. She may have dated one of the world's biggest musicians, but that didn't mean she owed anyone her love, her joy, her pain. And she certainly didn't owe them her privacy. *Not that she'd been afforded much of that*, she thought, scowling through the window at the newspaper stand across the street.

Her place in the public eye had been cemented at sixteen, when her song was chosen to represent the United Kingdom in an international song contest. Her place on the British tabloids hit list had been cemented when she'd had the audacity to fall in love with Jay Hutchison. And now, her place was New York, trying desperately to scrape the pieces of herself together after seven years had come to a close with one, *"I'm so sorry, sweetheart."*

She shook herself and turned to the romance section. Though she had no interest in an actual romance these days, she'd been devouring the summer romances she'd packed. She needed to remind herself that happy endings existed, even if only in books.

She picked up a floppy paperback and flicked through it, bringing it to her nose and breathing in the scent of ink and fresh paper. With a sigh, she held the book to her chest. She really had no business buying more books, but most of her collection was still packaged in cardboard boxes en route to New York.

A soft chuckle sounded from behind her and she looked up, eyes wide. A South Asian man with dark hair pulled back in a bun and tattoos coiling around one side of his face, neck, and arms stood there, twinkling eyes on her and her books.

He reached for the bookshelf beside them and grabbed a forest green hardback. He held it out to her. "Try that one. I swear deckled edges smell better." Blood rushed to Tessa's cheeks, but she took it from his outstretched hand and brought it to her nose.

He was right. The deckled edges made the book smell more like an old book, the smell so reminiscent of the antique bookstore that she and Jay used to frequent that homesickness flooded her.

"It does smell better," she admitted, turning the book over to scan the synopsis before handing it back. *Fantasy, heists, romance...* "Would it be unreasonable for me to grab a copy just because it smells good?"

The man laughed, the sound warm and rich like hot cocoa, and shook his head. Tessa tried not to notice how his hair danced around his face when he laughed. "Not weird. If it helps, the story is great too."

"You don't need to convince me," Tessa said, picking up the sequel for good measure. "I have a book-buying problem."

He leaned against the shelf and Tessa's eyes flashed to the small sliver of skin revealed by his t-shirt riding up. More ink lay below. She dragged her eyes back up to his face, hoping he hadn't noticed her gaze. "It's only a problem when they take up so much space that you can't navigate your apartment," he said, running his eyes over the stack and smiling. "Until then, it's an investment."

"You're my kind of enabler. Thanks." Tessa answered with a laugh, and the man grinned at her. Her stomach did somersaults, but the butterflies were nothing compared to the prickles of guilt that pierced her chest for even looking at him. *It's been two months,* she reminded herself. *And you're just looking.*

"Anytime." He hesitated, as if he wanted to say more. "See you around," he settled on, before giving her a soft smile and a wave and heading out of the stacks.

By the time Tessa made it to the counter twenty minutes later and gave up her pretense of not looking for him, he was gone. She shouldered her now ridiculously heavy tote bag full of books and cursed as she stepped out into the torrential downpour. Thirteen years in England had desensitized her to rain, but her books... Her grumbling stomach and the ever-dimming light decided for her. She hugged the tote bag close to her chest and darted out down the street, ducking into the first restaurant she came across.

She was a little bedraggled for the swanky hotel restaurant, but the hostess smiled widely. "Welcome. Do you have a reservation?"

"I don't, sorry. Do you have any availability?"

"Just for one?" Tessa nodded, and the hostess hummed, scanning the busy restaurant. "We have plenty of space at the bar if that works."

"That's great. Thanks."

Tessa followed the hostess and settled at the bar, quickly scanning the menu and ordering, trying to ignore the bartender's double-take as he took her in. She pulled the deckle-edged hardback from her tote bag and cracked it open, hiding behind it.

She was ten chapters in, her dinner long since finished, and already lost in the fantasy world, when a familiar deep voice said, "What's the verdict?"

The smile, when she turned, was familiar too, as the man from the bookstore stood behind her. The butterflies returned in full, unwelcome force. "So far, so good."

"You mind?" he asked, gesturing to the barstool beside her. Tessa shook her head against her better judgment, and he took a seat. "I'm River."

"Tessa." She reached out to shake his hand and ignored the fluttering in her belly. His hand was smooth and warm in hers.

"It looks like we have pretty similar taste," he said with a nod to the tote bag. He ran a hand through his hair, the fluorescents catching the side of his face and illuminating the tattoos scrawled across his golden brown skin. The black ink curved along his temples in a swirly pattern, but as the light caught it, Tessa realized it was made of hundreds of tiny words.

Before she could answer, the bartender greeted River by name, and they both ordered drinks and dessert. "Do you come here a lot?" she asked when he turned back to her.

"I'm staying here for a couple of weeks while they do renovations in my building. I can put up with a lot, but a lack of running water is my limit."

"How do you stay so close to a bookstore and not buy books every day?"

A wry smile flashed on his lips. "I've bought three today alone. My roommate is out of town and I'm expecting a scolding when he gets back."

"He doesn't like books?"

"He loves them, but he loves space more and you know New York apartments."

Tessa hadn't seen her apartment in person yet, but the shaky video her realtor had sent had been just clear enough for her to fall in love with the gorgeous West Village apartment. She wasn't due to get the keys for another week, and she couldn't wait to get in and settled. This was New York, so she knew it was smaller than the London penthouse she'd spent the past six years living in, but she didn't mind small —less space to be alone. Less space to think about what she'd left behind.

She drained her almost-finished whiskey and ginger beer and let the bitters wash away thoughts of Jay.

"So, what do you do?" she asked River, as the bartender set down more drinks and dessert. She'd been unable to decide between Black Forest fudge cake and tiramisu so River, who, by his own confession, could have eaten the entire dessert menu if allowed, had suggested they ordered both, split them, and added a crème brûlée for good measure.

"I'm a writer," he said, running a finger around the rim of his glass.

Her interest piqued, Tessa sat forward. "What kind of writer?"

"A romance writer," he said, his voice catching a little and his ears turning pink. "I, uh, I self publish under a pen name."

Tessa got the distinct feeling that River had no desire to share his pen name, and could she blame him? She had no intention of telling him who she was. She could guess why he seemed almost embarrassed to tell her. So much of the world still frowned upon romance as a genre, treating it with less validity than other genres. "That's so badass. I love romance. Clearly." She gestured to her tote bag with a smile. "Did you ever want to write under your own name?"

River nodded, and the smile that lifted his lips was sad. "Someday maybe. I've had a couple of offers from publishers wanting to pick up my books, but that wouldn't be anonymous and there's safety in pen names, you know? Especially in romance. There's so much stigma."

Tessa's brows knit together. "That's shit. I wish I could say I can't believe that's still the case, but…"

River chuckled. "Yeah, so much of publishing still lives in the Stone Age. What do you do?"

Tessa swallowed, tapping her nails against her glass. River didn't seem to recognize her, and it was nice to have a conversation with someone who wasn't aware of her reputation. "I'm a songwriter. The music industry is much the same."

He whistled. "I can imagine. Would I know any of your work?"

Tessa hesitated before rhyming off a few of her songs that had topped the charts, omitting Jay's music, and River's eyebrows climbed higher and higher.

"Holy shit, that's… Fuck, that's impressive," he said when he picked his jaw up from the table. "Wow."

"Thanks," she said with a soft smile.

"Two writers drinking whiskey in a bar might be the most NYC thing ever, huh?" River said with a laugh and

Tessa wanted to write about the sound, wanted to put the twinkle in his dark eyes to paper. They were several drinks in and the alcohol in her veins made him look a little hazy, like a grainy old photograph.

"What a disgusting cliche we are," she agreed, and she tried to ignore the guilt that fluttered in her stomach.

River nudged her knee with his, a mischievous look on his face. "I don't mind."

Tessa had been out of the dating pool for a while, but she was pretty sure he was flirting. Hell, she'd never really entered the dating pool. She hadn't been looking for anyone, least of all a man twenty-four years her senior, when she met Jay and she hadn't had to try with him. It had just happened. Sure, she'd had a casual thing here or there, but he was the first person she'd invested any time in. And for all the romance novels she'd torn through in her life, Tessa didn't have any idea how to flirt with the man before her.

Did she even want to flirt with him? She shouldn't. She was nowhere near ready for anything new. Her heart was still reeling, still raw. But she couldn't deny that River intrigued her. So maybe she could lean into it for one day, one night. She didn't have to marry him, for Christ's sake; she could just enjoy his company for now and walk away with no attachment.

She'd done the obligatory casual rebound hookup, and when it hadn't made her feel good, she'd tried again. A man from a dating app, the cute girl from her local coffee shop in London, since she would never see her again anyway, even a hurried tryst in the bathroom at Heathrow, and she had felt numb to them all. She missed Jay, even if she didn't want to, but she *really* missed good sex.

But River... She didn't know if it was the soft cadence of his voice that sounded like music, the whiskey or the whorls of black ink, but, for the first time in a long time, flames licked at her. She caught her bottom lip in her teeth and River's eyes snapped to them. He swallowed.

Tessa cleared her throat. "God, I couldn't possibly eat another bite." She pushed the plate of fudge cake away to give her something, anything, to do with her hands.

"Come on, you can manage one more," River said, the twinkle of a challenge in his eyes. He snagged the fork, and the remaining bite, from her plate and held it up to her mouth. "You know you want to," he teased and *fuck*, she was too stubborn to turn down the challenge.

She leaned forward and closed her lips around the tines, her eyes fluttering closed as the tart cherry jam flooded her tongue. She hummed as she pulled away, smiling. When she opened her eyes, the fork was still suspended and River's mouth had parted.

Tessa stilled, her eyes glued to his lips, and licked hers. "Delicious," she said, and her voice sounded not quite her own. And in the theme of not being quite herself, she leaned closer to him, testing him.

River dropped the fork, the sound barely audible over the rushing of blood in Tessa's ears. He took a shaky breath. "Do you want to—"

"Yes," she replied, too quickly to think it through.

CHAPTER TWO

Tessa

River took her hand in his as they made their way towards the elevator. The doors slid closed, and Tessa let the whiskey and loneliness take over as River turned to face her. She closed the gap between them and stood up on her tiptoes to capture his lips with hers.

It was nothing like kissing Jay. Perhaps she should feel guilty for thinking that, but Tessa remembered exactly why she and Jay were no longer together and pushed the guilt aside.

With Jay, everything had been controlled. Every touch designed to hit exactly the right spot, at exactly the right moment, always on his terms.

River felt like his namesake; wild and untamed; dangling on the edge of danger. Tessa would never have said she had a sweet tooth, but she might have to change her mind because he tasted like sugar, richer even than their long-forgotten cake. She ran her tongue along his lip

The Rule of Three

and he shuddered beneath her, his hands moving to grip her hips.

"Fuck, Tessa," he murmured, as they broke apart for air, and buried his lips on her neck. She whimpered, her head falling back, and leaned into his touch.

A ding was their only warning as the elevator jolted to a stop and the doors opened. Tessa pulled away, panting, and turned crimson at the family waiting on the other side of the door.

River just chuckled and led her from the elevator and down the hallway to his room. Or a suite, she realized, as the door swung open into a plush living room. Stacks of books littered the floor. She scanned the titles as she walked past them and he was right; they had similar taste. More books covered the coffee table, and what was unmistakably a bakery box.

"I told you I had a sweet tooth," River said with a sheepish smile, noticing her gaze.

"That must be why you taste so good."

River's eyes darkened, and he closed in on her. Tessa's hands found purchase on his thighs, rough denim beneath her fingers, and she squeezed hard as his teeth grazed her skin. He cursed and trailed his lips along her jaw before nipping at her lower lip.

"Please," she breathed, and he chuckled. His fingers danced along her shoulder, teasing the ruffled strap of her dress.

"You look like a princess," he said, so quietly she wasn't sure he meant to. While Tessa *did* favor a princess dress, clothing was the last thing on her mind. She reached between them and tugged on the white ribbon lacing up the front of her dress. Though it didn't reveal much, River sighed, a look of pure bliss on his face, and lowered his head to litter kisses along the edge of the dress. She squirmed and tried to pull him towards the couch.

River pulled back, his long hair tousled and his eyes wild, and said, "Not enough room."

Before she could ask what he meant, he had one arm under her knees, the other cradling her back, and he was carrying her to the bedroom. Under normal circumstances, she might have squealed, protested that she was too heavy, checked all the bashful boxes women of her size were expected to, but River's lips found her neck once more and she was otherwise occupied. He pushed open the door to what she assumed was the bedroom and crossed the room in three long strides before gently placing her down on the bed, her head on the plush pillows.

She had no time to miss him; in the blink of an eye, he was kneeling between her thighs and kissing her like he was high on the taste of her. She tugged on his t-shirt and he pulled away just long enough to tug it over his head and toss it to the side. He leaned towards her once more, but she placed a hand on his chest and he stilled. Her eyes widened as she took in his tattoos, her mouth watering. There was hardly an inch of him bare. She was, frankly, in too much of a rush to make out any discernible shapes, but she desperately wanted to taste him.

She pushed him back and flipped him onto his back, straddling his hips. He was hard beneath her and it took every shred of control she had not to just strip her dress right off. He groaned as she ran a finger down the center of his chest, wiggling her hips as she did so, causing River to curse and grip her thighs. The ruffles of her skirt rode up enough to show off the flora sketched across her own skin, starkly pale against his golden brown, and he ran a thumb across an inked sprig of sage on the inside of her thigh. Flames licked her where his fingers brushed.

She leaned forward to kiss him, capturing her name just as it fell from his lips. She rolled her hips and River rose to meet her. Electricity shot through her and she gasped into his mouth. He knotted a hand in her hair and gently pulled her head back, exposing her throat to his lips. Tessa's pulse went haywire as he dragged his teeth across her skin.

River kissed his way from her throat to her lips and nudged her back, never breaking contact. His hands danced around the edge of her skirt, and he pulled back, searching her face for confirmation.

"Yes," she begged, her voice breathier than it had a right to be. He pushed the fabric up her thighs at a snail's pace, his gaze glued to her face. Tessa's eyes fluttered as his fingers teased her bare hips, her stomach. He pulled the dress over her head and set it carefully on the bed beside them.

River's fingers looked perfect splayed across her lilac satin bra. He brushed his thumb across her nipple and she whimpered, her head falling back. He traced lazy lines across her skin, leaving sparks in his wake. Nothing about his movements felt planned or calculated, and Tessa couldn't tell where his fingers were going to land next. When he finally reached around to unclasp her bra, she pulled it from her body and tossed it to the side with far less care than he had shown her dress.

He wasted no time in burying his face against her, groaning as he grazed her nipple with his teeth. Tessa writhed in his lap, incoherent mumblings falling from her lips.

"*Please*," she gasped, fumbling with the button of his jeans. He placed several kisses along the curve of her breasts before pulling back and allowing her the space to unbutton them. He pushed them down his hips, and they were off in a flash, discarded to the side. She leaned forward to kiss him as he kicked his underwear off.

His hands gripped her hips, turning them until she was lying on her back, and Tessa thought she might see stars with her underwear still on at the newfound friction. River's fingers toyed with the scrap of fabric and she sat up, maneuvering herself under him until she was free of it. She was sure it wasn't the most graceful sight, but she didn't fucking care as River brushed a hand along her thighs. Tessa's eyes shuttered, but she opened them as a thumb brushed her lips, to find River's gaze seeking permission.

She nodded, all too enthusiastically, breathing hard at the sight of him hovering above her. Until he wasn't. Given how his fingers were teasing her thigh, she had expected them to creep higher, but she hardly had time to think as he lowered his head between her thighs.

"*Fuck*." She fisted the bedsheets, wriggling around so much that River pushed her thighs apart and held them in his grip. His tongue devoured her, flicking furiously against her, his teeth grazing her lightly.

"God, you taste fucking amazing, princess," he murmured, and then his tongue was inside her and Tessa had no control over the sounds she was making, no control over her shuddering thighs, but she tasted his name on her tongue as she cried it over and over. He kissed his way back to her lips, and she tasted some combination of herself and chocolate on his tongue.

River grappled with his jeans and pulled out his wallet. She heard the crinkle of the packet in his hand and he kissed her before asking, "You sure?"

Tessa took the packet from him and ripped it with her teeth with a breathy, "Yes." River's eyes shuttered as she rolled the condom down his cock. Her hand almost faltered as she felt the size of him, and her gaze snapped between them. She gasped, a moan falling from her lips as she took in the whorls of black ink that wound around his cock. She ran a finger along the lines, and River shuddered.

"Tessa," he gasped, pressing his forehead to hers. She withdrew her hand, brushing the tattoos on his face with her fingers instead. She wasn't sure who kissed who, but their lips met in the middle, and River pushed inside her.

He stilled and *God*; she felt so full. Her chest rose and fell as she panted, trying to catch her breath. Sweat gleamed on River's brow, the lamplight casting shadows across the tattoos on his face. She wrapped her legs around him, holding him to her, and, with a gentle wildness that just seemed so *him*, he moved inside her.

He gripped the headboard with one hand, her chin with the other as he kissed her, cursing into her mouth. The city sounds disappeared, the rain a distant memory; all Tessa could hear were the sounds of their mingling breaths and colliding bodies in the shadowed room, the creak of the headboard as River thrusted mercilessly into her. He pulled back, lifting her legs and angling her hips and *fuck*. Tessa shattered into a thousand perfect pieces, each one lashing her skin with a wave of heat. She cried out, grasping at River's forearms, not caring that her nails were digging into his skin.

He didn't stop, seeing her through the wave with slow movements. She shook beneath him, feeling both outside of her body and somehow so damn present.

Tessa caught her breath and pushed a hand against his chest, unable to find the words to ask him to roll over. She kept her legs tight around him while they rotated, so River was on his back, looking up at her with wild eyes. She leaned down to kiss him before grinding her hips, and River squeezed her ass. He guided her movements, working her into a frenzy, gripping her skin.

"Harder," she gasped, and River cursed. His hand left her for a moment before lightly smacking her ass. She cried out, bouncing faster. "*Harder.*" The next smack of River's hand stung and every nerve ending in her body exploded. She clenched around him, sobbing his name. He fell apart beneath her, holding onto her for dear life.

"Fuck, Tessa," he groaned into the crook of her neck, and she collapsed on top of him, fighting air into her lungs and shaking. River wrapped his arms around her and she was too worn out to protest the tender touch. They lay for a moment, a tangle of limbs and shuddering breaths. "You okay?" he asked, and she nodded, not sure she could even find words; not sure she could trust any she *could*.

River pressed a gentle kiss to her forehead, and Tessa's stomach fluttered. "Back in a minute," he said, but he hesitated before pulling away like he didn't want to detach himself.

Tessa rolled onto her back and stared at the ceiling, listening to him pad down the hall. The pillows smelled like River, sweet and woodsy, but there was another, more citrusy scent, twined around his. She snuggled back into them with a smile. Her heart stilled, and she sat up like a shot. *What was she doing?* She could not get comfortable here. She wasn't looking for a rebound, and River deserved better than that anyway. She shook herself and swung her legs around to the edge of the bed. She found her underwear on the floor and tugged it on, before leaning down and reaching for her bra that had, somehow, found its way under the bed.

"What are—are you leaving?"

Tessa didn't want to look up. If she did, she would see River's naked body in full and it would be much harder for her to walk out of the door. But she had to, and when she did... If she'd thought his body was going to make it hard, his expression made it damn near impossible. Even cast in shadows, his lips were down-turned, his brow drawn.

"I... Fuck." She blew out a breath. Her chest felt too tight. "I'm sorry. This was... You are... God, it's all fucking amazing. But I can't get into anything right now. I'm sorry. I've just gotten out of a really messy thing and I just... I promise you don't want to get mixed up with me anyway. It's better this way, really, trust me. I—"

"You're rambling," River said, his voice too soft, too understanding. She clutched her bra to her chest, suddenly far too exposed.

"I should just go."

River ran a hand through his hair and perched on the edge of the bed, his shoulders hunched. "It's pouring outside. You shouldn't leave in this." He patted the space beside him. "Stay. No strings. I'll sleep on the couch."

Tessa swallowed. She shouldn't stay. Rain or not, she should get a cab back to her hotel and move on with her life. She wasn't sure why she nodded, wasn't sure why the fleeting expression of relief that flashed on River's face made her pulse race.

"I'll get you a shirt." She tried not to stare as he walked away, but her eyes betrayed her. *Who gave him the right to look like that, anyway?* When he stepped back into the room, the closet door closing behind him, he was wearing a pair of plaid pajama shorts that sat low on his hips. He passed a folded shirt to her, so soft he must have worn it a hundred times. She slipped the burgundy fabric over her head and wrapped her arms around herself. River was tall and broad enough that it just about covered her ass.

"Do you need anything?" She shook her head, and River paused for a moment before nodding. "Okay, well, I'll be just out here if you need me."

He started for the door, but Tessa reached out and snagged his hand. "Stay," she said, though every warning bell in her head sounded. He stared down at their joined hands, silent for a moment, before his eyes flicked to her face, searching it.

"Okay," he said, simply. The smile on his face should have meant nothing, it *did* mean nothing, but Tessa's belly fluttered at the sight.

They climbed onto opposite sides of the bed and Tessa fought herself for all of thirty seconds before leaning into him. River slung an arm around her shoulders and cuddled into her back. She had to be a masochist. There was no other explanation.

"Goodnight, princess," he whispered, his breath tickling the back of her neck. She closed her eyes, relishing in the feeling of being wrapped up by him just once.

"Goodnight."

Tessa snuck out of his arms before the sun crested the New York City skyline and tried not to miss the piece of her she left behind.

CHAPTER THREE

River

River Sage picked out three desserts from the cafe to sweeten the bitterness coursing through him. It had been two days since he'd woken up to an empty bed, but he couldn't stop thinking about Tessa.

"I can't get into anything right now. I'm sorry."

The words alone had been disappointing; the look on Tessa's face had gutted him. She had looked haunted, guilt etched on every freckle on her cheeks, as if it physically pained her to step away; or perhaps it pained her to want to stay.

It had been a while since he'd felt such an instant connection to someone, if he ever had, but the moment he saw her sniffing that book, he'd been gone. Everything about her piqued his curiosity; her long blonde hair, golden eyes, and freckled face, which felt almost familiar; the contrast of the ruffled princess dress and the ink on her arm. And when they tumbled into his bed and he traced the rest of the ink on her body with his fingers… He wanted to know the stories behind every tattoo. He wanted to sink himself into every corner of her, litter every inch of her body in kisses, and—

"Hello, Earth to my best friend who I haven't seen in almost *two weeks*."

River looked up. "I'm sorry, what?"

"I said, are you okay? You've hardly touched your cookie, or your muffin, or your… What even is that?"

"A salted honeybun." Though River hadn't taken a single bite, his fingers were already fucking sticky. He brought them to his mouth to lick off the syrup and immediately pushed the plate away. Honey and salt, that's what she tasted like. The image of her lying beneath him flashed in his mind. He could almost hear her little whimpers.

"River, what the fuck is going on?"

He sighed, rubbing the spot between his eyebrows. He was in some deep shit. "It's a long story."

Cass frowned, the corners of his eyes crinkling. "We have time."

River opened his mouth and closed it. He knew Cass was just concerned, but he really didn't want to talk about Tessa, especially with him. He needed to move on. Cass's brow fell at the hesitation. They could talk about anything, *would* talk about anything if the other needed it, but River's romantic life was skirted around. Or rather, River's lack of romantic life. Sure, he'd had nothing remotely serious in years, but they didn't need to talk about that. It was the only boundary the two of them hovered around.

Their food arrived, and he busied himself with his sandwich.

"Have I done something?" Cass asked after a pause. River shook his head. "Is it… Are you…?" His voice was too gentle and River looked up into slightly panicked dark eyes.

"No," he cut him off firmly. He took a deep breath and looked past Cass's shoulder into the crowded cafe. "I… I met someone."

He watched a small child drop a cupful of crayons on the floor and burst into tears before Cass said, "Oh." His voice was perfectly level and River didn't dare look at him. "Is that a good thing?"

He shrugged, running his finger through a droplet of spilled coffee. "It didn't work out. It's nothing."

"River."

He looked up. Cass's eyes were wary. "It's not nothing, clearly."

"It's fine," River replied, too quickly. "It's just…" He sighed. "She was amazing. There was definitely something between us, but she recently got out of a relationship, so she didn't want to start anything. Just shitty timing." Cass reached out and grasped his hand. "And she snuck out in the middle of the night," he added as an afterthought.

Cass winced. "That's… Ouch."

"Yeah." A dull pain throbbed between River's brows. He rubbed his face, laughing humorlessly.

"I'm sorry," Cass said softly, tracing light circles on his hand. "I… I guess it's been a while, huh?"

That was, perhaps, a gross understatement—if a gentle

one. River's romantic history comprised exactly two people. Eight years ago, he had a thirtieth birthday panic that he was going to die alone. Not that Cass would have let him, but that wasn't what he'd meant.

He met Eliana in a coffee shop when they both reached for the same espresso macchiato. The perfect New York meet cute. And while it hadn't been the sweeping romance he'd dreamed of, it had been enough. Until he'd found her in bed with her assistant and a surprising amount of indifference at being caught.

He hadn't given up right away; he'd gone on more first dates that year than he had combined at that point, but there was never enough of a spark to justify a second date.

Because before Eliana had been Cass. Hell, even during Eliana, there had been Cass.

They'd been best friends since birth, inseparable since the day River came into the world. Cass was the calm to his wildness, the steady glow that lit up his shadows. They'd weathered their darkest storms together, and none of the things that should have shredded the golden thread that tied them together had so much as touched it. Except one, but that was River's storm, and River had found a way to let it wash over him and live beside it.

It had been almost sixteen years since Cass had told him he couldn't do it, couldn't love him like River had grown to love him. *"It's not you,"* he'd cried, haunted by his own words. *"It's me. I don't think I can love anyone like that. There's something... missing."* River had nodded and held him close, had sworn it was okay and, after a while, it had been easier to pretend it was.

It shouldn't have surprised him; Cass had spent his life looking for some missing piece. He didn't know what, but he swore he'd know when he found it; that last little thing he needed to make his life complete. Once, they'd thought dating was the answer. Clearly not.

River had tried since then. He'd tried to find someone, anyone, who made him feel a fraction of what Cass did. He'd even tried to ignore the feelings and just settle with someone who had wanted him. That had worked about as well as expected. So he had casual hookups, pretended they filled some gap within him, and when he couldn't pretend anymore, he fell into bed with Cass. He'd long left behind the hope that one day they might try again, and he was okay with it. Really. What they had was more than most people found in a lifetime.

But still, River was forever chasing the butterflies only his best friend had ever given him. Eliana hadn't given him so much as a flutter, and he'd stopped looking after a while. But then he'd seen Tessa's tongue trapped between her teeth as she picked books off the shelf. He hadn't meant to walk over, his feet taking him of their own accord. Up close, butterflies swarmed his stomach. He'd stood like an idiot, counting the shades of gold in her hair, and when she turned around…

He shook his head, trying to shake thoughts of Tessa with it, and cleared his throat. "Yeah, it's been a while. But it wasn't meant to be. It's cool."

Cass watched him as he drained the last of his coffee and pushed cake crumbs around his plate. "We can… we can talk about this kind of stuff, you know?"

"Of course," River lied, forcing a smile onto his face that he knew Cass would see right through. And he saw through Cass's answering smile, before swiftly changing the subject.

They weren't just friends; they had never been just friends; but they wanted different things. And for River, that would be enough. It would have to be.

So when they paid the check and headed off to the movies, and Cass threaded an arm around his waist to tuck him into his side, River let himself sink into his best friend and enjoy what they did have.

CHAPTER FOUR

Tessa

Tessa had spent too long in the UK; she was cursed with being overly polite.

The movers stood huddled around the mountain of boxes in the hallway, exchanging confused glances. "Are you sure?" the man at the front asked and Tessa nodded.

"Of course. They're super heavy. I've got them from here."

"Okay…"

She pressed an envelope of cash into his hand and the group stepped into the elevator, leaving Tessa standing in the hallway with two dozen boxes and several tote bags of incredibly heavy books. She stared at them and shook her head. *Why the fuck did I do that?*

At some point, she really had to figure out how to function around actual human beings. She tried to pick one box up and barely managed it an inch from the ground. She cursed. "Fine, we'll do it a few at a time." She gathered a stack of books into her arms and stomped into the apartment.

The realtor's video hadn't done it justice. The apartment was bright and airy, and much roomier than she had expected. The front door opened into the open-plan kitchen and living room and, though the kitchen was small, she thought she might squeeze a little dining table in. There was a deep windowsill in the living room that would make the perfect reading nook.

When she and Jay had been apartment hunting, back when they'd planned to move to New York together, the penthouse they'd picked had a similar window.

"You can look down onto the street and daydream for hours, sweetheart," Jay had told her, picking her up and swinging her around. Tessa had forced a grin and ignored the prickle of fear that flooded her when he'd popped the celebratory champagne.

She'd set up her office in the second bedroom, with bookshelves lining an entire wall and her beloved piano taking up another. She stacked the books carefully, in no particular order. Organizing them would be a whole day's job, perhaps when she'd had more than a few hours of fitful sleep.

Several trips later, her arms ached as she headed back out to the hallway for another round of books. Okay, maybe she conceded that perhaps, in some circumstances, she owned a few too many books, or at least too many hard-backs, but—

Tessa stopped dead in the doorway. Standing in the hall, crouched down amongst the boxes with a very familiar deckle-edged hardback in hand, was River. He had keys gripped in his other hand, and the door to the apartment across the hall was open to reveal stacks of books all over the living room.

He stood, the book still clutched in his hand. "Hi."

God, that voice. It had kept her awake for days, winding its way through her bones. "Hi." Her answer was barely audible.

"So, we're neighbors, huh?"

She couldn't get a read on him, like he'd shut himself off to her. His expression was guarded, his voice perfectly steady. Hers was a squeaky mess as she responded, "Looks like it, yeah. What are the odds?" she finished with an attempt at a casual laugh, but it sounded pained.

Of all the eligible people in New York, how had she stumbled upon the one person she would be sharing a hallway with?

"You're supposed to be British," River blurted, and Tessa raised a brow.

"What?"

Pink-tinged River's cheeks. "Mrs Fletcher—the old woman downstairs—she said the new neighbors were a couple. An Australian man and a British woman."

Tessa frowned, leaning against the doorframe, at some attempt at being casual and not her usual awkward self. She wasn't surprised that her realtor had been gossiping, but something must have gotten lost in translation.

"I am British. Kind of. My dad's Welsh," she explained. "I have dual-citizenship, but we lived in DC until I was thirteen, then we moved to London."

"Ah. And the Australian?"

She looked away and cleared her throat. "Dead to me, as far as I'm concerned."

"Shit, I'm—"

She waved him away with a snort. "Really, it's fine. It's a long story." A story they were saved from by the ding of the elevator.

The tall Black man who stepped out was the most attractive person Tessa had ever laid eyes on. He was taller, though not as broad, as River, his rich dark skin glowing under the fluorescents like it was lit from within. His jaw was the kind of sharp people paid money for, his lips full with a lazy smile that fit so perfectly, it might have been a permanent fixture.

He had a box in his hand and greeted River by saying, "They didn't have chocolate, but I got you caramel."

He turned to face her and his eyes lit up.

"This is our new neighbor," River began, "Tessa—"

"Tessa fucking Reid. Holy shit!"

Tessa winced, but the man—River's roommate, presumably—certainly didn't seem bothered by her reputation. He was grinning, his smile blinding. He turned to River, rolling his eyes at his confused expression. "She's engaged to Jay Hutchison." River blinked in recognition but, otherwise, his face stayed completely neutral. "I love your writing," the roommate added, turning back to Tessa. "Especially anything you do with Aaron Peters. Seriously, it's like magic."

"Thanks," Tessa offered with a smile. With a deep

breath, she added, "And it's just me. Not engaged anymore."

His eyes widened. "Shit, of course. I'm sorry." He took in the boxes. "You're our new neighbor? What are the odds?"

"Really, *really*, small," Tessa said with a strained laugh.

River took pity on her. "This is my roommate, Cassian King."

Cassian wrinkled his nose and shoved River with his shoulder. "What have I told you about calling me your roommate? It's weird. We've been best friends literally since birth." He held a hand out to Tessa. "Hey, I'm Cass."

She couldn't help smiling at him. Whatever energy he was putting out was infectious. River had a darker, more mysterious, energy; Cass appeared to be pure sunshine. "Tessa."

"That's a lot of books," he said, with an impressed whistle. "Did your movers just leave them here?"

"Oh, they're so heavy, and such a hassle, really, so I told them just to leave them."

The two men stared at her. "Isn't moving them into your apartment literally their job?"

She groaned. "Yes, but it turns out I have issues accepting help even when I'm paying for it."

Cass snorted and set the cake box on the floor before crouching down and picking up the boxes with ease. "Then we're taking it out of your hands. Where to?"

Tessa tried to protest, but they ignored her. Between the three of them, they had the rest of the books in the office in two trips. Cass paused by her piano. "This is gorgeous," he said, peering at the engraving.

She didn't look at it, but felt a pang in her chest. The piano had been a gift from Jay, to celebrate her first Grammy. It was a work of art, engraved with quotes from all of her favorite fairy tales. She hadn't touched it since that night, had written solely with her guitar, but she couldn't leave it behind.

"Don't worry, I won't keep you up. I don't play at night."

River stood awkwardly in the corner, but if Cass picked up on anything strange between them, he said nothing. He had such an at-ease vibe that Tessa, who wasn't sure she had ever been relaxed for a day in her life, didn't quite know what to do with it.

"We should let you get settled," River said finally, shuffling to the door.

"Yeah, thank you for your help. Seriously, I'd still be lugging books in without you."

Cass flashed her a winning smile. "Anytime. Hey, you should come over for dinner sometime. We'll get takeout."

"Um, sure," Tessa agreed, knowing full-well she could never take them up on that. She walked them to the door and waved, watching as they crossed the hall and closed the door to their apartment. She walked back through the apartment in a daze, sank onto the piano bench and traced her finger across the engraving.

"Tessa, I... I love you, you know that, right?"

Jay's face swam before her eyes. She let her head fall into her hands.

It hadn't been perfect, nothing was perfect, but it had been enough. She thought *she* had been enough. *Seven years.* Jay was all she'd known since she was nineteen, and perhaps she hadn't actually known him much at all. She had ignored every red flag; the concerns of the few people around her who seemed to care enough to worry about her. She had ignored the malice in the press, ignored the so-called journalists who called her naïve, a gold-digger, worse. She'd ignored the empty bottles and the secret hospital visits. She'd ignored too much.

And now, she was just Jay Hutchison's midlife crisis, trying to learn how to be on her own again. And that meant forgetting how River's lips felt against the hollow of her throat.

She was in deep shit.

River

River glared at the blinking cursor, the empty document, and let his head fall into his hands. *What a fucking mess.* What were the odds that, in a city with millions of apartments, Tessa would end up just a few steps from his front door?

The irony didn't escape him that the one person he'd dared to really have romantic feelings for since Cass (Eliana sure as shit didn't count) he couldn't be with.

Glancing to the door, he slid his headphones from his

ears and listened, soft snores confirming Cass was fast asleep on the couch.

Turning back to his computer, River opened the browser and typed in her name, ignoring the feeling that he was committing a gross invasion of privacy.

Her name brought up a barrage of articles about her recent breakup. Jay fucking Hutchison; beloved of middle-aged parents and hipsters everywhere. And, perhaps most of all, Cass. No wonder Tessa had looked vaguely familiar. Cass had been following Jay's career since he was a kid, though River noticed he'd neglected to mention that to their new neighbor.

In River's opinion, Jay was vastly overrated, but he liked some of his newer songs. Scrolling through Jay's Wikipedia page, he found Tessa listed as a co-writer on most of his recent music; the songs that even River, who hardly cared for rock music, hummed along to.

It was hard to tell, from the scorn in the tabloids, what really happened between them, but River had seen the shadows on her face when she told him she couldn't get into anything right now. He had seen the way she fidgeted with her sleeve, eyes cast downward. He didn't need the tabloids to tell him that, whatever happened, it had done a number on her.

Tessa didn't seem like the kind of person who would break up a marriage, but how well did he know her, really? Not well, he realized, as he clicked onto *her* wiki page. She'd only been nineteen when she and Jay had started dating. He'd been forty-three. She'd been three years into a whirlwind songwriting career after one of her songs was chosen for the UK entry of some international contest, but she hadn't been the one to sing it; in fact, River couldn't find anything to suggest she'd ever performed her own music.

His mouse hovered over the *Controversies* section of her page and he clicked off. That was a step too far. He sure as hell wouldn't want *his* controversies slapped on the internet for anyone to read.

He'd thought, had hoped, it would have been easy to forget about her. New York was a big city; avoiding her should have been easy. Until he'd come home and found her in the hallway in a dress straight out of a fairy tale and full of the shy awkwardness he'd caught only a hint of a few days ago. It was endearing, too endearing. How many more facets of her were there to learn? River wanted to learn them all.

But he couldn't. And she didn't need the mess he brought to the table anyway. She'd been through enough.

He sighed into his hands. If River knew how to do anything, it was to keep people at a distance, and if that's what it took to keep her safe, he could do it.

CHAPTER FIVE

Tessa

Radio silence has echoed in the dramatic world of Jay Hutchison and his ex-fiancée, Tessa Reid. Believed to have been using Jay to grow her own career as a mediocre songwriter, Tessa has said nothing against the allegations that she was the one to wreck Jay's marriage to Stephanie Hutchison seven years ago.

Not caught up on the drama? Here at ABZ, we've got a rundown on the timeline of the alleged gold-digger and the world's most beloved rockstar. And if you don't believe us that Tessa had ulterior motives from day one, you don't have to—let's see what her family had to say…

Tessa stared at the article on the screen and willed the tears in her eyes to back the fuck off. They were all the same. She didn't know why she kept looking. She had to know, though, if anything new had surfaced to sink her reputation further into disrepair. God knows her manager did nothing to keep her informed.

She closed the computer with a thud and stormed into the kitchen. The place was still a wreck, boxes still littering the floor, but the kitchen was organized. Not for long. She pulled a mixing bowl from the tiny cupboard and an armful of ingredients from the pantry.

Some people drank; some did drugs or turned to sex; some tried yoga and meditation. She had tried it all, and she always reverted to one thing; Tessa was a stress baker. Something about the control involved in meticulously weighing each ingredient, of turning a bunch of random shit into something cohesive, calmed her down.

She chewed on her lip as she measured the flour, the sugar, and the baking powder. When it came time to mash the bananas, she took every ounce of the frustration coursing through her and mashed them into fucking oblivion.

For hours, she baked in silence; the sounds of the city and hum of the oven her only soundtrack.

When the timer dinged and she withdrew the last tray from the oven, the kitchen looked like a bakery awaiting hundreds of customers. Banana bread, zucchini bread, four dozen cookies, two carrot cakes, a slab of fudge, three flavors of muffin, and a tray of pistachio shortcake. The apartment smelled like pure sugar. She boxed up a little of everything to take with her to the studio the next day and sat back on the barstool with a huff.

When she'd stress baked back in London, the treats

were given to Jay's staff, or taken to the studio for Aaron, who never turned down sugar.

Aaron, Tessa's favorite co-writer, producer, and closest friend, had moved to New York not long before she had. Tessa, Jay, and Aaron had planned the move to New York to work on Jay's next album, but fuck knows what Jay's plan was now that he didn't have Tessa to write for him, or Aaron to produce his record. As far as she knew, Jay was still in London. But Aaron was here, so Tessa had moved anyway. There was nothing left for her in London.

She and Aaron had been writing together since she was seventeen. Aaron had introduced Tessa to Jay, but they'd still taken her side in the breakup. These days, Aaron was the closest thing to family she had. Really, they were the only person she had.

Tessa would eat a little of the baking herself, though she didn't have a sweet tooth. But she knew someone who did and, since she and River were going to be neighbors, she should probably apologize for sneaking out of his bed before sunrise. They could be friendly, at least.

Her hands full of sugar, she resorted to balancing on one leg and tapping River and Cass's front door with her foot. Tessa had never been particularly coordinated, so it didn't surprise her in the slightest when the door opened and she wobbled on her leg, tipping forward. Strong hands wrapped around her, steadying Tessa and stopping the boxes from crashing to the floor. She looked up into River's face and sucked in a breath at how close he was.

His expression morphed from amusement to confusion to blankness in seconds.

"Thanks," she offered, her cheeks burning. River nodded, his eyes guarded. He stepped aside to let her in, and Tessa's nose filled with the sweet, smoky scent of him as she took in their apartment. There were more of the stacks of books she'd spied from the hallway on her move-in day covering the living room. Snapshots of, she assumed, River and Cass's life filled the rest of the room. A shelf filled with old cameras stood beside another, bowing under the weight of yet more books. Framed photographs covered every wall, and Polaroids littered the surfaces. She knew books were River's thing and wondered if the photographs were Cass's. There was no TV, but perhaps they just didn't like it.

"Are you opening a bakery?" River's words were cool, and Tessa stilled. *Okay, maybe they* couldn't *be friendly.* Was he really *that* mad at her for leaving?

She didn't answer straight away, distracted by Cass walking into the room and melting the frostiness in the air a little. River stood as still as a statue, his arms crossed.

"I'm a stress baker," she explained, setting the trays down on their table. "And I don't like sweet stuff as much as some people," she inclined her head towards River with an attempt at a smile. He turned away. "So I figured it wouldn't go to waste here." She tucked her hands behind her back and looked away from him.

Cass laughed and snagged a white chocolate cookie. "Your reputation precedes you," he said, looking over at River. He frowned when he saw River's expression. "How did you already find out about his sweet tooth?"

Interesting, Tessa thought. He hadn't told Cass about their night. "Mrs. Fletcher," she replied, smoothly. She'd introduced herself to the old woman the night before and had been pulled in for tea and an hour of chatter about what wonderful neighbors River and Cass were.

Cass laughed. "At Christmas, she makes the most incredible—"

"I have shit to do," River interrupted and stalked from the room. Seconds later, a door slammed.

Cass sighed and rolled his eyes. "I swear, he isn't always like this," he assured her. He wrinkled his nose. "Okay, well, that's not strictly true. He kind of *is* like this with pretty much everyone, but not usually friends."

"Wow, I bring you baked goods and get upgraded to friend?"

"This is a damn good cookie," he said with a laugh, polishing it off. "But yeah. I figure you could probably do with an extra friend or two about now."

He gave her a warm smile and Tessa's heart seized in the way it did when a book had a happy ending, and she willed herself not to cry in front of Cass. She barely knew the man, for crying out loud. She cleared her throat and said, "Thanks. I don't… I don't really have many people here." Or anywhere.

"Does your family still live in London?"

Tessa shrugged. "I'm not sure. We don't keep in touch." She knew Jay had helped keep them away from her, but as far as she knew, they hadn't tried to contact her in years. Tessa didn't think of her family often. Walking away from her mom and dad six years ago had been a relief. Walking away from Rhys had been excruciating, even if he'd been the one to plunge the knife in her back, the final nail in the coffin of Tessa's toxic relationship with her family.

Cass searched her face. She was sure it showed every shred of the conflicting emotions that her family brought up. "Well, you have the Sage-King family now," he said with the kind of finality that made it a fact. And it was the kind of fact that made her want to run.

"Sage-King?"

"River Sage, Cassian King," Cass confirmed, reaching for another cookie.

Tessa wracked her brain for why the names were familiar before her eyes landed on the one organized shelf of books—romance books, by Sage King. "River's pen name." She'd read all of his books. He wasn't just an indie romance author; he was *the* indie romance author. She'd often wondered why he remained anonymous.

Cass grinned. "You figured that out fast. See? You were meant to be our friend."

Tessa knew her inability to let people close to her wasn't healthy, and she was self aware enough to know she had leaned on Jay—who had stuck around through everything with her family—more than she should have. Aaron had always been patient with her; extending a permanent hand of friendship and never complaining when Tessa didn't grasp it as often as she probably should have. Most people hadn't been so understanding. She didn't have friends, didn't have people. Since cutting out her family, it had been just Tessa, Jay, and Aaron.

"Thank you," she said, her voice small and shaky, and offered him what she hoped was a smile. His dark eyes shone with understanding, as if he could see the war waging in her head. She cleared her throat. "I better go so River can stop hiding in his room to avoid me."

Cass laughed and shook his head. "I don't know what the fuck is wrong with him. I'll talk to him."

"Don't worry about it." Tessa waved him away as she stepped into the hallway.

"Hey, come to dinner on Saturday. We can order from the Indian place downstairs. It's amazing." Tessa glanced behind him, to the closed door River was hiding behind. "Seriously, I'll talk to him, Tessa. He'll be fine."

She wasn't so sure. "Can I let you know?" There was plenty of time before Saturday night to arrange a last-minute writing session. Aaron preferred to work in the morning, but she was sure they'd be up for something.

Cass chuckled, as if he already knew she was going to try to wriggle out of it. "Sure. What's your number and I'll text you so you have mine?"

Tessa rhymed off her number before waving goodbye and shutting the front door behind her. She cleared up the kitchen while a pot of tea brewed, added Cass to her contacts when his message came through, and then threw herself on the couch with a cup of tea and switched her phone off. *That's enough people for one day,* she thought, picking up a romance from the stack beside the couch.

CHAPTER SIX

River

R iver's head was pounding as he prodded at the elevator button. He'd had the day from hell. Cass stood beside him, pissed off, as he had been since he'd been an ass to Tessa yesterday. River hadn't had an answer when asked to explain himself, but he'd put his foot down on Cass inviting her over for dinner.

"I already did," Cass said, *frowning. "Tomorrow night. If you don't want to be here, go somewhere else."*

And that was that. Cass didn't get mad easily, and River knew he was mostly upset that he wouldn't talk to him. So they'd gone for a frosty dinner, where he'd been disturbed by a message from Eliana.

> Going to be in the city tomorrow night,
> want to hang out?

By *hang out*, he knew she meant *hook up*. Eliana seemed to think getting him into bed was the key to getting him back, as if she wasn't the reason they weren't together anymore.

Sorry, I have dinner plans. Maybe next time, he'd texted back. Apparently, he would be having dinner with Cass and Tessa, after all.

He rubbed his temples as they exited the elevator and rummaged around in his laptop bag for his keys. Cass was silent as he opened the door and they stepped into the apartment, but he spun as soon as the door was closed. "Are you going to tell me what the fuck is going on with you?"

River let his bag drop onto the couch and sighed. He might as well just tell him. It was inevitable; he was Cass. "Yeah. Just let me make tea."

Though he didn't speak to his parents much these days, he still defaulted to tea whenever he needed comfort. His mom, a second-generation immigrant, hadn't taught him much about her Indian heritage growing up. Everything he'd learned had been in the kitchen, and the ritual of tea making had gotten him through many an anxious spell.

He spooned black tea leaves into the strainer and poured hot water over them before closing the teapot with a soft clink. Cass gathered cups and the last of Tessa's cookies and they set everything down on the coffee table.

"Do you remember," River began as they settled, "when we were at lunch the other day and I told you about the woman I met?"

"Yeah, of course."

River took a moment to pour the tea before sighing and saying, "It was Tessa."

Cass took a moment to process, eyes wide. "That's…

complicated." A frown appeared on his lips and disappeared just as quickly. "You didn't think to mention she was Tessa Reid?"

He snorted. "I had no idea who she was until you mentioned her ex. She was just… Tessa."

"So it's not that you don't like her, it's that you like her too much."

River shrugged. "I guess."

Cass blew on his tea and sipped before saying, "You have to fix this, River. From the sounds of things, she's pretty much on her own here. She needs friends." He looked away, as if realizing he was suggesting River once again stay friends with someone he wanted more from. But he needn't have. River liked Tessa enough that being her friend would be easy. Tamping down his feelings might not be, but that was his problem.

"I'll fix it."

"Excellent." Cass put down his cup. "Let's go."

"Now?" River asked, scrambling after him as he strode for the door.

"I don't want dinner to be awkward tomorrow, so yes."

A breeze flitted through the air as they stepped into the hallway and they paused; the door to the roof stairs was slightly ajar. He and Cass often sat on the roof. It was the perfect place to think, to write or edit, but no one else ever went up there. They exchanged a glance and River sighed as Cass started towards the door.

He followed him up, and they both stilled at the top, their eyes adjusting to the golden hour. Tessa was silhouetted by the sunset, her arms wrapped around her knees. Her blonde hair and floaty dress fluttered in the wind, and she had her laptop and a notebook open in front of her.

They stepped out onto the roof.

"Tessa?" River said softly, trying not to startle her. Her head snapped up, her amber eyes glowing.

"Hey. It's gorgeous up here." The New York skyline, for all its faults, was beautiful. *Not*, River thought, *anywhere near as beautiful as she was, though.*

"You mind if we join you?" She shook her head, so he and Cass made their way across the roof and sat down beside her. He ran his eyes over the notebook and laptop and realized she must have been writing. She had some kind of piano simulator on her laptop, and messy scribbles in her notebook.

"Is everything okay?" she asked, looking at them warily.

Cass gave him a *fix this* look.

"I want to apologize for how I acted the other day."

She peered up at him, her lips down turned. "You don't have to apologize. Just because…" She looked quickly at Cass. "You're not obligated to like me."

"I told Cass everything," he explained. "And I do like you, I just… I didn't know how to act when we met again. I'm sorry."

She took in his expression for a moment, her gaze like a brand, and seemed to believe whatever she saw there. Her shoulders relaxed. "I get that," she said, laughing, and the city seemed to brighten. "I was so surprised to see you standing there. What a mess, huh? For what it's worth, I'm sorry I snuck out without waking you."

River shrugged, but his heart leapt at the words. And

wasn't that the most dangerous thing it could do? "It happens. I get what you meant now, when you said you couldn't get into anything."

Tessa chuckled, her hair dancing around her face. "Yeah. Kind of hard to summarize without context. And, honestly, I liked that you didn't know who I was. It's been a while since I've been just Tessa, instead of Jay Hutchison's mid-life crisis." She finished with a wry smile.

River took a deep breath. "Hey, maybe... maybe we could try to be friends?"

"I'm taking that choice out of your hands," Cass chimed in, his easy smile back in place. "We're already friends. You both just need to get on board."

She stared at them, searching their faces, backlit and glowing. "I'd like that," she said, finally, and butterflies fluttered in River's stomach.

"I know it's probably going to take a while until you're able to let us in, given everything that's gone on, but we're here and ready when you are," Cass said, squeezing her hand.

Shadows crossed her face, but she swallowed and nodded. "That sounds nice."

"Excellent." Cass stood up and brushed off his jeans before offering her a hand. "Shall we hug on it and then maybe go downstairs and finish the carrot cake?"

She wrinkled her nose as she stood. "I'm not really a hugger..." Her eyes flicked over them. "But in the interest of trying not to be so closed off, maybe I could try."

"We're not going to force you to hug us, princess," River said with a laugh, the nickname slipping out. He paused, but the corners of her mouth lifted, so he figured he hadn't fucked up their new friendship in record time. "We can shake on it or just eat the cake. The cake is the main event here."

She considered them for a moment, chewing on her lip. "And what if I do want the hug now?"

"God, you're contrary."

River tugged on her hand, pulled her into his arms, and Cass nestled behind her, wrapping her up tight.

They fit together perfectly, his whole body urging him to relax into them. Cass's cedar and citrus scent mixed with Tessa's honey and salt, and he wanted to drown in it.

"The princess thing," Tessa said, her voice muffled between them. "Is that sticking?"

"Definitely," Cass confirmed and River hummed in agreement.

"Noted," she answered and, when they pulled apart, she was smiling.

The air had cooled considerably in the half hour they'd been on the roof, and there were goosebumps on Tessa's bare arms as they descended the stairs.

"Do you really still have cake left? I was sure you'd have finished it all," she asked as he wrenched the door open.

"Technically, there are only two slices left," he admitted. He had devoured Tessa's baking with a kind of fervor that would probably be embarrassing if Cass hadn't seen him do it before. Everything was fucking delicious, which hadn't surprised him in the slightest.

"And you're offering to share? Damn." She shook her

head with a teasing smile. "You know, I have more. I baked a lot the other—"

"Say no more," River said, holding up a hand. "You've already convinced me."

She laughed aloud as they stepped out of the stairwell and strode to her apartment, and he'd be damned if that wasn't the best sound he'd ever heard.

CHAPTER SEVEN

Cass

C assian King was an excellent liar. He had to be in his line of work, but that didn't mean he liked it. He'd been modeling since his college days, but he'd grown to hate standing in front of the camera and lying through his teeth to sell a product, service, or himself.

It came in handy, though. Like when he found himself sitting with River and Tessa, pasting a smile on his face, and pretending that his heart wasn't, in fact, trying to beat its way out of his chest. It meant nothing. And perhaps if he kept lying to himself, he'd believe it.

"Why don't you have a TV?" Tessa asked, glancing around their living room.

River paused the ripping of his chapati and shrugged. "We don't really watch much TV. We have movie nights, but Cass has a projector in his room."

"Movie nights are better in bed," Cass added, and Tessa nodded in agreement.

She glanced between the two of them. Cass knew she'd been trying to figure out their dynamic since she'd arrived. The line between friendship and more had always been hazy between him and River, but it felt hazier amongst the twinkling string lights and soft music in the living room.

Cass busied himself with his favorite dal. "You know, you can just ask, princess," he said, between mouthfuls.

"Ask what?"

"Ask what you're missing between us."

She gaped at him. "You're a mind reader now, too?" Tessa had been impressed to learn that he'd taken most of the photographs littering their apartment. It was just a hobby, but he'd taken a few classes and learned a lot while modeling.

"Not a mind reader, just observant. And you are too, which is why you want to ask," he pointed out and she sighed.

"Fine. What am I missing between you two?"

Cass looked at River, who suddenly seemed very interested in his dinner, before answering. "We really have been best friends since birth. We're only nine months apart, so we did everything together growing up. We tried dating when we were teenagers, but something was missing." *For me*, he thought, *never for River*. "And now we're friends, with occasional benefits, and roommates. But we're not like *just* friends, you know? We're more than that." It was the same explanation he'd given a million times before, but it sat like lead in the pit of his stomach. He pulled the bottle of bourbon sitting on the table towards himself and topped up his glass.

River was staring resolutely at his plate, but the muscles in his jaw were stretched tight. Cass reached out a hand and let it fall. He and River had shared everything for as long as he could remember. They'd been each other's first friend, first kiss, first relationship. First heartbreak. They knew each other inside out, and they could talk about everything. Except that.

He knew River had seen them married with kids before Cass had ended things. Cass had tried for years to fully explain it, but could never quite put how it felt in words. He'd done the research, he knew he was somewhere on the aromantic spectrum, even if he wasn't sure where. But Cass had never been one for labels; he was just Cass. He'd only ever labeled himself to make things easier for others to swallow.

River had been his other half his entire life, but Cass had always felt like there was some big missing piece. A space between them that wasn't filled when they dated, and sure as hell hadn't been since they'd broken up. The day he'd ended things was still branded in his brain. It wasn't that he hadn't wanted to be with River, but River deserved someone who loved him wholly and didn't need anything else.

If he sometimes wondered if he'd made a mistake, River never had to know. And River certainly didn't need to know that something about the way he and Tessa smiled at each other made every one of Cass's nerves stand on end.

"How did you get started in songwriting?"

Cass started at River's voice.

Tessa seemed to recognize his attempt to change the subject and took pity on him. "Honestly, I don't remember a time when I wasn't writing. My dad's parents were musical, so they got us playing young, and the writing just came naturally to me. I started taking it more seriously when I was twelve, and my parents saw an opportunity to make some money." She shrugged, but her whole body seemed to tense when she talked about her parents. "My dad knew someone who knew someone who was scouting for the song contest and that was that. My song was picked, I signed with Empire Records, and I just never stopped writing."

"Did it feel different, doing it professionally?" River asked.

"Oh, yeah. There was a whole new level of pressure. The first few years were slow, but things kind of blew up when I started writing for Jay. It was… a lot, but the writing was still magical. Still is." She smiled. "I still write exactly as I did when I was twelve years old, even when I'm working, but I get to make a living from it. There are a finite number of notes, chords, combinations, words, and they're all mine to play with."

She lit up as she talked about it, the same way River did when he was excited about a writing project, her eyes like sparkling whiskey.

She looked up at the two of them, both smiling at her enthusiasm, and stilled. "Sorry, I'm a little much sometimes when I talk about writing."

"Never apologize for that," River said, quickly, and Cass nodded in agreement. "There's nothing cooler than watching someone talk about the thing they love most."

The smoggy skyline bled into pink and orange as the

night moved on, and, after her third yawn, Tessa stood up and said she was calling it a night.

"Tonight was really nice, thank you." She gave them a tentative smile, like she was still a little nervous about letting them in. "I, uh, expected New York to be pretty lonely, but you've been super welcoming. Thank you."

"No thanks needed, princess," Cass said, unable to resist tugging her into a vise-like hug. She was still for a moment before relaxing into him. "We're happy to have you."

He hoped she couldn't feel his racing heart. He didn't want to let her go, but he did. She hugged River, looking up at him with the softest of smiles, and Cass hated every single step she took back to her apartment.

River

The apartment was heavy when Tessa left for the evening, like she took her sunshine with her and left behind a storm cloud that was just itching to burst. River and Cass didn't bother to dance around it. They knew themselves well enough to recognize that something was off between them, and though River wasn't sure what it was, they knew how to fix it.

They tore into each other with a fever. Since their very first time, sixteen and fumbling in the dark in River's childhood bedroom, this part had always been easy. And twenty-one years later, he and Cass knew each other's bodies with a familiarity that still blew River away. Cass knew that one spot on River's ribs that was ticklish and avoided it expertly; River knew how much Cass liked it when he dragged his teeth across his skin. He kissed the hollow of Cass's throat and watched him shudder beneath him, as he had a thousand times before.

They landed on River's bed and grappled with each other's clothes until there was nothing between them; not fabric, not space, not the chasm left behind in Tessa's absence. River luxuriated in the feel of Cass's lips. He knew he shouldn't let this mean so much, but he did every single time. And when he started to feel too much, he dropped to his knees and took Cass's cock between his lips, teasing the metal piercing with his tongue.

His best friend cursed, knotting his fingers in River's hair and arched off the bed. River was relentless, teasing Cass and gripping tight to his thighs until he fell apart and River drank him down greedily, relishing in every curse and moan that slipped from his tongue.

Cass reached into the drawer beside the bed and rummaged around before tossing a small bottle of lube to him. River flipped him over and sighed as he sank into him. He rolled his hips and Cass gasped as he moved inside of him.

"Don't go getting gentle on me now," he said, through panting breaths. "I know you're frustrated. Take it out on me. I can handle it."

He knew he could, knew Cass would take anything he had to give him and enjoy every second of it. River cursed and drove into him harder, his whole body aflame with every thrust.

He angled his hips and Cass cried out. River's name tumbling from his lips was his undoing, and he fractured into a hundred pieces, gasping and panting, holding onto Cass as he came down.

His knees buckled and Cass wriggled out from under him, tilting his head up to kiss him. "Come on," he said, his lips brushing against his. "Shower."

They showered in relative silence, aside from Cass's happy sigh, when River massaged shampoo onto his scalp. They still liked to take care of each other after, still liked to cuddle and fall asleep in each other's arms. River had occasionally worried that Cass did so just because *he* liked it, but whenever he'd brought it up, Cass had brushed him off.

They climbed into bed, and Cass tugged the blankets over them.

"Night," River murmured, his head resting on Cass's chest. He could hear the thud of his heart, the steady rhythm lulling him to sleep.

Cass kissed the top of his head. "Goodnight." Warmth spread through River from the spot Cass's lips had touched, through his whole body. He was almost asleep when the crying started. Loud, wreaking sobs.

He shot up, bleary-eyed, Cass following suit. "I think it's Tessa," Cass said, his voice gravelly, and they exchanged a glance before jumping out of bed.

CHAPTER EIGHT

River

They didn't bother dressing, darting through the dark apartment and across the hall in their underwear. Cass knocked on the door and the wait until they heard Tessa's shuffling steps felt like an eternity.

She paused by the door—reasonable, given the late hour—until River said, gently, "It's us, princess."

"Hey. Everything okay?" she answered with forced brightness, pulling the door open. She'd clearly scrubbed her face of tears, but the tracks remained. Her eyes were red rimmed, her lip bitten raw, and her voice croaked.

"Can we come in?"

She stepped aside and closed the door softly behind them. They settled on her couch, barely big enough to hold all three of them.

"Did something happen?" Cass asked softly and the fake smile slipped from her lips.

"I'm sorry. I had a bad dream. Did I wake you?"

"No, no, it's okay," Cass told her and River nodded in agreement when she didn't look convinced. As if instinctually, they both threaded arms around her. It took a moment, but Tessa's body relaxed and nestled into them.

"This… It happens sometimes. I can look into soundproofing—"

"Hey, we're here, okay? Don't worry about it, we just want you to be okay." An emotion River couldn't put his finger on crossed her face at his words.

"Do you want to talk about it?"

She sat up straighter, but let them keep their arms around her. River wasn't sure he could let go of her now, anyway, until he knew she was going to be okay. "I have trouble sleeping sometimes. It's been pretty bad lately, and when I get overtired, I have nightmares."

"What kind of nightmares?"

Shadows dredged her eyes, and River recognized that Cass's question made her want to shut down. He saw himself too clearly in her. "You don't have to tell us," he assured her, trying to ease her panic. "But you should talk to someone about it."

She met his eyes and, whatever she saw in him, perhaps the burning worry, made her bite her lip and nod. She tensed, before saying, "Jay had, *has*, a drinking problem. It wasn't new when I met him, he'd been drinking too much for decades, but…" she trailed off, clenching her fists tight. "He wasn't himself when he was drunk." The words were whisper quiet, but as soon as he heard them, River was murderous. It took a remarkable amount of self-control not to grab his phone and book a ticket to London.

"He hurt you?" Cass asked, and River recognized the same dangerous anger in his voice that he himself was feeling. It took a lot for Cass to get angry, and River had rarely seen his eyes so dark.

Tessa half shook her head. "Not physically," she said quickly. "He just… He was mean, for lack of a better term. He would get really mad at himself for drinking, for not doing better. And I didn't help the situation, I got mad at him too. He wanted to punish himself, and the worst punishment he could think of was to hurt the thing he loved most. So he just lashed out." She shrugged, and the movement alone made River want to destroy the man who had so thoroughly broken her she even remotely blamed herself for what he had done.

"I know how it sounds, but he's not a bad guy," she added.

He and Cass exchanged a glance. "Tessa—"

"He's not." Panic crept into her voice, and her eyes widened in the flashes of light that peeked through the curtain. "He's not necessarily a *good* man. He was unfaithful, and harsh, and he…" she trailed off, shaking her head as if she could finish her sentence. "But he's not bad. I probably should have left long before I did, so that's on me."

"Why didn't you?" Cass asked without a shred of judgment.

She toyed with her hands. "He was all I knew. I didn't have anyone else, and even when I *did*… My parents weren't good people either. It is what it is." Had anyone ever been on Tessa's side? River's heart splintered.

"It doesn't have to be anymore," River said, gently

stroking his thumb along her palm until her breathing settled. "How often do you have the nightmares?"

"I've been having them on and off for a couple of years. They always got bad when Jay was out on tour, or when something new came out about me in the press. They've been pretty consistent since I got here. I'm not good at sleeping alone." She took a shuddering breath. "A new article about me dropped last night. My manager sent it over just before I went to sleep. That's probably what triggered it."

"It was bad?"

She nodded and grabbed her laptop from the coffee table. She opened it to a celebrity news website and River's stomach dropped at the headline.

RACY PICTURES SURFACE OF JAY HUTCHISON AND EX-FIANCÉE: WHAT WON'T TESSA REID DO TO STAY RELEVANT?

"Oh, shit," Cass murmured, and River closed the laptop. They didn't need to read further.

Tessa trembled in their arms, a single tear running down her face.

"You think Jay leaked them?" Cass asked, shadows crossing his face. He hadn't been entirely truthful with Tessa, though River understood why. He could see Cass trying to rewrite the image of Jay in his head, from the musician he'd idolized so much growing up that his posters had covered his bedroom walls, to the man who had treated Tessa so badly.

She shook her head, the tears falling thicker. "I can't think that. I can't have been *that* wrong about him. It was probably Steph. Jay's ex-wife," she explained. "She's always hated me. She blamed me for them getting divorced, but Jay ended things between them a year before we even met."

"And they… they got back together recently?" Cass asked.

Her hair glinted gold as she shook her head. "No, but Jay… Steph was in London and they hooked up." She swallowed. "He told me, wanted us to work things out. I can't even count the number of times he cheated, but something about it being her was just the last straw. And now I'm here. Seven years down the drain, just like that.

"At least the press hasn't figured out where I live yet, I suppose. If this had happened back in London, they'd be camped outside the apartment." She sighed and pinched the bridge of her nose. "They'll almost certainly be waiting at Aaron's studio tomorrow. They've caught me there a couple of times already." Panic crept into her eyes.

"You know, River and I would be happy to take you anywhere, if it'll help you feel safe. And hey, how about we stay with you tonight? If you're comfortable with that." Cass offered.

She looked between them, chewing on her lip. "I don't want to be a bother."

River shook his head. "It's not a bother."

"We should warn you we're both cuddlers, though, so you have to be prepared for that," Cass added and the shadows cleared as a short laugh burst from her lips.

River tried to ignore the way his heart raced at the sound, the butterflies going haywire in his stomach.

It's not the time.

She's off limits.

She's going through a whole lot of shit and you don't need to add to it.

He recited the thoughts like a mantra.

"I think I can handle cuddling," Tessa answered, and Cass kissed her temple before jumping up. She looked a little startled at Cass's casual affection, but didn't seem to mind it.

"Excellent. I'll go lock up our place."

They watched him go and River couldn't help but wonder if he'd ever seen him so comfortable around someone so quickly as he was with Tessa. Cass was easy to get along with—everyone liked him. It wasn't unusual for him to be affectionate, but something about the energy between him and Tessa reminded River of the energy between Cass and *him*. Like the thread of friendship had been there all along, just waiting for them.

He liked it a lot. It was normal for him to be glad they'd made a new friend. It had nothing to do with being happy that his best friend liked the first person to turn his world upside down in over a decade. Nothing to do with that at all.

He shook it off. "Do you need anything? Water, maybe some tea?"

Tessa hummed and pulled out of his arms. He regretted asking immediately. "Chamomile tea sounds good, actually. Do you want some?"

She made to get up. "I'll get it," River told her.

She followed him anyway. "I have a kettle," she said quickly, glancing at the microwave and he laughed. He understood: he'd been burned by American tea-making skills more times than he could count.

"My mom's Indian. I was making tea before you were born. I can handle chamomile, I promise."

Tessa bumped him with her hip. "You're not *that* much older than me."

"You're what, twenty-six?" She nodded. "Cass and I would have graduated high school the same year you graduated kindergarten," he pointed out as they stepped into the small kitchen. Tessa filled the electric kettle with water and scoffed.

"There's a big difference between six and eighteen and twenty-six and..." She quickly did the math. "Thirty-eight?"

River thought her perception of age differences might be a little skewed, considering she'd been engaged to a man twice her age, but he just said, "Thirty-seven for a few more weeks, but true," and pulled three mugs from the mug tree on the counter.

They worked in tandem to make the tea. Tessa had only been in the apartment for a week, but the cabinet was already full of different teas, from loose leaves to bags. She passed the chamomile buds to River, and he measured them into the strainer and set it gently into the teapot. Tessa poured over the water and immediately, the subtle scent of chamomile filled the air. He breathed it in and sighed contentedly.

The front door creaked open and Cass walked back into

the apartment, pausing at the sight of them and sniffing. "Hmm, that smells good." He'd brought their phones and chargers back with him, and he set them on the kitchen island before tossing River an orange bottle.

"Thanks," River said, taking a pill from the bottle and swallowing it dry. He rarely forgot to take them, but his focus had been elsewhere before bed. Though he didn't consider himself actively depressed anymore, taking one pill a day gave him a little extra breathing space and helped keep him even. He tried not to miss them.

"Do you want a cookie?"

He raised an eyebrow at Tessa. "It's one in the morning." She raised one back. "Okay, maybe I do."

She laughed and slid a container across the counter to him. He resisted the urge to take more than one.

By the time their teacups were empty, and the cookie crumbs cleared away, the clock was nearing two and Tessa was fighting sleep. "Come on." He took her hand and tugged her towards the bedroom, Cass following behind them with a yawn.

Tessa's sheets were as soft as he imagined clouds might be, or perhaps he was just tired, but he fought a groan as he laid back against the pillows. Tessa took the space between him and Cass without prompt. "Thank you for tonight," she said with a deep sigh. "I... I'm not good at this whole letting-people-in thing."

"You're trying, princess. That counts for a whole hell of a lot," he told her and she smiled up at him.

"Okay, I'm ready for the cuddling." They laughed, but when River rolled her into his chest and Cass curled up behind her, his breath caught in his throat. She fit perfectly between them, like she was meant to be there. He saw Cass's brows meet in the middle and wondered if he was thinking the same.

But Tessa just sighed contently and snuggled into them both. "Goodnight," she murmured, and her eyes fluttered closed.

River and Cass lay awake for a while, holding her while she slept, and, when River finally drifted off, he dreamt of puzzles with missing pieces.

CHAPTER NINE

Tessa

When morning dawned and the three of them awoke with the rest of the city, Tessa knew something had fundamentally changed between them. They hadn't thought twice before coming for her, caring for her. She'd never had anyone, not even Jay, treat her with as much tenderness as they had, their arms around her like a safety blanket. And the sleep... God, she couldn't remember the last time she slept so well unmedicated.

Much to her surprise, River was a morning person. While he pottered around making coffee, honest-to-God *humming*, she and Cass lay bleary-eyed on the couch wrapped in a holey afghan that Tessa had bought purely for decorative purposes. "Is he always this much in the morning?"

"Yes," Cass said shortly. He was a little surly in the morning, and she was relieved to see he wasn't cheery *all* the time. "He's like sunshine for the first two hours of the day and shadows for the rest."

Tessa forced one eye open to peer at him. "That was awfully poetic for seven a.m. I might steal that."

He yawned. "It's all yours."

River wandered over and pressed warm coffee cups into their hands. Tessa inhaled the bitter coffee and wrinkled her nose as she watched River adding three sugars to his own. "What are your plans today, princess?"

She sipped at the scalding coffee before answering. "I have to go into the studio in a couple of hours to write a bit and record some demos of the songs with Aaron."

"Do you have any idea how cool that makes you sound?" Cass asked, and she laughed.

"I promise it's not all that. I just go into the booth, sing along to an acoustic track, and call it a day."

"You're working with *Aaron Peters*. That's pretty fucking cool." Cass woke up enough to nudge her with his foot.

"Aaron *is* pretty cool," she relented. "You know, if you're not busy, we should be done writing by eleven if you want to come meet Aaron while we rec—"

"We're totally coming," he interrupted. "Right?"

"Of course. It'll be nice to see you do your thing," River agreed.

"Perfect. We could get lunch after. Aaron's been raving about a Mexican place near their apartment."

It was only fair to share her work with them. She'd admitted to reading, and loving, River's books over dinner, and she'd seen some of Cass's work. And, of course, had the great pleasure of seeing the face that scored him his modeling job, not to mention the body—she'd been too shaken the night before to notice, but even sleepy morning Tessa could appreciate the sight of the two half-naked men in her apartment. *Half-naked men that were firmly off limits,* she had to remind herself.

Tessa turned on her phone and promptly regretted it. She had taken to turning it off overnight, when she and Jay started dating, but it had been switched off during the day too more often than not these days. Every time the screen lit up, there was another barrage of notifications; messages from her manager, from old acquaintances looking to cash in on her fifteen minutes of notoriety. She had changed her number since moving stateside, but people somehow found it.

Her email account wasn't any better. Most people dodged spam emails, but Tessa dodged interview requests and inflammatory articles. She swiped through, ignoring the repeated requests from her manager for a meeting. She was just about to close the app when one email caught her attention.

(1) Rhys Reid
No Subject
Hey Tessa, I know you probably don't want…

Her stomach somersaulted; her heart raced. She hadn't heard from Rhys since she'd left him crying on her doorstep six years ago. Her parents had tried to reach out in the first year, but never Rhys. Maybe he was mad at her, maybe he felt guilty, or maybe he just didn't care. Tessa wasn't sure she wanted to know. She didn't click on the email from her twin, but she didn't delete it either.

"I'm going to go get ready. There's sliced banana bread in the freezer, if you want it," she told River. "You just need to—" He was already on his feet. "Pop it in the toaster," she finished with a laugh before heading into the shower and scrubbing her skin raw. Even the sweet scent of lavender soap did nothing to calm her nerves after the email.

She watched the bubbles swirl down the drain and squared her shoulders. She wasn't going to let anyone else make her feel shit. It was mind over matter, that's all.

She left River and Cass in her apartment with a spare key, her stomach fluttering at how at home they looked, and jumped on the B train towards Aaron's studio in Brooklyn. They lived in a modern brownstone, and had converted most of the condo into a soundproofed studio. They buzzed her up, and she strolled through the eclectic apartment into the large studio. Aaron was sitting with their back to the door, headphones on, and peering intently at a computer screen.

Tessa set her bag on the floor by a ratty old armchair that had followed them across the Atlantic because Aaron swore it was their lucky chair—Tessa didn't want to know more—and nudged them in the back. "Hey," she said, and they spun around, removing their headphones.

A grin spread across Aaron's face. "Hey, T. How are you getting on with unpacking?"

"Okay," she shrugged. "I still can't believe how quickly you managed to pull this place together."

"I paid someone to do it. I can't take the credit," Aaron admitted with a laugh as Tessa pulled out her favorite acoustic guitar and took a seat on one of the floor pillows sitting in front of the plush couch. She wasn't entirely convinced the thing wouldn't swallow her if she tried to sit in it.

"Hey, I have a couple of friends coming by this afternoon. Is that okay? They want to meet you, see how we record." Aaron frowned at her.

"What?"

"You're making friends now?"

She frowned back, defensively. "I'm giving it a go."

She turned the worn pegs, tuning her guitar by ear.

"I'm really enjoying the breadcrumbs," Aaron drawled sarcastically. "But are you going to tell me about them or what?"

Tessa rolled her eyes, but nerves fluttered in her belly. Right now, River and Cass and the strange and intense little friendship they'd formed belonged only to the three of them. Letting someone else in on it felt like turning on the lights after creating something in the dark. Maybe letting River and Cass into her life was a terrible idea and she just couldn't see it; but Aaron might.

"Their names are River and Cass," she started with, pausing to brush a piece of lint from her guitar.

"Okay, that's a start," Aaron replied, their blue eyes twinkling like they were fighting a laugh. "Can I get a little more? Like how you met?"

Tessa sighed, quietly strumming a chord progression. "It's a pretty convoluted story." Aaron just stared at her expectantly until she put down her guitar and leaned back against the couch. "I met River in a bookstore."

Aaron listened without saying a word, their brows climbing higher and higher as Tessa told them the story of sneaking out of River's hotel room, only to find out he was her neighbor. When she recounted the night before, Aaron's jaw dropped.

"I'm sorry, back up; they slept with you and you just cuddled?"

"Friends can cuddle." Why did she sound so defensive?

"We've never cuddled," Aaron pointed out, and Tessa snorted.

"Of course we haven't. We had to sit on opposite ends of the couch when we watched movies in case Jay came home and got mad." She could still remember flinching every time she heard a door, and the sense of relief when one of Jay's staff walked in instead of her fiancé.

"Yeah, well, you got away from him in the end," Aaron replied, shaking their head. "Have you heard from him?"

"Nope." Every time her phone rang, Tessa still tensed, expecting Jay's name to flash up, but he'd respected her wishes to leave her alone so far. "Have you?"

Aaron tossed a guitar pick between their hands and nodded. "A couple of times. He's been trying to convince me to work on the album."

"I don't mind you working with him," Tessa pointed out, but Aaron scoffed, dropping the pick on the desk.

"*I* mind," Aaron replied. They hesitated before adding, "He's asked about you, you know. Checked in to make sure you're okay."

"Oh." Tessa ran her thumbnail along a groove in the wood of her guitar, not sure what else to say.

"I told him to go to hell," Aaron said, giving her a sympathetic smile. "You know, it's okay to miss him. Even after what he did to you."

Tessa huffed, surprised by the tears threatening to fall. She blinked them back before replying. "I don't know. I guess I miss him a little. I'm still kind of sad, but mostly just pissed off." She took a deep breath, forcing air into her lungs. "I opened up to River and Cass a bit last night about how he treated me. I didn't tell them everything," she added, quickly. "But I told them a little."

"You trust them that much already?" Aaron asked, eyes wide.

They weren't nearly as surprised about it as Tessa was. "I think I do. I trust that they're not going to run to the press anyway."

"That's amazing, T. I can't wait to meet them." Aaron raised a brow. "Just friends?"

"Just friends," Tessa confirmed. "I like them and there's definitely something between River and I, but it's not happening. I'm not going to ruin things with one of my three friends. Besides, he's clearly still in love with Cass. It's a bad idea all around."

Aaron laughed to themselves as they swiveled around in their chair to grab their notebook. "If you really believed that, you wouldn't be so desperate to convince me. Or maybe you're desperately trying to convince yourself— either way, I'm not buying it."

Tessa's stomach fluttered. Thinking about that wouldn't

do her any good. She threw a patchwork pillow at Aaron and picked up her guitar. "Let's get some work done."

River

River was starting to suspect that Tessa was made of some kind of magic. He tried to pretend to be interested in what Aaron was telling Cass about the mix, but he couldn't take his eyes off her. She was singing like the rest of the world had disappeared for a moment, swaying along with the track in time to the beat, her eyes closed.

Her voice rang out clear and strong through the mic, and fuck, she was *good*. He knew already, of course, that she was a damn good writer; he'd heard enough of her songs over the years to know that, but he couldn't understand why she wasn't singing them herself with a voice like that.

The song she was singing, a folky pop breakup song, was like a poem right out of the mind of Robert Frost, as if she'd written it in the depths of some faraway forest. He tuned back into the conversation enough to hear Aaron telling Cass about the song.

"It's based on some old Russian fairytale, or something like that," they explained. "But romanced up in the way she always does."

"It's gorgeous," Cass admired with a whistle.

"She really is the best of the best right now," Aaron told them. "We've been writing together for years, but she's the mastermind behind the songs. I work on the production and help with the music, but the lyrics are all her."

The song drew to a close, and Tessa looked over at Aaron, who gave her a thumbs up. "*Roadside Poppies* next?" they called, and she nodded. Aaron pulled the track up.

"I had a new idea for the melody on the bridge," Tessa said, staring at what he assumed were lyrics on her phone.

"Give it a go, we can re-do it if necessary. We have time."

Slow, melancholic, piano music played softly through the speakers and Tessa began a sad story about a road trip gone wrong.

"How does it work after you record the demos?" Cass asked.

"We'll send them off to Empire—her label—and they'll share them around their artists to see if anyone wants any of them. She writes for specific artists too, but today's tracks are all up for grabs."

They tuned back into the recording to listen to Tessa's new bridge idea and River leaned back in his chair to watch her. Thankfully, her back was to them while she sang, or she would have seen how intently he was watching. She couldn't, but Cass could, and when the song faded out, and River tore his eyes away, he found Cass watching him with an all too knowing expression.

They recorded four more demos before running through them again to add some harmonies. It was a surprisingly efficient process. River had always imagined it took hours for a single recording. He was saying as much to Aaron when Tessa stepped out of the booth.

"It can do, for a final track. No one outside of the industry is going to hear these," she told him. "They don't have to be perfect."

River thought they had different ideas of perfection.

She leaned over Aaron's shoulder to listen to the harmonies and pulled her hair down. It tumbled around her shoulders in golden waves and River looked away.

It's not the time.

She's off limits.

She's going through a whole lot of shit and you don't need to-

"What did you think?"

He started as Tessa's voice interrupted his mantra. She had turned around and was leaning back against the desk, biting her lip. *Was she nervous?*

"You're fucking amazing, princess," Cass told her, grinning. She smiled back, but her eyes were still wary. River supposed this was all new for her, inviting people into her world instead of keeping them on the outskirts.

"You're incredible," he assured her, and her shoulders relaxed a bit. "Honestly, we knew you could write, but your voice is next level."

"Yeah, why don't you perform your songs? Do you just prefer writing?"

She shrugged at Cass's question and sat down on the armchair to tug her shoes back on. "I prefer writing."

"Liar," Aaron called from the desk, and she scowled at them.

"It's not a lie. I *do* prefer writing. Would I like the chance to perform? Sure, but my label doesn't want me. It is what it is."

River frowned. "Why the hell wouldn't they want you?"

"I don't fit the *Empire Image*," she said, rolling her eyes. "The last time I told them I was interested in a performance contract, they told me to learn to keep my mouth shut and lose sixty pounds."

Anger flooded him at the thought of anyone speaking to her like that. Tessa's body was nothing short of incredible. Her soft skin, stretch marks, curves, bumps, and all, had been playing through his mind on a loop since the second he'd fallen asleep beside her. How anyone could look at her and not think she was drop dead fucking gorgeous was beyond him.

"Fuck that," Cass growled, and she laughed.

"That's exactly what I said, which, if you're wondering, is the exact opposite of what they meant by keeping my mouth shut."

"God, is everyone in your life a dick?"

She considered this. "Pretty much, yeah."

"Sitting right here," Aaron grumbled.

"*Except* Aaron," she finished. Aaron turned back to the screen before them, placated.

"You have us now. Cass is never a dick, and I'm only a dick like… seventy percent of the time?" River offered, and she laughed.

"I'll take it. Shall we grab lunch?"

Aaron took them to a nearby hole in the wall Mexican restaurant. It was dead for lunchtime, which was just as well. It was so small that they took up half the room. They shared nachos and River kept an eye on Tessa, watching as she relaxed into having people around her. Now and then, she seemed to catch herself and withdraw from the conversation for a moment, her eyes wide. He brushed her leg with his under the table and she looked up at him, smiling instantly, and joined back in the conversation.

River tried to ignore the thudding in his chest, replaying his mantra over and over, but every second he spent with Tessa, the harder it became to listen.

It's not the time.

She's off limits.

She's going through a whole lot of shit and you don't need to add to it.

CHAPTER TEN

Tessa

Tessa had expected her time in New York to drag, but November snuck up on her faster than she could blink. She'd also expected to be lonely, but on the rare evenings River and Cass didn't congregate in her apartment, she was most likely at theirs. She regularly woke up from nightmares in their arms, and on nights when they could tell she was a little shaky, they didn't even try to leave. She couldn't deny that she'd had some of the best sleep of her life sandwiched between them.

River's birthday found her stumbling through the streets of New York, clinging to Cass's arm, a few too many margaritas into the night. Tessa was not a *going out* kind of person. She never had been, since she wasn't a *people* kind of person, not to mention how much she loathed being photographed everywhere she went. River, it turned out, also didn't enjoy going out much, but he made one exception every year for his birthday and he and Cass would get dressed up and go to a bar or club. He and Tessa had gotten a head start on drinking while Cass had spent the day shooting a designer campaign.

The afternoon passed in a whirlwind of lime, salt, and tequila, and by the time Cass got home, Tessa wasn't entirely convinced she could walk in a straight line.

She said as much as Cass looped her arm around his to steady her. "Princess, I have literally never seen you walk in a straight line. You can't blame the tequila for your lack of coordination."

She poked him in the chest. "I'm a good dancer, I'll have you know."

"Are you really?"

She frowned. He looked like a hazy angel. *What was he saying?* "No. That's definitely the alcohol talking."

Wedged between River and Cass, Tessa made it to the bar without incident. It was a miracle, really; River held tequila about as well as she did. Though he wasn't wobbling all over the place, he stopped every few feet, trying to talk to passersby.

The bar was busy, the crowds of rowdy patrons congregated around tables, or the small stage at the front where the karaoke set up was. Tessa had visited many an Irish pub in her day and it smelled somewhat like home, if she was still considering London home. She glanced at River and Cass. She wasn't so sure these days.

They took over a big circular booth, and Tessa paused before sliding in to shuck off her coat. "Can you hold this?" She passed her purse to River.

When it was off, she reached for her bag and stilled at

his expression. His eyes roamed her, black save for the flecks of gold reflecting the sparkly lights, taking in the crop top and skirt set she had bought for the evening on a whim. The emerald green set looked like nothing else in her closet, but she'd been drawn to it when she'd spotted it in the window of a nearby boutique. She loved green, and she couldn't deny her body looked hot as fuck in the two piece set, even if the shop assistant had flicked her eyes over Tessa's body and all-but sneered.

"Fuck," River whispered, so quietly she was sure he hadn't meant to. His eyes snapped to hers and he took a deep breath. "You… you look…"

She'd put on her coat before he'd seen the outfit. She laughed and took the bag gently from him. She needed a drink. "Thanks." She slid into the booth beside Cass, and River sat on her other side. Heat radiated from him, and his empty hand, resting on his thigh, was calling to her. Yeah, she *really* needed a drink.

River

Beautiful. She looked beautiful. Of course, River tripped over his own damn tongue and didn't say that; not that he should. He figured he should probably take it easy on the alcohol at that point—the booth was forcing Tessa to sit close to him and *fuck*, he just wanted to hold her hand.

Seeing Tessa and Cass together was something close to

torture. Cass had an arm casually slung around her bare shoulders, his dark umber skin contrasting against hers. He was all perfect angles and relaxed smiles, Tessa soft curves and a nervous energy, and they looked perfect together, glowing under the twinkling lights. *Fuck*, he so desperately wanted them both.

He could feel the tension rolling through Tessa beside him. As if she, too, was struggling to keep her hands to herself. So, against his better judgment, he took the hand she had resting on her thigh and he rubbed his thumb across the top until it relaxed in his. When the server passed their table, he flagged her down and ordered more drinks. He needed it, and he was sure Tessa did too.

Several empty glasses later, and River couldn't remember why he had been worried. Tessa was leaning into him, her hand still clasped in his, and a smile played on her lips like a game he would love to learn to play. Another God awful karaoke song finished, and they clapped half-heartedly.

"How many times are they going to let someone karaoke that damn song? There's only so much Shania Twain a girl can take," Tessa groaned, burying her face in his shoulder.

"You should sing!" Cass all but shouted. Though he was much less drunk than they were, he'd long since passed tipsy.

Tessa just laughed and shook her head, her hair tickling his jaw. "Not a chance."

In his drunk state, River's mouth opened before he could engage his brain. "Hey, sing with me, princess."

She looked up at him, her hazy amber eyes dazzling. "Seriously?"

"Yeah, it *is* my birthday, after all. I want to sing with you." River, in fact, had no interest in singing. He just wanted to hear her, to see her lose herself in a song. If that meant standing on the small stage and singing to a room full of people… honestly, he thought he might have done it sober for her.

"Fine," she said, rolling her eyes, but there was no real annoyance on her face. "But I'm putting my foot down on Shania Twain."

The DJ manning the karaoke set was also putting her foot down on Shania Twain, it seemed. She passed them a tablet to choose a song and said, "Anything but fucking Shania Twain, I swear to God."

"Your choice, birthday boy," Tessa said, leaning into him and stealing his breath as her body pressed against his. He swiped through the duets section, the words blurring together. He couldn't tell if it was the alcohol, Tessa, or a combination, but he finally picked a popular pop duet that he vaguely knew and Tessa hummed in approval.

He might have had the foresight to be nervous about singing in front of so many people, but he couldn't take his eyes from her as she joked with the DJ and passed him a microphone with his favorite soft smile.

Cass cheered them from the booth as the song began, and he saw the switch in Tessa, saw the sparkle in her eyes get brighter, but she didn't lose herself to the music as she sang; she lost herself to him. Holding his hand and swaying to the beat, her eyes stayed glued to his as she sang. River was so caught up in her he almost missed his cue.

River liked to dance, and he liked to sing along with the radio when he was driving; he *didn't* like to do any of the above in front of people. But the bar could've been filled with a thousand people, and he didn't think he would have noticed. He tugged Tessa closer to him, her back to his chest, wrapped an arm around her, and rested his chin on her shoulder as they swayed and sang along. He realized, as the lyrics made it through his drunk goggles, that he might have chosen the most sensual song on the list of karaoke options, but it was hard to care when Tessa's voice trilled and her cheeks glowed rosy red—not in anything close to embarrassment, but in joy.

She spun around as the song faded out and pressed her face against his chest, laughing. "That was fun," she said, breathily through the applause, looking up at him with eyes full of mischief. He couldn't find the words to do anything but nod.

They handed the mics back to the DJ, who whistled. "Damn, you're good. Singer?" she asked Tessa, who shook her head.

"Just a songwriter."

Drunk as he was, River filed *that* away to bring up later. *Just* a songwriter. Which of the assholes no longer in her life had made her feel that way?

"We do open mics here, you know. We have one next weekend. You should come play."

Tessa chewed on her lip. "Oh, I don't know…"

"You should do it, princess," River told her, rubbing a

hand across her back. He knew he should stop casually touching her so much, but fuck, it was addictive.

She looked unsure, but nodded anyway. "Sure, yeah, I'll give it a shot." She gave the DJ, who introduced herself as Inga, her contact details and they stepped off the stage.

"That," Cass slurred as they slid back into the booth, "was absolutely the hottest thing I've ever seen."

"You're welcome," Tessa replied with a laugh, sliding into Cass's open arm. "I'm always extra friendly when I'm drunk."

River slid in beside her and Cass extended his arm until it rested on his shoulder. River reached up to hold his hand as he looked up and caught Cass's sad smile. Cass, who knew him better than anyone, well enough to know that, though the liquor may excuse Tessa being so *friendly*, it didn't explain his behavior, and that River was all but drowning in his feelings for Tessa.

But it was his birthday. For one night, he would silence the mantra and let himself hold her.

Cass

Cass collapsed on the couch with a yawn, leaning over to turn on the stereo as River grabbed a clean fork and dug into the chocolate birthday cake on the counter. Tessa had made him three birthday cakes, one for each meal. If she hadn't already stolen his best friend's heart, the cake would have done it.

Now she was perched on the edge of the coffee table, her shoulders slumped. River took a seat beside her. "You okay?"

"Yeah, of course," she answered too quickly, sitting up straight. He raised an eyebrow, and she sighed. "People kind of drain me, you know?"

River slung an arm around her shoulders, and she leaned into his chest. "I feel that. We can't all like people as much as Cass—the world would crumble."

Cass rolled his eyes and laughed before closing them and letting his head fall back against the couch. Extrovert though he may be, crowded bars weren't really his scene.

He heard the telltale beep of Tessa's speakers, and a slow song filtered into the room.

"Dance with me, princess." He cracked an eye open to see River stand and offer a hand to Tessa. She hesitated, but stood and clasped her hand in his. He pulled her in close to him, their bodies swaying in harmony to the rhythm of the music. Her skirt shimmered as he spun her, tiny flecks of silver glitter catching the light. They were like something straight out of a fairy tale. Cass swallowed, unable to look away even though he knew he should. He shouldn't let himself feel these things.

But it was River's birthday, and one night wouldn't hurt.

"Do you know what I realized today?" River asked.

Tessa looked up at him through her dark lashes, her amber eyes like flames in the warm glow of the apartment lights. "What?"

"Cass and I have been best friends for a long time—"

"Literally forever," Cass interjected.

"Exactly. And we've never known someone who fits so perfectly with us. Do you know what that makes you?"

Tessa swallowed and shook her head.

Cass knew, of course. Had suspected from the moment they'd held her on the roof and he'd realized how perfectly she fit between them. Their missing piece—not the romance he'd once believed was the answer, but Tessa.

River leaned forward and rested his forehead against hers and Cass saw her eyes widen. The alcohol must have been making River feel reckless, but when he reached out a hand and gestured for Cass, Cass let himself be a little reckless too. He took it, joining the two of them and circling his arms around Tessa from behind.

"That makes you our best friend now too. And, much like the nickname, it's already a done deal. You're stuck with us forever, princess," he said, softly.

Tessa pulled away from River slightly to look back at Cass, her eyes wide and lined with silver. She searched his face, and then River's, the smile on his face so serene, so certain. She chewed her lip, and Cass wondered if he had come on too strong—if they needed to back off a little.

"It would be an honor to be your best friend," she told them, finally, and his heart soared from his body.

They were no longer swaying, and River held her tighter, one hand settling on Cass's back. "That means we're yours too, you know," he told her. "Cass and I have always taken care of each other, and we're going to take care of you too. You're our person now."

They held her close as the song faded. "It's been a long time since I trusted people," she said as the next began. "I'm glad those people are you."

Cass let himself lean into them, let himself hold them and, for a moment, he forgot to pretend it didn't mean what it did.

Tomorrow. He would lie to himself tomorrow.

CHAPTER ELEVEN

Tessa

My flight got cancelled because of the
storm. I've booked another shoot and
moved my flight to Tuesday. :(

Tessa frowned at Cass's message as she punched the
elevator button. Cass rarely took work outside of
NYC, but he'd gone to LA for a shoot and New York had
treated them to the worst snowstorm the city had seen in a
decade.

Tessa had been in the middle of recording with Aaron
when they'd received the emergency weather notification
and she'd hurried home before the trains shut down. She'd
stopped only to pick up enough groceries to last River and
her for a few days, which meant she had enough sweet
treats to last him maybe five minutes.

Things had been... tense since River's birthday. She
hadn't forgotten the feel of his fingers on her waist when

they sang together, or his forehead against hers as he and Cass held her close. That moment had a starring role in her dreams these days, and it wasn't just River she was dreaming of.

Tessa was doing everything she could to pretend that it wasn't happening, but things had gotten worse since Cass had left for LA. She hadn't realized how much of a buffer he was between them, and she hadn't realized nearly how much she'd miss him. Hearing he'd be gone for another five days made her heart ache in a way she was adamantly pretending it wasn't.

Besides the obvious that she couldn't have them, Tessa couldn't help but feel guilty about how quickly she'd replaced Jay's face in her dreams. Sometimes, when she closed her eyes late at night, she wished she'd stayed with him and missed the days she swore she could fix him. At least then, she'd known where she stood. Somehow, the bottles, bruises, and biting words made more sense to her than the tangle of feelings in her chest whenever she fell asleep in River and Cass's arms.

She sighed as she walked into her apartment and dropped the groceries on the counter. Music was playing from the bedroom, which meant River was probably writing in her bed.

He hadn't left once since Cass had gone to LA, and they'd both burrowed into bed whenever they'd been home, watching snow drift past the window and cuddling to stay warm. It was the definition of masochism, but she couldn't seem to make herself stop.

She shed her coat and boots by the door and tiptoed

through the apartment. River hadn't responded to their group chat with Cass, so she could only assume he was engrossed in whatever he was writing, and she didn't want to startle him.

She knocked once and pushed open the door. "Hey, did you—" She stopped in her tracks, her knees almost buckling.

River wasn't writing. He must have been just out of the shower, his dark hair wet and curling around his tattoos, and his hand around his cock. Tessa dragged her eyes slowly up his body, before meeting his wide eyes. They stared at each other, neither of them speaking. She should leave, close the door, let him… finish. But—"I can't seem to make myself leave," she admitted, breathily. She clenched her fist, needing to do something with her hands, something other than reaching out and touching him. Because that was a terrible idea.

"I can…" River trailed off, looking away and reaching for the blanket to cover himself. He paused, swallowing. "Or you could stay."

He looked up at her, his eyes full of longing, his arm half-extended as if he was fighting the urge to touch her as much as she was him.

Tessa's feet seemed to move on their own, pulling her towards him. She sank onto the bed, facing him. "I think if you touch me, I'm going to lose it."

River's eyes glowed onyx, with an edge that set Tessa's fight-or-flight response on edge. *Danger*, every alarm bell blared, and it took all she had not to squeeze her thighs together. "I'm not going to lay a finger on you," River murmured and Tessa swallowed, his dark, sensual tone making her knees shake. "I'm going to tell you what to do with *your* fingers, princess. And you're going to do as you're told."

She couldn't stop the whimper that fell from her lips. For as much as she liked to have control over every little thing in her life, handing these particular reins over to River sounded like the best and worst idea she'd ever had. "Okay," she whispered, and the wild gleam in River's eyes was almost enough to make her come.

"Take off your dress." His eyes followed her every move as she stripped the fabric from her body. "Tights." She pulled the thick winter tights off and spread her legs, her barely there thong doing nothing to hide how much she wanted him. She hooked her finger in the straps and waited for him to nod before sliding them off, leaving her bare to him.

River groaned, his fist closing on the blankets. Tessa drew her eyes from his hand to his cock and licked her lips. "You want me to touch myself?" he asked, his voice gravelly.

"God, yes."

River brushed her foot with his own, and she almost jumped out of her skin. "You first, princess. Show me how you take care of yourself."

Tessa wasn't shy about sex, but she'd never shared this part of herself. She trailed her fingers slowly up her thighs and sighed as she grazed her clit. She paused; if they were going to do this, then she might as well do it right. She took a deep breath and bit her lip. "Bottom drawer of the night-stand, red satin pouch."

River raised a brow. He seemed hesitant to look away from her, but obliged, leaning over the bed and sliding open the drawer. He cursed softly as he took in her small, but certainly mighty, collection of toys. "You have no idea how much I want to see you use all of these," he murmured, grabbing the satin bag and handing it to her.

She slipped the small bullet vibrator from the pouch. "That could be arranged." Tessa gave him a wicked smile of her own, and he seemed to shake with restraint. She held her breath as she pressed the button, hoping like hell she'd charged it after last using it, and breathed a sigh of relief when it buzzed to life. She dragged it across her nipples, down her belly, and gasped as she finally, *finally*, grazed her clit.

She moved the vibrator in small circles, slowly increasing the deep, rumbly vibrations, imagining it was River's fingers. Her eyes threatened to flutter closed, but she forced them to stay open as River palmed his cock. She watched him stroking, his eyes glued to her. God, she wanted to taste him.

His breaths turned ragged, his lip trapped between his teeth. Tessa remembered so perfectly how those teeth had felt grazing her skin, his mouth in the crook of her neck, his hand against her ass…

She gasped, his name tumbling from her lips before she could stop herself, and tumbled over the edge. Her free hand fisted the covers, her legs shaking, stars bursting in front of her eyes. It wasn't until she came down that she noticed River had gone still, his eyes black.

"Tessa," he whispered, soft as a feather. He extended a hand towards her and then pulled it back at the last second. Against every shred of judgment she had, Tessa reached for him and pulled his hand towards her, holding it to her chest so he could feel her racing heart. With his other hand, he brushed a thumb across her cheek, her jaw, pausing at the edge of her lips. "This is a bad idea," he said, barely audible.

Tessa nodded slowly, unable to take her eyes off him, unable to move more than that for fear that her heart would give out. "A terrible idea." And yet, she couldn't stop her tongue from darting out to lick his thumb at the corner of her mouth. His breath caught in his throat and he ran his thumb across her lower lip, his eyes trained on her mouth.

"Tell me to stop, princess," he begged, edging closer to her.

Tessa took a deep, shuddering breath that rattled in her chest. His eyes flicked to hers and she shook her head and whispered, "I don't want you to stop."

He paused for a moment, and she could practically hear him trying to talk himself down. She should move away, give him space. She opened her mouth to say so, but he pounced on her and all that fell from her lips was a gasp.

Fuck, she'd missed how sugar tasted on his tongue. She devoured him as he gently spun her and pushed her back until she was pressed against the pillows. His pushing was the only gentle thing; his hands knotted in her hair and his teeth grazed her lips like she was to be his last meal.

"Fuck, princess," he groaned, running his tongue along her bottom lip and looking up at her through dark lashes. Tessa fought to steady her breathing, to hold air in her lungs. A curl fell across his forehead and she reached up to brush it away, her fingers stilling on his cheek.

"I never should have left that night," she said before she could think twice. River blinked, his eyes softening.

"It worked out well in the end," he murmured against her lips.

River sat back, his eyes molten, roaming her body. He reached out a hand and brushed the curve of her belly, tracing her stretch marks. For a split second, Tessa wanted to hide away in her self-consciousness, but any shyness disappeared when River wrapped his hands around her hips and whispered, "You're so fucking perfect." She thought her heart might still but, somehow, it kept racing. "Oh princess, the things I want to do to you."

"Please do them," she groaned as his fingers danced dangerously close to where she wanted him.

He nudged apart her thighs and leaned down to kiss her. "You sound so pretty when you beg," he whispered against her lips and she cried out as he bit down on her lip. "Condom?"

"I—" Tessa glanced at her nightstand and groaned. "I don't have any." River glanced at the door like the last thing he wanted to do was go next door to his apartment to get one. "I'm on birth control," she said softly, and his eyes snapped to hers. "And I haven't been with anyone else since we met." There had been many nights when she'd been in the mood and settled for her own hands because the only man who remotely caught her attention was off-limits.

Men, if she was being honest with herself. *But now wasn't the time to be honest with herself.*

She watched River's chest rise and fall. "I've only been with Cass. It's only been us." Tessa nodded, entirely trusting of her two best friends. She wasn't sure she had been entirely trusting of anyone since she was nineteen, but she was getting there with River and Cass. "Are you sure?"

She caught his fingers and brought them to her lips. "Yeah."

River paused for a moment before tilting her chin up and kissing her, gentle, but deep. He positioned himself between her thighs and held tight to her hand as he pushed inside her with a groan.

Tessa's world splintered for a moment, the room fading to black. All that existed was River inside her, his forehead against hers. He rolled his hips, and she cried out, squeezing his hand.

"River?" she gasped, and he looked at her in question. She tugged on his hand and set it on her throat. "I fucking love how much you take care of me, but I don't want you to be gentle this time."

It had taken her a while to open up to Jay about her proclivities, for fear of judgment. He'd never judged her, though it had taken them some time to find their rhythm. But River hesitated for less than a second before wrapping his hand lightly around her throat and leaning into her lips to whisper, "You might be the girl of my dreams, princess."

He knotted a hand in her hair and tugged her head back,

exposing her throat further. His hand barely gripped her, but she whimpered as the burn in her lungs she loved began. He shifted inside her and rubbed his thumb across the center of her throat; Tessa writhed beneath him, gasping.

"Tessa," he said, but she could hardly concentrate enough to answer. He laughed lightly. "Stay with me, baby," he said, loosening his hold on her throat until her eyes opened and she managed some kind of incoherent, *"Hmm?"* He littered kisses across her cheek as if he was trying to memorize each freckle. "Safeword?"

"Red."

"Promise you'll tell me if you need me to pull back?" She nodded, but he searched her face. "Promise me."

"I promise," she said, wriggling beneath him. He smirked at her impatience.

"Play nice."

She ran her nails down his back until he shivered and said, defiantly, "No."

River took the challenge and tugged her head back hard, pulling on her hair and gripping her throat until she saw stars. "Oh, you asked for it," he answered, a wicked gleam in his eyes.

He rolled his hips, once, twice, as if teasing her body, before pulling out of her entirely and spinning her around so she was lying on her stomach, holding onto her throat all the while. He pushed her legs apart and wrapped his free arm around her middle, trapping her to his body as he entered her in a swift, hard stroke.

She cried out, and he released his thumb from her throat to rub along the underside of her chin, his cock driving into her like crashing waves. "You feel so fucking good. I could just drown in you."

Tessa was too overwhelmed with sparks and waves and *him* to find words. She grasped the blankets in her fists, sobbing, as every single graze of River's fingers, every thrust of his cock, coiled within her and she broke into pieces. River held her somehow tighter, hit her somehow deeper, and she called out his name, crumbling in his arms. Her body turned to jelly as wave after wave crashed over her.

River growled as she tightened around him. He whispered her name like a prayer, soft against the moans and gasps and stormy night as he came inside her and *fuck, she'd never felt anything so good.* He bit down on her shoulder and, somehow, she shattered further. She was nothing but his, nothing but a mess of beautiful broken pieces that River was an expert at putting together and breaking apart.

He slipped out of her and released her throat, replacing his fingers with his lips, placing desperate kisses across her skin. He gently turned her until her face was nestled against his chest and held her close to him, rocking her so lightly she wasn't sure it was intentional.

"Are you okay, princess?" he asked, still catching his breath. He ran his fingers across her jaw as if he couldn't bear to be touching anything but her.

"Better than okay," she answered, her voice hoarse from the most blissful screams. "I mean… fuck."

He chuckled, a mix of exhaustion and awe. "Yeah, fuck."

Tessa yawned and closed her eyes as she burrowed back into the blankets. She heard him fumble on the small table beside the couch. Moments later, she felt his touch between her thighs as he cleaned her off. Part of her wanted to protest, wanted to keep him on her for as long as she could, but she put that part down to her orgasm-addled brain and, instead, said, "Thank you," with another yawn.

He tossed the tissues and lay down beside her. River wrapped his arms around her and pulled her in close to him, as Tessa pulled a blanket over the two of them. She leaned back into him, relishing in the warmth of his body, the beat of his still-racing heart.

As she drifted off in his arms, she couldn't help thinking that this, the cuddling and comfort, felt somehow so much more dangerous than everything else.

CHAPTER TWELVE

Cass

Not even the sea view from his hotel room could make Cass feel at home when River and Tessa were three thousand miles away.

He'd declined every invitation to go out with the other models on the shoot since he'd been in LA. He usually faked it, pasted a smile on his face, and pretended to enjoy himself at whatever bar or club they dragged him to. It was good marketing to be friendly with other models—everyone in the industry had connections.

Instead, he'd returned to his hotel with takeout every night, and tried to pass the time until he could call River and Tessa. God, he missed them. He had always hated taking jobs away from New York. River had occasionally joined him in the past, but Cass was usually so busy that there wasn't much point in River tagging along. Besides, coming home from a long day of work he hated to see River sitting behind his computer doing the job he loved always stung.

Cass had never wanted to model, and he'd enjoyed it less and less as the years went on. At first, he liked the attention. He'd always been extroverted by nature, in stark contrast to River's introversion, and River had been content to stay home and write while he went to all the networking events his agent arranged. But these days, more and more, he loathed the industry, between the impossible beauty standards and fetishization of Black models that made him want to scrub himself clean after the directors called him things like *exotic* and *dark chocolate*. Perhaps he should have stood up for himself more, but he'd been too scared when he started out and he was too used to it now, too exhausted, after so many years.

So he smiled and posed and let it all roll off his back, because what else was he going to do? He'd never really known what he wanted. He'd followed his mom's footsteps all the way to med school, taking on the odd shoot after being scouted by a modeling agent at a club, when he had the time. But after the dark years, holding his breath in waiting rooms and crying by River's bedside, Cass had no interest in spending any more time in hospitals.

He'd fretted for weeks after dropping out, unsure of how to break the news to his parents, but they'd taken it well. Melanie and Kurtis King were the best parents he could have asked for. They were children of first-generation Senegalese immigrants who had struggled to put food on the table and their own parents put all of their hopes and dreams onto them. Cass's parents had sworn not to do the same to him. They'd been nothing short of perfect parents, but Cass couldn't help but feel like he'd let them down—and let himself down by falling into a career he didn't care for at all.

They'd moved back to Senegal two years ago, and he missed them more than he thought possible. He and River hadn't had the chance to fly out and see them yet, though his parents had surprised them for Cass's birthday. Maybe he could convince River and Tessa to take a trip in the Spring. He couldn't wait for his parents to meet Tessa; he knew they would love her as much as they loved River.

His parents tried to be there for River when his own parents hadn't been, but River had pulled away, too scared to let anyone get too close. And now… well, they just didn't talk about it. River took the pills, went to therapy, and never faltered.

As far as he knew, River hadn't fully opened up to Tessa. Yet. Cass gave them three months before they gave in and admitted they were crazy about each other. And when they did, he would be happy for them. He would.

Cass couldn't blame River for holding off on spilling his heart. He wasn't the only one keeping secrets. Cass hadn't found a way to mention that he wasn't *just* a big fan of Tessa and Aaron's work; he'd been obsessed with Jay Hutchison since he was a kid. He'd even met Tessa's ex at a post-show meet and greet a few years ago, and been drunkenly propositioned. *"My girlfriend would go crazy for you,"* Jay had slurred after Cass spent three solid minutes gushing about the lyrics on his latest album. *"What are you doing after this?"* Before Cass had been able to reply, another fan had lunged excitedly at Jay and security had promptly ushered both Jay and the drunk fan out of the room.

My girlfriend. Tessa. He had no idea how to broach the subject of him being a fan of Jay with her. He was still wrapping his head around learning that his idol was, in fact, a terrible person.

He stripped off and collapsed onto the bed, pinching the bridge of his nose. His shoot had run on later than expected, and River and Tessa had already gone to bed by the time he'd finished. It was the first time in a long time he was going to sleep without speaking to them. He'd called every night he'd been away, and, back home, he and River spent almost every night with Tessa these days.

He pulled the comforter over himself and closed his eyes. He could practically feel them beside him, the weight of them pressing into him. *Home.* That's what they were. And he wanted them so badly he couldn't even think straight.

It's normal to be attracted to them both, he reasoned with himself. He'd been attracted to River since they were teenagers, after all. That hadn't changed when he'd fucked everything up.

Tessa had caught his eye long before he stepped out of the elevator. He'd been following her career since she'd started working with Aaron, and even more so when she'd started dating Jay. He'd seen her pictures; he knew she was gorgeous. But when they'd met, and he'd seen the way her smile lit up the whole damn city, he was gone. Something about seeing her and River together, like two planets perfectly in orbit, made his heart stop dead in his chest.

The two of them swam before his closed eyelids, and he groaned as his cock stirred. It was becoming a problem. It had been a long time since Cass had been remotely interested in hooking up with anyone except River. It had been years since he'd actually done so—not that River knew that. But it wasn't River's face alone that had him palming his cock and sighing with relief.

It was Tessa's face, too; both River and Tessa's hands he saw when he stroked himself. He could feel every one of Tessa's guitar-given callouses, every scratch of River's stubble. He buried his face in a pillow as he came, gasping their names, panting.

He cleaned himself up and climbed back into bed, shivering; it was colder than LA had a right to be. He pulled the covers around himself and stared at the ceiling.

He should be able to sleep; he'd been working like crazy and had hardly slept since leaving NYC. But when Cass closed his eyes, Tessa's rosy cheeks and River's dark eyes appeared behind his eyelids. His body was too awake, too alert.

More. *God*, he needed more.

CHAPTER THIRTEEN

River

R iver had expected to wake up to an empty bed, but his heart still sank at the sight of the wrinkled sheets and no Tessa. He'd been hoping he was wrong. He rolled over with a sigh and grabbed his phone. Three a.m. and... a text from Tessa.

> I promise I'm not running away this time.
> Just getting some air. I'm on the roof if
> you wake up.

He smiled and held the phone to his chest. Progress.

He threw on some clothes, grabbed a blanket, and headed up onto the roof.

It was bitterly cold, but Tessa was wearing his t-shirt, her snow boots, and, by the looks of it, nothing else, sitting on the crumbling wooden bench they kept covered most of the year. His feet crunched through the snow and he settled the blanket around her shoulders. "You're not dressed for this, princess."

She turned her head and grinned up at him before gesturing at the city. "Look at this. It's magical. I've never seen it so quiet." Most people had taken shelter from the flurries, and the thick snow muffled the sound of the traffic.

River sat beside her, and she leaned her head on his shoulder. He peered down at her face, her expression peaceful and snowflakes on her lashes. *She* was magical. She met his gaze and bit her lip, wariness in her eyes.

"Do you regret it?"

She ran a hand through her hair and shook her head. "No. God, no, last night was… I don't even have words. I don't regret it, but it was a mistake."

River's relief at Tessa's lack of regret was short-lived. *Mistake*. His face must have fallen, because Tessa looked immediately stricken. "Oh God, I'm fucking this up. I don't mean *mistake* like… It's just, I don't want to jeopardize our friendship. What we have, the three of us… I've never had anything like this before, and I don't want to lose it."

She reached out and grabbed his hand, clinging onto it like some kind of lifeline, and his traitor of a heart soared. "I still don't know how to fully let you both in. I'm so scared." Her voice cracked, and he pulled her in close.

"You're not going to lose us. I promise. But I get it. You've been through hell and back and everything has changed so quickly."

"Yeah." She sighed, her breath visible in the cool air. "I like you, River, and I trust you. Hell, I have since the bookstore. I'm just not there yet, you know?"

She liked him. He tried his best to calm his racing heart and said, "I know how scary it is to let people in, and I'm so proud of you for trying," he told her earnestly, and her answering smile made him pause. He was asking her to trust him, to let him in, but he hadn't been entirely honest with her.

He had been through years of therapy to help rid himself of the shame, but it settled in beside him, his body tensing, the moment he realized he had to share his past with Tessa. He was used to people thinking badly of him, but he wasn't sure he could handle *her* thinking badly of him.

"Hey, are you okay?" Tessa asked, concern filling her eyes.

River rubbed his face with his hands. "I just realized I've been encouraging you to open up and talk to us and I haven't shared my own shit."

"You don't have to share anything," she assured him. "I know you'll tell me when you're ready."

"I want to tell you, I just… Fuck, it's scary."

"River," she said, gently, stealing his hands back in both of hers. "There's nothing you could tell me that would make me not want to be your friend."

Since that first night on the roof, Tessa had worked her ass off, learning to open up to him and Cass. He could do the same. He took a deep breath. "Just before I graduated college, I kind of spiraled. I… I was already pretty self-destructive back then. After Cass and I broke up, I kind of went off the rails. Drinking, sleeping around, you know. I was just hollow and, eventually... I got addicted to coke."

He had to look away from her. There was no judgment

on her face, just a touch of surprise. "No one knew, not even Cass, until I accidentally overdosed when I was twenty-five. Or maybe it wasn't an accident. I'm still not completely sure, to be honest." He took a moment to catch his breath.

"After I got out of the hospital, my parents set me up with therapists, addiction specialists, you name it. They tried to get me to move back home, but they didn't like Cass. They didn't want him around and I would never leave him. My parents are pretty obsessed with their image, and having a son who wasn't straight doesn't fit that image.

"They stopped trying, eventually. Everyone did, except Cass. He was always there, never giving up on me." He paused and took a long draw of his coffee. "A few days after his twenty-seventh birthday, I was driving back from a meeting out of the city and got pulled over. They searched my car, and I was arrested, charged with possession with intent to sell. I never dealt, but I had picked some up for a friend, so it didn't look good.

"I pled guilty to possession, and they dropped the intent to sell charge. I did just over thirteen months. It was brutal. The detoxing alone…" River blew out a breath. He remembered the agony like it was yesterday. If not for the fact he'd been on suicide watch thanks to his previous overdose, he wouldn't have survived it. At the time, he couldn't imagine a time he would have been glad to survive it, but now, he was grateful for the wake-up call.

But the real work began on release day. Almost all the guys he'd kept in touch with had been in and out of prison time and time again, thanks to the utter lack of support given to addicts after release. He was lucky; most people didn't have a Cass.

"When I got out, Cass was waiting for me and drove me to a rehab clinic down in Maryland. I was already in recovery at that point, but I needed a shit ton of therapy.

"He got an apartment near the clinic, visited me every few days." River swallowed. Tears always prickled his eyes when he thought about how much Cass had been there for him, always. "I don't think I would have made it without him. He was the only one who thought I could do it at that point."

"But you did," Tessa murmured, and he looked up to find her eyes lined with silver. A tear slipped down her cheek and he brushed it away.

"I did. I've been drug-free since my arrest, ten years this past March, and damn glad every day." He and Cass had celebrated by taking a trip to Maine for a few days, shutting off their phones, and spending every second by the sea.

Tessa leaned into him and wrapped her arms around his middle. "That's fucking amazing, River. You know that, right? You're amazing. Cass too, and he's getting the biggest hug when he walks through the door later."

River chuckled and rested his chin on her head. "Like you wouldn't have given him one anyway."

"True," she agreed. "So that explains why you're not close with your family. Do you ever see them?"

"We go up to Poughkeepsie once a year and have dinner with them, a few days into the New Year," River scowled at the thought of the annual dinner from hell—it wasn't far away. "They hate that I bring Cass, but he's non-negotiable.

You're coming too, this time." He nudged her, and she pouted, but didn't protest.

"They've never tried to make up for giving up on you?"

"They don't think they did." He shrugged. "As far as they're concerned, it's my fault for being a stain on the family name."

"That's bullshit," Tessa growled. "You worked your ass off to get better, despite them leaving you behind."

"They tried. I was just too much."

"It's been ten years," she argued, spitting mad on his behalf. He smiled, shaking his head.

"Didn't you once tell me you've never forgiven anyone in your life?" he asked, recalling a conversation about a book they'd both read, in which the theme had been forgiveness. Tessa had scoffed and said, *"The institution of forgiveness is just a breeding ground for disappointment and I refuse to take part."*

Tessa frowned. "That's different."

"Different how?"

"Because they hurt you. I… okay, I think I understand your hatred of Jay now."

He couldn't help himself; he pulled her into his arms and pressed his lips to her cheek. But Tessa turned her head, and his lips grazed hers instead. He should have pulled away instantly, but he hesitated, and so did she, and damn, she tasted so good.

They pulled apart, and Tessa squeezed her eyes closed. "I didn't mean to do that."

He reached out to stroke her cheek and thought better of it. "I'll try to remember that's how you respond to emotional vulnerability in the future," he joked, trying to ease the tension.

"Oh God." She buried her head in her hands. "You just opened up about your life story and I can't even keep my hands to myself. I'm sorry."

"It's been a weird twenty-four hours. And if it makes you feel better, I think about kissing you at least three times every day." Three was seriously underestimating it, but he didn't want to overwhelm her.

She laughed lightly and looked up at him. "Thank you for sharing that with me. I'm so fucking glad you made it through all of that and I get to call you and Cass my friends."

"Likewise. It was worth making it through everything to have you and Cass." He couldn't imagine it now, not getting the chance to meet her. "I promise I'm not going anywhere, Tessa. Maybe we can't be the kind of friends who sleep together without feelings getting in the way, but you're my best friend, okay? Besides, Cass would kick my ass if I let anything come between that."

She laughed. "I'd like to see that."

He held out a pinky, and she twined hers with it. "Are we okay?"

She loosed a long breath, her shoulders relaxing. "Yeah, we're okay."

"Good. Let's go in before we freeze to death."

He tossed her the apartment keys and gathered up the blanket, shaking off the snow as they descended the stairs. The hallway was like a sauna compared to the icy air.

Tessa's footsteps slowed as she approached the door.

"Hey, River?"

He looked up, and she paused, turning to face him, chewing her lip. "Yeah?"

"What if we could be?"

"Could be what?"

Tessa took a deep breath and leaned back against the door, the keys clutched in her fist. "What if we could be, you know, friends who could sleep together without feelings getting in the way?"

His breath caught in his chest. Of all the things he expected her to say... He swallowed. "Would you want that, if we could?"

"Would you?"

He stepped across the hallway, stopping just out of her reach. Up close, he could see the rise and fall of her chest, a shade faster than it usually was; he could see the way her fist was clenching and unclenching around the keys. "I asked first," he said, softly.

She kept chewing her lip, and he was desperate to taste it. "Maybe," she replied, her voice hardly more than a whisper.

He took a step closer, unable to stay away. "Just maybe?"

She closed her eyes and took a deep breath. "Yes, I would want that."

River considered her, the flush on her cheeks, her shallow breaths. He placed his hand on the doorframe as her eyes opened and she looked up at him with an almost shy expression. "Would you want that?"

Did he want that? Could he even manage it without

getting caught up in the feelings? He was already so *gone* over her. "Yeah, princess, I want that," he said, because how could he ever say no? "But we can't pretend the feelings don't exist, we just have to… learn to live alongside them, I guess."

Tessa frowned, but nodded. "We can only try, and promise to talk it out when we need to."

"Yeah, as long as we're honest and talk to each other, we should be good."

"What about Cass? Is this going to be weird for him?"

River knew Cass wouldn't care that they were sleeping together. He would be happy for them. "He won't care," he told her, but why did the thought of telling him turn his stomach?

Tessa chewed her lip. "Do you think we could… see how it goes for a little while before we tell him? I don't want to hide, I just… it's a lot."

River nodded, relieved. "Of course. He'll probably just figure it out. He already knows how I feel about you, and he notices everything." He rolled his eyes but laughed. "When he figures it out, we'll come clean about everything to him. How does that sound?"

Tessa breathed a sigh of relief. "Yeah, that sounds good."

"So we're doing this, princess?" he asked, and she smiled up at him, the little worry on her face melting away.

"Yeah, we're doing this."

"Thank fuck," he groaned and lowered his mouth to hers.

CHAPTER FOURTEEN

River

She was sunshine and daisies and everything beautiful in the world and, as she leaned further into the door and tugged on his collar to pull him closer, he thought his legs might give way. She tasted so fucking good.

She tangled her hands in his hair, her keys jingling near his ear, and ran her tongue along his lower lip, tasting him and moaning.

"You need to open that door now, or I'm going to do filthy things to you in this hallway," he managed between gasping breaths.

Tessa pulled away long enough to fumble with the lock, and he reached out a hand to help. She stilled and looked up at him with dark eyes, licking her lips, and dropped the keys, kicking them just out of reach. "Oops," she whispered.

River chuckled and pushed her further into the door until there was no space between them, only far too many clothes. "You're dangerous."

She pressed soft kisses up his throat and slid his jacket from his shoulders until it fell to the floor with a thump. He tugged at the bottom of his t-shirt, but she pushed him back, spinning them so that his back was against the door, and sank to her knees before him.

He hardly had time to think before she had his zipper down. "You have no idea how long I've wanted to do this," she all but moaned. She wrapped her fist around his cock, running it up and down his length a few times, before leaning forward and taking him in her mouth.

His head fell back against the door with a crack, but all he could feel was her; her mouth, warm and wet and perfect around him. "Fuck, princess," he panted. His hands knotted themselves in her hair of their own accord and he looked down to find her watching his face with bright eyes.

She pulled back slightly, swirling her tongue around the head of his cock. "River," she said, the words vibrating through him. He cursed, fighting his hips as they seemed to want to fucking impale her.

"Yeah, baby?"

She paused and met his eye, a wicked gleam in hers. "Please fuck my mouth."

He'd died and gone to heaven. That was the only explanation for the way she moaned as he tightened his hold on her hair. "Don't be gentle," she added, and he thought he might come from her words alone.

"Jesus, do you have any idea how perfect you are?" He brushed his thumb across her lips. "Promise me you'll slap my legs if I'm too rough?"

"I *want* you to be too rough. But I promise." She licked her lips and opened her mouth for him. *Fucking hell.*

River entered her mouth slowly, testing how much of him she could take comfortably. Her eyes flutter closed as he neared the back of her throat, her grip tightening on his legs. He stilled, but she opened her eyes and kept her gaze on him as she took him further and, honest-to-God, *hummed* contentedly.

"Fuck," he groaned, pulling out of her mouth and pushing in again, a little harder, a tight grip on her hair. Tessa moaned, spurring him on, and he stopped holding back.

He gripped the doorframe with one hand, holding himself up because *God*, he could have collapsed with how good she felt, and held her head still with the other, fucking her mouth and throat harder than he would have dared if she hadn't asked, if she hadn't been moaning and holding him to her.

Yesterday's mascara ran from the corners of her eyes, and she blinked up at him, her eyes alight with desire, with *need*. He closed his eyes, his head falling back, and cried out her name as she took a hand from his legs and trailed one finger across his balls.

She cupped them, rolling them in her hand, and every-thing around him dulled. "Tessa, baby, I'm going to... Fuck," he cursed, as she squeezed gently and he came, his vision shuttering and his hips stilling.

Tessa continued to suck him as his legs buckled, drinking him down and licking her lips when she pulled away. "God, you taste amazing," she said, and he stared down at her in disbelief. She couldn't possibly be real.

He caught his breath and tugged her up. "Bring the keys, princess. I plan to thoroughly worship you, and I need you naked to do so."

He had the door open in seconds and his lips on hers as they fell into her apartment, the door slamming behind them. He all but ripped his t-shirt from her until it fell in a puddle at their feet.

Tessa pulled away from him to step over it, and he pulled his shirt over his head. She took his hand and led him towards her bedroom, giving him the perfect view of her ass. Her lace white underwear hardly covered her flushed skin, or the inked black florals that covered her left side.

He reached forward and gently swatted her as they walked through the doorway into her bedroom. She gasped and spun around, and he pushed her back into the doorframe so he could sink his face into the crook of her neck. Tessa squirmed beneath him as his tongue lavished her skin, his teeth grazing her throat.

She cried out, his name tumbling from her mouth as he trailed kisses down her chest, moving down her body until he was kneeling before her. He pulled her underwear down and nudged her thighs apart.

She looked like a goddess standing over him, her golden hair spilling across her naked body, her whiskey-eyes glowing in the low light. She gasped as he leaned forward and bit down on her thigh, his tongue immediately licking the spot. Before she had time to calm her breathing, he parted her thighs further and buried his face in her pussy.

He didn't know whether he loved the taste of her lips or her pussy more. She was fucking divine. She grasped the wall on either side of the doorframe, shaking as he devoured her, so sweet on his tongue. It took no time at all for her to fall apart, crying his name, quivering. He held onto her thighs, steadying her, and looked up to see her back arched and her eyes closed, the picture of bliss.

He might never look at doorways the same.

All it had taken was one taste, and he was already hard and ready for her again. If he didn't get inside her soon, he was going to explode. He stood and picked her up, ignoring her protests as he carried her to the bed and laid her down on her front so he could run his hands across her back, massaging the sore spots left behind by the doorframe and giving her time to catch her breath.

She sighed happily, and he traded his hands for his lips, running gentle kisses along her back.

River lifted her hips enough for him to run a finger lightly over her clit until she was whimpering. He slid a finger inside her, then two, and groaned at how tightly she enveloped them. His fingers curled, and she cried out, tightening around them. He rubbed gentle circles inside her, bringing her down slowly, and then withdrew, leaning over her to kiss her shoulder.

"You still with me, princess?"

She mumbled incoherently, but turned her head and pushed up so she could look at him. Her eyes were hazy, black smudged beneath them.

He kissed her, a hand below her chin, and they pulled

apart, breathless. "Condom?" he asked, and she bit her lip and shook her head.

"I want to feel you," she whispered against his lips.

He kissed her hungrily, then turned her until her front was pressed against the comforter. River trailed his lips down her back, tracing her tattoos. He grasped her hips, and she lifted them for him, glistening and ready. He pushed into her slowly, and she whimpered, her head falling onto the bed. Fuck, she felt amazing. He swore he could die happily inside Tessa, like they were made to fit together.

He teased her, rolling his hips oh so gently, brushing his thumb lightly across her ass until she was begging him for more.

"Please, River," she sobbed into the blankets and he bent down to kiss her forehead before taking pity on her and slapping her ass. She cried out, and he slammed into her, using the mattress as leverage.

She clenched around him, falling over the edge and crying unintelligible words. She came down slowly and seemed close to coming again when he slipped out of her and his cock pressed against her ass.

"Sorry—" he began, but Tessa moaned and pushed against him and he paused, his mouth going dry. He leaned over her, brushing his lips against her cheek, and rubbed his cock against her ass. "Is that what you want, princess? You want me to fuck your ass?"

"God, yes," she moaned instantly, and he chuckled against her ear.

He dragged his thumb through her wetness and pressed

into her, and she clenched around him, gasping. "Have you done this before, baby?"

She nodded. As much as could, pinned beneath him anyway. "Yeah."

"Good." He slapped her on the ass and said, "Go further up on the bed, on your knees."

She crawled slowly up the bed, and he groaned at the view as he followed her. She reached over into the bottom drawer of her nightstand and tossed him a bottle of lube. He stilled her before she could settle on her tummy again and pressed a gentle kiss to her lips. "Safeword, princess," he prompted.

"Red," she managed through shallow breaths.

"And you promise you'll use it if you need to?"

"Promise."

"Hold on to the headboard." He poured a generous amount of lube on her ass and over his cock. He rubbed the head over her entrance and she took a deep breath as he pushed slowly into her.

Her back arched, and she whispered, "Fuck," as he sheathed himself in her and stilled, breathless.

God, she was so fucking tight. He placed his hands on top of hers on the headboard and she flexed her fingers until they were threaded through his. "Okay?" he checked, and she nodded quickly.

"You feel fucking amazing," she moaned, and he slowly rolled his hips. "More, please," she gasped. "I can take it, I promise."

He chuckled and squeezed her hand. "Oh, I know you can." He wasn't sure *he* could.

She leaned forward and pressed her lips to his hand before wiggling her hips and making him curse. He blew out a breath as he started moving behind her, everything in the room fading to nothing except her and how good she felt. He was aware of the headboard knocking on the wall, but he couldn't hear it over her cries and their gasping breaths.

Tessa shuddered beneath him, screaming his name and *fuck, he wanted to see her face when she came.* He pulled out of her long enough to spin her around so she was lying on her back. He lifted her leg over his shoulder and pushed into her ass again as her head fell back against the pillows and he felt her tighten around him.

"Open your eyes, princess," he growled, and she met his gaze with a hazy gold stare. She bit her lip and cried out as she came again and he fell apart alongside her, leaning down to kiss her hungrily as he came, groaning her name.

He collapsed on top of her and made to roll off, but she wrapped her arms around him and held him there. "I don't want to crush you."

"I like it," she said, the words muffled.

He chuckled and rolled them so she was tucked into his chest. "Compromise."

She hummed and turned around so she could look up into his face. She snuggled into his chest before saying, "That was… I don't even have words. Amazing, incredible, and outstanding don't even scratch the surface."

He brushed her hair back from her face and kissed her. "You might be the death of me."

"It'll be my pleasure," she replied with a laugh. She sniffed and buried her face in the pillow, breathing deeply.

"What?"

She offered the pillow to him. "It smells like Cass." He sniffed the fabric, and his heart dared to race at the light earthy scent that clung to Cass, sandalwood, and citrus. "I miss him," Tessa added, snuggling her head into the pillow when he handed it back.

"Me too," he agreed with a sigh. Cass not being there had felt like a constant ache. "Just a couple more days. And hey, we couldn't have done *that* with him here, could we?"

She raised her eyebrows as if considering that. "Hmm, that's a nice visual. Going to fall asleep with that one in my head," she said with a chuckle, and the image of Tessa between him and Cass flooded his mind. He swallowed and tried desperately to push it out. She was joking, surely.

"You need to sleep before you give me ideas," he told her, reaching around to swat her ass.

She laughed and lifted her head to kiss him before burrowing under the covers with a yawn. She winked at him before reaching to turn the lamp off. "Sweet dreams."

CHAPTER FIFTEEN

Tessa

I t hurt to sit down. And stand up and lie down. Everything hurt after two days of near constant sex, but Tessa wasn't complaining. The aching thighs, stinging ass, and complete exhaustion that washed over her every time she so much as breathed only reminded her how fucking amazing things were between her and River.

They were curled up on the couch, River with a book in hand and Tessa with a cup of coffee as she watched snow falling outside the window like fluffy confetti. The heady tension that had been plaguing them since they met had been replaced by a steady comfort, even if they were still struggling to keep their clothes on. And though her heart raced anxiously at least once every ten minutes while she thought of all the reasons this was a terrible idea, River's touch calmed her.

Tessa groaned as she sat up, stretching her poor spine, and River reached out to rub her back. She leaned back into him, his deft fingers warm as they rubbed her shoulders, left bare by the tank top she had thrown on after their last shower.

She whimpered as he worked his fingers into the back of her neck, her head falling back and her muscles relaxing beneath every deep push of his fingertips. He tugged gently on her neck, turning her to face him and pressing his lips softly to hers. God, would she ever tire of the taste of this man?

Her tongue swept across his, tasting sugar, cardamom, and rose, thanks to the Gulab Jamun he had ordered from the other side of the city when she told him she'd never tried it. It tasted even better secondhand.

She turned her body, ignoring the twinges of pain, so she could straddle his lap, and shivered as he tugged her tank top up. "Wait, stop," she said, pulling away from him and quickly pulling her tank top back down. River stilled, panting beneath her. "Jesus Christ, what is wrong with us? We need to pause. Cass is going to be home any minute and my body is going to shut down if I don't let it rest."

He chuckled, and she tried her damndest not to notice how good the vibrations felt. He reached for one last kiss before pulling back and releasing her waist. "I'm going to miss being able to do that whenever we want."

Tessa opened her mouth to answer, but paused at the jingling of keys. She squealed and shot up, rushing to the door. It swung open, and she jumped into Cass's arms.

"Oof," he gasped, dropping his bag and holding her tight, spinning her around. God, he felt amazing, steady as an oak in the midst of the wild forest that she and River so closely resembled. "I missed you too, princess."

He set her down and pressed a kiss to her cheek, before pressing one to River's. "Have you two just not left the apartment while I've been gone?" he asked, raising an eyebrow. River and Tessa exchanged a glance.

"What do you mean?" Tessa asked him, forcing her voice to remain steady.

Cass dug around in his bag and pulled out a stack of letters and packages. "The mailboxes were practically overflowing."

"There's been a snowstorm, and we've been busy with work," River lied through his teeth. They'd been busy with each other.

Cass shed his jacket and yawned.

"Rough flight?" Tessa asked, standing on her tiptoes to rub his shoulders and resolutely ignoring the tingle his answering groan sent through her.

"Nah, just long. My seat buddy was *very* friendly and spent the entire flight telling me about his grandson's figure skating competition."

"How much can there really be to say about figure skating?" River asked, handing Tessa her pile of mail.

She flipped through the envelopes as Cass said, "You'd be surprised. I'm exhausted."

"How about we order take out and have a movie day in bed?" River asked and Cass quickly agreed.

"Sure," Tessa answered, frowning at the return address on a large envelope. Her manager usually let her know if she was sending any documents over.

She tucked it under her arm and followed Cass and River to her bedroom, where they settled under the covers. As the two of them scrolled through a list of movies, Tessa tore the envelope open and shook out the contents. A folded sheet of paper and another, smaller envelope fell onto the bed.

She unfolded the paper, recognizing her manager's messy scrawl.

> Tessa,
> This arrived at the office and I wasn't sure whether to forward it on to you, but I figured if it was me, I would at least want the option to read it.
> Looking forward to catching up when I'm in NYC next month.
> Rebecca

Tessa frowned and set the note aside, picking up the envelope. Her eyes drifted across the paper and her chest tightened as they took in the address. She'd recognize those slanted *T*s anywhere.

She flipped the envelope over and sure enough, the return address read *Rhys Reid*. She stared at it, at his handwriting, warring emotions already rising within her. She had never opened the email, had left it safely tucked away, but it was hard to ignore something as tangible as a letter.

"Princess?"

She looked up into two faces lined with concern.

"What's wrong?"

Tessa swallowed and set the letter down with shaking hands. "It's from my brother."

They glanced at the envelope, surprise coloring their faces. They knew she hadn't spoken to her family in six years. She didn't know how much they knew beyond that, though; everything about her was easily accessible online, but they'd never mentioned looking.

"Are you going to open it?" Cass asked gently. She shook her head, picked the envelope up, and dropped it in the bottom drawer of her nightstand.

"No. I don't care what he has to say." *Liar.*

She pulled her knees up to her chest and held them close. A moment later, River's arms wound around her waist and he pulled her into his lap. Cass lifted her legs onto his and rubbed gentle circles on her knees.

"Why don't you talk to your family?"

She chewed her lip and leaned back into River. "You don't have to tell us," River added. "But it might help to talk about it."

She blew out a shaky breath and toyed with her split ends. "It's... it's kind of a long story."

"We have all the time in the world for you, you know that."

She looked between them. There was none of the hunger for gossip that terrified her on their faces, and she knew well enough to know that whatever she told them wouldn't leave the room. Their eyes shone with worry and care.

She swallowed. "I guess to fully understand, I have to tell you what happened when my song was picked for the contest."

They'd been in London for a couple of years, but she'd been lucky enough to make a close group of friends. They were excited for her; *everyone* was excited for her. Though she was too young, by the contest's rules, to perform the song herself, she was the youngest songwriter to be featured in its history. The little song she'd submitted on a whim, about the first girl to break her heart, was finally making people take her writing seriously. Sure, it had been nothing more than puppy love and she'd had to change the pronouns, but it was still hers.

She'd sat backstage at the contest amongst the glitter and champagne and watched along with the rest of the world as the UK's chosen pop star stood and sang her song and she'd known at that moment that no other career would do for her.

They didn't win—the UK never did—but her song was praised worldwide and she signed her first songwriting deal just a couple of weeks later, the youngest songwriter ever to be signed by Empire Records.

It was a big enough deal for the press to sniff around; sure, she was only sixteen, but the British tabloids were hardly known for their morals.

"They, uh, they found my friends and spoke to them. They couldn't offer them money, since they were minors, but they gave them concert tickets or something and they just… spilled all my secrets. I was on the front page of every tabloid." She hated how weak and watery her voice sounded, but River laid his head on her shoulder and Cass scooted closer and she felt a little stronger.

She couldn't blame her school friends for turning on her.

She'd only known them for a couple of years, but it still stung. Tessa had been far from angelic at sixteen, if she was being honest. She tried everything; drinking, sex, drugs. Nothing in excess, but everything more than she should have, trying to find something to make her feel better about how things were at home.

And her so-called friends had receipts; pictures and videos they shared with the press. Nothing was spared from the pages of Britain's filthiest tabloids. Which meant nothing was spared from her parents, including her sexuality. Tessa was still questioning at sixteen, still unsure of a label, but her parents couldn't handle that (*"How are we supposed to explain this to people, Tessa?"*) and so she'd been forced into the box of bisexual.

It had taken years before she'd felt comfortable enough to take herself out of the constraints of the box and simply identify as queer. Her feelings were hers and hers alone, and no one else needed the details unless she wanted to share them.

"I stopped letting people in after that. I didn't make any more friends, aside from Aaron, and I became super protective of my privacy," she continued. "My only other friend, really, was Rhys."

"Your brother?"

She lifted a shoulder in a half-hearted shrug. "My twin." River and Cass couldn't hide their surprise.

He'd been her best friend, her other half, but they'd grown even closer when she'd gone through hell. Rhys had stayed up night after night when she cried herself to sleep, had stood in her corner when she fought with her parents, begging them to allow her to homeschool.

They'd relented, eventually, not because they cared about how miserable she was at school, but because it meant she could spend more time writing, and they desperately needed the money. Her dad had blown through all of their savings with a hidden gambling addiction. Every penny she made writing, which wasn't much at the time, went straight to paying off their debt, but it was never enough. Nothing was ever enough.

It had been a blessing when she'd gotten the call that a major player wanted to write with her. Her manager promised her the royalties would be incredible, and they made her sign an NDA before walking into the studio. She hadn't been expecting Jay. She knew enough of his music to know that he probably wouldn't be interested in working with some nineteen-year-old indie pop songwriter. But he was working with Aaron at the time, trying to revive his career after his past couple of albums hadn't done well and his career had been labelled stagnant. Aaron had played Jay one of Tessa's demos when he mentioned he was struggling to find a songwriter he connected with, and Jay had requested her within the hour.

"We hit it off the second I walked into the room. He was hesitant given my age—I had to make the first move," she rolled her eyes at the memory, and realized with a jolt that thinking of Jay no longer meant the sharp pain or heavy ache that had plagued her for so long.

They'd kept things quiet for a while. Tessa still struggled to trust anyone, and, though it took time, when she slowly let him in, she didn't want anyone else popping their bubble. She hadn't even told Rhys.

"I introduced him to my family on my twentieth birthday. It was about as awkward as you would expect, and my parents weren't happy about it. Well, my mom was happy— I think she thought I could use him as some kind of sugar daddy to help pay off their debts. Anyway, they got into a huge screaming match and my dad ended up going out. He lost the last of our savings that night. They asked me for more money and I said no. I'd had enough. I was working three jobs while I was writing just to help them out, and Rhys was too busy with uni to work. I'd just moved out and London isn't cheap. I told them they had to figure it out themselves."

She took a deep breath. The story didn't hurt so much if she stopped at that point, but it didn't stop there. "Rhys went to the press, told them all about Jay and me. Gave them pictures, intimate details he'd clearly stolen from my journal. They paid him a fortune."

River and Cass tensed, but she didn't, couldn't, look at them. Where the ache left behind by Jay had settled into a sense of quiet nostalgia, Rhys's betrayal still stung like a thousand cuts.

He'd shown up on her doorstep in floods of tears, begging her to forgive him, trying to explain himself. He'd been mad at her for not telling him, for shutting out their parents. She had slammed the door in his face and cut them all off. Her parents had tried to reach out, but she hadn't spoken to any of them since.

It had been carnage. The world had loved Steph, the

perfect wife for the world's most beloved rockstar. "Fuck knows why," Tessa said with a frown. "She has the personality of a shoe. But people were devastated when they found out she and Jay had separated and I became the scapegoat."

The British public were far from forgiving, and they'd never really forgiven Tessa's teenage transgressions. Being with Jay was the icing on the cake.

"I know you both hate him, and I get it, I do, but… I wouldn't have survived that year without him. He saw me at my absolute lowest and, instead of running for the hills, he told me he loved me all the more for being so strong." The drunken nights hadn't been so bad then; he'd been sweet, and she'd been sad, drinking up his drunken kisses like it was all she had. Tessa could never have guessed how things would turn out. "Even with it ending how it did, he was the first person to make me feel like the person I am is enough, and it was all worth it, if only for that."

When the press had been beating down her door, literally, he had shown up personally with a hoard of security and taken her away. She'd only planned to stay with him until the craziness died down, but she never left, and it never had died down.

"Do you miss him?" Cass asked quietly, and Tessa considered it.

While she couldn't deny she stood taller now that he was gone, she couldn't pretend she didn't miss him. "I think so, yeah. Not in a romantic sense, that ship has long sailed, but I miss having him in my life. He wasn't always a good partner, or even a good friend. But he was my person." They'd brought out the best in each other for a long time until they'd brought out the worst. She wished she could turn back time and leave before it got so bad. Maybe then they could have stayed friends.

"I'm so sorry you went through all of that," River told her softly, pressing a kiss to the top of her head. "Not a single one of them deserves you. But it's fucking amazing that you made it through it all, and I'm so glad you did."

"You have us now." Cass kissed her hand. "And we're not going anywhere. That's a promise. You're stuck with us."

She glanced between the two of them. Her heart was raw, beaten and bruised by the people who should have loved her most, but it was healing. It was healing because she was trying; because she was talking and letting in the people who had her best interests in mind.

Maybe one day she would heal enough to open the letter, but for now…

For now, she had people.

CHAPTER SIXTEEN

Cass

I t had taken Tessa three shots of tequila to pick up her guitar and climb up on the tiny stage for her first New York City Open Mic. But as soon as she started strumming, her hands stopped shaking, her spine straightened, and the music flowed from her like magic. She played one of the songs they'd heard her recording with Aaron, and Cass, River, and Aaron cheered so loudly when she finished that her cheeks were scarlet when she made it back to their booth.

They toasted with more shots, and by the time they left the bar, Tessa was yawning as they stumbled back to Cornelia Street. She leaned into River as the elevator ascended, while Cass looked around the tiny mirrored box and fought the urge to pinch himself. He was standing in an elevator with Tessa Reid and Aaron Peters. And somehow, they were his friends. *What the fuck.*

Tessa struggled with keys until Aaron rolled their eyes

and grabbed them before she dropped them. They slotted the keys into the door and opened it. "I've watched you play classical piano after half a bottle of whiskey and a handful of pills—you're losing your touch, T."

"I think that's called growing up," Tessa pointed out, before walking into the kitchen island and cursing. "Or maybe I'm just out of practice."

She collapsed onto the couch and kicked her heels under the coffee table.

"Move over, princess," River said, nudging her with his knee until she shifted enough for him to squeeze in beside her and pull her onto his lap. He unwound her jacket from her body and set it aside. Tessa looked up at him with a soft smile that made Cass's heart race. River brushed her hair from her face, his thumb lingering by the corner of her mouth, and Cass wondered what it would be like to run his fingers across her lips.

"Are you okay?" Cass jumped as Aaron's voice sounded from beside him. He looked away from River and Tessa, shedding his jacket and hanging it over a chair.

"Yeah. Just zoned out for a second," Cass lied. Aaron gave him a smile that had *bullshit* written all over it, but Cass ignored them. "I'll make drinks." He turned away from Aaron, taking a deep breath as he stepped into Tessa's kitchen and reached into the cabinet for glasses.

Aaron took a seat at the end of the couch, picking up the paperback Cass had left sitting on the armrest before they'd gone out and flicking through it. It was one of River's more recent releases; a filthy workplace romance River somehow made as sweet as he'd made sexy. Though Cass knew each of River's books inside out, he still re-read them every couple of months.

"I haven't read this one yet," Aaron said, running a finger over the illustrated cover. They'd been making their way through River's backlist since the moment Tessa had mentioned his pen name. Aaron wasn't a reader, but they were devouring River's books—Cass often woke up to find Aaron had messaged their group chat at three a.m. with comments that were usually along the lines of *this is the dirtiest thing my eyes have ever seen* or *fuck you, for making me cry when I should be sleeping.* For someone who didn't read much, they'd really nailed the unhinged reader thing.

"I think that's my favorite," Tessa said, nodding to the book in Aaron's hand.

River smiled down fondly at her. "I didn't know that. Why's it your favorite?"

Tessa shrugged. "I wish I had a better answer than just saying a sexy older love interest really does it for me, but I am who I am."

River chuckled and tightened his hold on her. Cass had to force himself to look away from them. They fit together so beautifully. Friends didn't look at each other like River and Tessa did and Cass would know; River looked at Tessa like he looked at Cass.

Cass tuned out the conversation as he finished making drinks and carried them over to the coffee table. He squeezed into the spot between Aaron and River and Tessa —Tessa's couch barely fit three, let alone four—just as Aaron asked River, "Why the pen name? Do you just like the anonymity?"

River shrugged, wrinkling his nose. "At first, yeah. I was worried about my parents finding out what I wrote, then I was worried about people finding out about my past if I used my real name, but now I wish I had. I like my pen name, but I'd prefer to use my actual name." Shadows crossed River's rich brown eyes, and Cass swallowed down the guilt.

River had been using the pen name Sage King since they were in high school, when he'd posted short stories on a journaling website. When they'd dated, they'd joked that he was just practicing for when they got married and River legally changed his name to King, finally getting away from the family name that had done nothing but made him feel like an outsider. Back then, both River and Cass thought they'd be married long before River ever published for real. And now, River was forced to work under a last name that he would never legally have, and it was Cass's fault.

River had built an incredible career, and Cass was so fucking proud of him. He deserved to have the name he wanted on his books. But whenever anyone suggested it, River shied away from the idea of publishing under his own name.

"Can't you rebrand under your real name?" Aaron asked.

"I could," River agreed, not immediately batting away the idea like he usually did. Cass raised his brows as River's cheeks colored. "But I don't know, it's—" He paused as Tessa let out a soft snore. The three of them looked at her as she nestled into his chest, fast asleep, fisting his t-shirt. "Can you pass me the blanket?" River asked, and Cass handed him the soft pink blanket strewn messily over the back of the couch. River set it gently around Tessa, staring down at her with so much love in his eyes that Cass had to remind his lungs to draw in air.

"It's a big change," River continued, his voice softer. "And my parents would be fucking pissed if I used my real name to publish romance. As far as they're concerned, it's basically porn."

"Shit, you two really lost the parental lottery," Aaron said, nodding at River and Tessa. "What are your parents like?" they asked Cass, who couldn't help but smile.

"Amazing. They've always supported everything River and I have done. I got really lucky." He'd learned at a young age that not all parents were as loving as his were, and he'd never taken it for granted. "Did you ever meet Tessa's family?"

"Unfortunately." Aaron frowned, pushing back their sandy hair as it fell across their face. "Rhys was okay. He wasn't particularly nice to Tessa, but I don't think she actually realized it. He was really critical of her, and let her pick up all the extra work to help out her parents without stepping in, but he could be nice when he wanted to be." Aaron winced. "I, uh, hooked up with him a couple of weeks before he went to the press about Tessa and Jay. Not my best decision—and not one I've told Tessa about, considering the timing."

"I haven't told Tessa that I met Jay at a meet and greet and he invited me to have a threesome with them, if that makes you feel better," Cass offered, and River blinked in surprise, as if he'd forgotten. Cass didn't think he would *ever* forget about that.

Aaron's jaw dropped. "Seriously? Wow. You know, as someone who had a few threesomes with Tessa and Jay, I'm just going to say it: you missed out."

Yeah, Cass fucking knew that.

Aaron's gaze settled on Tessa, their lips turning up in a smile. "She would've loved you just as much back then. Anyway, Rhys wasn't a great brother or friend, but he wasn't as bad as their parents at least." Aaron's blue eyes darkened, their mouth settling into a thin line. "She's never admitted it, but I'm pretty sure they were abusive. There are a few of her songs that allude to it, and I saw bruises on her a few times —before she met Jay, so I can't blame *those* bruises on him."

It took a second for Aaron's words to sink in but, when they did, Cass looked up and saw the same shock on River's face that he felt. "She told us that Jay never hurt her physically," River said, quietly, gripping the edge of Tessa's blanket.

Aaron sighed, their shoulders slumping. "Shit. She mentioned she'd talked to you and I hoped she'd finally admitted it to someone. I've tried to get her to talk about it I don't even know how many times, but she was always adamant that she was just clumsy. As if being clumsy was enough to put her in the hospital with broken ribs and a concussion," Aaron growled.

Cass's heart turned icy, anger chasing the cold as it spread through his veins. River's eyes were thunderous; he looked ready to pick Tessa up, tuck her gently in bed, and get on a plane to go hunt Jay down. And Cass would have been right there beside him.

"How long did he…?" River's voice cracked as he trailed off, as if he was unable to form the words *hurt her*; as if saying them out loud made it too real.

"I don't know for sure, but I suspect around three years." Aaron swallowed and Cass recognized the shadows on their face; guilt. "It's my biggest regret that I didn't step in, but I had no idea what to do. I was so worried that if I pushed her to leave, she would stay with him and he'd stop her from seeing me. And everyone else was too scared to step in in case Jay fired them. I called his mom once and told her what I suspected was happening." Aaron took a deep breath. "She believed me, which says it all, I guess. She flew over from Australia without telling them she was coming, and Tessa answered the door with a fractured jaw and tried to blame it on slipping in the shower. We couldn't get through to her, but fuck, I wish I'd tried harder."

He'd fractured her fucking jaw? Cass pushed down the fury. It wouldn't do Tessa any good.

Cass wound his arm around Aaron's shoulders and squeezed. "You're not much older than she is and Jay is… well, Jay."

"And she's so fucking stubborn," River added. "She would never have left until she was ready."

"That's true. I'm glad she has you two. She's happier than she has been in a long time, and I know you're the reason."

"She's not the only one who's happier," Cass said, smiling at River, but his best friend was too busy looking down at Tessa to notice. She let out a sleepy sigh, rubbing her face against his chest, and River pulled the blanket tighter around her, leaning down to press a soft kiss against her hair.

"They look good together," Aaron said, quietly enough that only Cass heard them. He turned to find Aaron looking, not at River and Tessa, but at Cass, with a knowing expression.

"They do," Cass agreed, swallowing. Between Tessa's pastel princess dress, long golden hair, and winding floral tattoos, she really did look like a fairytale princess. And River, dressed in dark green, with his long dark brown hair, beard, and head to toe tattoos, was the dark and twisty prince. They were a perfect match, right down to their careers. Cass loved books, but he'd never been able to understand what writing was like for River the way Tessa could.

"In fact," Aaron continued quietly. "I'd say the three of you look pretty good together."

Cass tried not to let himself think about that. Because if River and Tessa were the fairytale prince and princess, where the hell did he fit into the story?

CHAPTER SEVENTEEN

Tessa

Tessa read the text one last time before stepping out of the cab.

> Hey sweetheart, I'm in New York this week. I know you probably don't want to see me, but I would really love the chance to talk to you.

If not for Rhys's letter, she might have said no. She couldn't, wouldn't, open that door again, but she could manage lunch with Jay. She couldn't deny she'd been curious about his lack of trying to contact her since she'd moved to New York. Boundaries never were his strong suit, but she hadn't heard a peep.

She hadn't told River and Cass that he'd texted her. She knew they wouldn't have been okay with her meeting him for lunch, and she knew they would try to talk her out of it. Tessa was already wavering as she stepped onto the street, her stomach churning at the crowd of photographers standing in a huddle outside the fancy sushi place Jay loved, and she might have turned back to the cab if it hadn't sped away so quickly.

The door was within arm's reach before they spotted her. It started with a single shout and then the blinding flashes and clicks that still haunted her nightmares. She pushed through the crowd, forcing air into her lungs, and stepped into the restaurant.

As soon as the door closed behind her, the chatter hushed. She was vaguely aware of people holding up their phones, but her eyes zeroed in on the back booth where, even with his back to the door, she recognized Jay. She walked through the whispers and pointed cameras—so much for keeping this from River and Cass—and paused as she reached the booth.

Jay sprung up as he took her in, reaching for her and dropping his hand. "Hi," he all but whispered as she slid into the booth opposite him.

"Hey."

"I wasn't sure you'd come."

"I wasn't either," she admitted, her heart racing as she took him in. Jay hadn't changed, though he never had in the seven years she'd known him. He had a team of people around him making sure he looked the picture perfect rockstar. He spent hours each day with his personal trainer, and Tessa hadn't realized how hard he was until she was sandwiched between River and Cass. Though Cass was muscular, he wasn't nearly as jacked as Jay. Coupled with River's softness, it was the perfect combination.

Jay's skin was glowing, just a shade more tan than his natural pale, his black hair sitting perfectly in contrast.

"I'm glad that you did," he answered. "I—"

The server interrupted him and they placed their order, not even bothering to check the menu. Jay had dragged them here for sushi every time they'd been in New York and, though she didn't particularly like sushi, she'd never let on. They had their drinks in less than a minute and it didn't escape her notice that Jay had ordered water.

"How have you been? Settling in okay?" he asked, toying nervously with his hands.

She busied herself with a sip of too-hot coffee before answering. It seemed wrong, somehow, to answer truthfully. If she was being honest, she was doing better than she ever was. She had people now, the press had settled, and she'd been writing like crazy. Not to mention, she was regularly having the best sex of her life.

But all of that had started once she and Jay had ended, and she couldn't pretend she didn't feel a whisper of guilt. So instead she just said, "I've been okay, yeah. How have you been? Did you go home and stay with your mom?"

Jay was quiet, running his finger around the rim of his glass. "I didn't stay with my mom, no," he said, finally. He took a steadying breath and looked up, his blue eyes wary. "I, uh, I went to rehab."

Surprise rippled through her, and she fought to keep her face neutral. In all the years she had known him, Jay had never admitted to having a drinking problem. *"I don't drink that much, Tessa. I have a lot going on,"* he would shout, whenever they spiraled into an argument about his alcohol consumption. By the end, she'd just stopped mentioning it.

For him to have sought help was so far beyond what she expected. She wasn't sure what to say. "That's… Fuck," she said, leaning back. "That's great. How was it?"

His lips lifted into the barest hint of a smile. "It was… Christ, it was hard, but I'm sober now. Six months yesterday, actually."

Her first instinct wasn't to believe him, but, God, she wanted to. It would explain why he'd stayed away, why he was back now. The tears that sprung to her eyes surprised her; she knew she shouldn't be, but she was proud of him. "I'm so fucking proud of you," she said, her voice cracking.

Relief colored Jay's voice as he answered, "Thanks, sweetheart."

She blinked away the tears, unwilling to cry in the middle of the restaurant. Jay took a deep breath. "Tessa, I need to apologize."

"You don't—"

"I do," he interrupted. "The way I treated you… I will never forgive myself for how I hurt you, Tessa."

Tessa closed her mouth, fought the urge to interrupt, to retreat into some kind of void where she wasn't confronted with feelings; Jay's, or her own. She'd read enough to know that this, making amends, was part of the process, and for Jay, she could sit through it without clawing her skin off.

"I need you to know that absolutely none of what happened between us, what I did, was remotely your fault. I loved you so much—I do love you—but I was so bad for you when I was drinking. I had no idea how to love you how you needed." He shook his head, sorrow etched in every line, every freckle on his face.

Tessa blew out a breath and clasped her hands. "Honestly, I don't think I knew how I needed to be loved, Jay. But you... you made me feel safe when I really needed it."

"Until I didn't," he whispered, his eyes like a haunted house. "I hurt you. Fuck, the things I said to you. And that night, after the Grammys..." He rubbed his face and Tessa wondered if the same memory was playing in his mind.

The bathroom door creaked open and Tessa jumped, dropping the bag of ice in the sink with a clatter like dice. Jay's eyes zeroed in on the ice, and then on her cheek, bright red from the cold, swollen and purple from the night before. His face crumpled and Tessa looked away, picking up the ice and tucking the cubes back into the bag.

"I'm sorry," he croaked, his throat no doubt sore from the screaming match that led to the bruise on her cheek.

"It's fine."

"It's not fine, I... fuck, sweetheart, I'm sorry."

She didn't flinch when his arms wrapped around her, when he reached for the bag of ice and held it to her skin. She was perfectly safe when he was sober, and she'd thought she was perfectly safe even when he was drunk and spitting mad. She hadn't expected him to hit her so hard across the face that the momentum threw her to the floor. And she had no idea what to do with it.

"I love you so much, sweetheart. Never again."

She leaned in closer to him, his eyes bloodshot in the bright bathroom lights, and rested her unbruised cheek on his heart. "I love you too."

That had been the first time. It hadn't been the last.

"You didn't mean it. You never meant it," she said quietly, not entirely sure if she was trying to convince him or herself. "It's okay, Jay."

Tessa had lied to River and Cass when they'd asked if he'd hurt her physically. She could just about justify staying through the years of emotional abuse, but there was no part of her that could justify staying for three whole years after he'd started hitting her. She'd sworn to herself after getting away from her parents that she'd never let another person lay a finger on her, but by the time Jay had, she was so broken down she had no idea what leaving looked like.

"It wasn't okay. And I hate that I made you think it was."

She took him in—his eyes were clear, free of bruises from sleepless nights, his hands were steady. For a moment, he looked like the man he'd been when she'd first walked into that writing room at nineteen. "No, it wasn't okay. But... but I forgive you. Okay? I have to. I can't keep carrying around the weight of everyone who's ever hurt me. It's exhausting." Her phone buzzed on the table, Cass's picture flashing on the screen. She declined it and turned it over, though Jay's eyes didn't miss it. "We're good. I mean it."

"Yeah?"

"Yeah."

"Would it be inappropriate to say I missed you?" he asked with a smile and she laughed.

"We were together for seven years. It would be weird if

we didn't miss each other a little." Her phone buzzed again. River this time. She frowned at it, declining the call.

"You can get it if you need to. It's okay," Jay said as their food arrived.

"No, no, it's fine. I just didn't tell them I was going out."

Out for lunch, I'll call later, she wrote in their group chat before turning her phone off. She could only assume that the pictures of her and Jay had surfaced already. Cass had set up a google alert with her name to keep an eye on what was said about her.

Tessa knew they would be mad at her for not telling them she was meeting Jay, and this wasn't the place for that conversation. There was a donut shop on the way home, so she could probably distract River with sugar.

Tessa looked up and noticed Jay's eyes glued to her phone, her lips pursed. *Oh boy.* She cleared her throat, stealing his attention back. "I made some friends." She gestured to the phone. "River and Cass live in the apartment next door. River is an author and Cass is a model, and they're... really nice," she finished lamely. She didn't know why she was trying to make Jay like the sound of them. They would never *ever* meet, as far as she was concerned. She wasn't convinced River wouldn't end up back in prison if they did.

"That's good. Really good," Jay lied through his teeth, the shadows in his eyes betraying exactly what he'd thought upon seeing their pictures on her phone. Old habits died hard, and Tessa's heart raced at the sight of those shadows.

"Aaron and I have been hanging out a lot, too," she added hurriedly, trying to change the subject. She wasn't lying. She and Aaron actually were hanging out outside of their writing sessions. They'd had coffee dates and Aaron had even come over to the apartment for a movie night. They got on so well with River and Cass that Cass and Aaron had gone to see a show together (River and Tessa, who'd had little interest in the standup gig, had taken full advantage of an entire night to themselves.)

Jay cleared his throat and forced a smile on his face. "That's good. They seem to be settling in well."

"Yeah, their studio is amazing. So, are you staying in New York or going back to London?" she asked Jay as their lunch plates were cleared away and the server left behind dessert menus in their place.

"I'm not sure. I like New York, but it's kind of exhausting. It would be easier for work, though."

"You could always…" Tessa trailed off as a shadow loomed over them. A familiar citrus and sandalwood scented shadow. She squeezed her fists in frustration before looking up. *Overprotective busy bodies.*

Cass *almost* flinched at the glare she leveled him, but flashed her the same lazy grin she'd become a pro at pretending didn't make her heart fucking flutter. "Hey, princess."

"Hi. What are you doing here?" she asked, shortly, and his lips twitched in amusement.

"You're not answering your phone. We were worried."

"I texted you."

"Just wanted to check on you."

She took a deep breath. "Jay, this is Cass. Cass, Jay."

"Tessa's told me so much about you, it's nice to—" Jay cut off, frowning. "Have we met? You look so familiar."

"Cass is a model," Tessa reminded him, but Jay shook his head.

"No, it's not that…" Jay's eyes lit up. "Madison Square Garden, four or five years ago, right? You came to the meet and greet, and we were talking when that guy tried to grab me."

Tessa couldn't hide the surprise from her face as she looked up at Cass. Guilt shone in his eyes. "You never told me that."

"It never came up," Cass replied, shoving his hands in his pockets.

"I told you about him," Jay cut in. "Remember? It was the night before we flew to Italy for the EMAs."

Tessa remembered vividly. She'd been waiting in Jay's dressing room when his security team had come to usher her away. They took security threats, even if they were just grabby fans, seriously. Jay told her on the drive back to their hotel all about the guy he'd wanted to bring back with them. It wasn't unusual for them to invite a third into the bedroom, but fans were generally off limits, given the security risk.

Tessa gaped at Cass. "I didn't even know you were a fan." When they'd met, Cass had mentioned being a fan of her writing, and of Aaron, but he hadn't mentioned Jay at all.

"I *was* a fan," Cass replied, heavily exaggerating *was* before turning to Jay with a cold smile. "Tessa's told me a lot about you too." Jay's expression quickly turned wary, and Tessa couldn't blame him. Cass could be intimidating when he wanted to be and the sight of him towering above Jay, rain glistening on his skin below the spotlights, made her mouth a little dry. Even if she was a little pissed off at him for showing up at the restaurant.

"I'm just going to run to the restroom," Jay said, and Tessa shot him a grateful and apologetic smile as he escaped the booth.

Cass slid into his vacant seat, and Tessa growled at him. "What do you think you're doing here? And why the fuck didn't you tell me about the Jay thing?"

He reached across the table to snag her hand. If she had even the slightest idea of how to stay mad at him, she might have pulled away, but she melted into his touch. "Princess, we were worried. What else were we supposed to do when you didn't answer your phone?"

"You could have tried trusting me."

He raised an eyebrow at her. "Kind of hard to do when you didn't tell us and we had to find out you were going to lunch—with a man who has physically hurt you in the past —from Twitter."

Tessa sucked in a breath and sat back as his words resonated. "I never told you that."

Cass winced. "Fuck. No, you didn't. I shouldn't have said that. I'm sorry. I'm just worried."

"How did you know?"

He turned over her shaking hand and traced her lifeline with his finger. "Aaron mentioned it." At Tessa's frown, he added, "Did you think no one knew?"

She knew they did. As hard as she'd tried to lie, Tessa knew no one had bought her flimsy excuses for the bruises and broken bones. It was easier to pretend than to ask for help. No one had ever stepped into help with her parents; there was nothing to suggest anyone would help with Jay.

Sure, Aaron had tried to talk to her about it, but Jay could have—would have—ended their career in a heartbeat if he'd known Aaron had even suggested Tessa leave.

Even Jay's mom, who had treated Tessa like a daughter since their first meeting, had tried her best to help. When Tessa had been unwilling to talk, Sharon Hutchison had made no effort to hide her disappointment in her son. Tessa didn't know what she'd said to him, but Jay had treated her better for all of a week after his mom left before Tessa had been photographed in a coffee shop and he'd decided she was smiling too much at the barista. Her fractured jaw hadn't even healed before she was back at the hospital with a broken rib.

Tessa didn't know how to answer Cass, so she just shrugged and Cass cursed, sliding out of the booth and in beside her, wrapping her in his arms. "I'm sorry, princess. I didn't mean to bring all this up. I just… I panicked when I saw you were with him. River did too."

She let her head fall onto his shoulder with a sigh. "I'm sorry. I should have told you I was coming. I'm fine though, I promise. We're in a perfectly public place, as evidenced by the fact you heard about it on Twitter, and it's just lunch."

Cass frowned but nodded. "What are you doing here, anyway?"

"Can we just talk about it when I get home? And about you keeping shit from me too."

Home meaning her apartment, for her *and* River and

Cass these days. Home had become synonymous with wherever the three of them were together, and more often than not, that was curled up under piles of blankets on her couch or in her bed, reading or watching movies. Sometimes, these days, several days would go by without them even stepping foot into their apartment.

Footsteps echoed, and Jay reappeared. Cass gave her one long, lingering look before standing. "Yeah, okay. We'll talk at home." He leaned down to press a searing kiss to her forehead and gently brushed her cheek with his thumb. Tessa's stomach did somersaults. "Just keep us updated, yeah, princess?"

"Yeah." She nodded and watched Cass walk out. He looked back as he neared the door and smiled when he caught her eye. She smiled back, waving, and turned to Jay. "Sorry about that. They can be… protective."

He picked up his water glass and sipped slowly. "Just friends?" he asked quietly. His voice was completely void of emotion, but Tessa knew him well enough to know he was upset and trying to hide it.

She swallowed. Outbursts had often followed that tone, when he could no longer keep his emotions in check. "I don't think we're at the point where we can talk about that kind of thing," she replied carefully. She could have said yes, could have assured him they were just friends, but that didn't feel wholly accurate.

Jay nodded but said nothing, scanning his dessert menu. Tessa knew he wouldn't order dessert—he never did—but she mirrored him just for something to do.

"I didn't just ask you to meet me to apologize," he said, causing Tessa to jump after a moment of taut silence.

She set her menu down and found him staring at her. "Oh?"

"Tessa, I love you—"

"Jay," she interrupted, but he held up a hand and, though she hated herself for it, she closed her mouth.

"Hear me out. You're the love of my life, sweetheart, you know that. We've been through so much together. We can't just let it all go to waste. I'll do anything—whatever it takes to make you trust me again." He reached into his pocket and pushed the ring she'd last seen when she'd pulled it off her finger and thrown it at him towards her. "Say yes, Tessa."

She stared at the ridiculous diamond, glinting under the light. She'd always hated the ring. It was too big, too flashy, and nothing like she would have ever picked for herself. But for a while, at least, she'd loved everything it represented. She was going to have a family again, even if it was just her and Jay. Sure, she'd always wanted kids, but she wouldn't risk having them with a man like her dad. She would have been content, just the two of them.

She reached for the ring, weighing it in her palm. How had she been so delusional about the false promises it offered for so long?

She set it back down and pushed it back to him. "That isn't what I want. I don't want to try again."

He blanched, balling his hands into fists so hard they turned white. "Because of him?"

Tessa leaned back from the table before answering, her

heart thudding. "Partly, yes. And also partly because of River and Aaron. But mostly because of me moving here, getting some distance and realizing that I deserve to be treated with a bit of respect, Jay. I deserve to go through my life without being scared to say the wrong thing in case I make you mad. I thought…" Her voice cracked, and she looked away, holding back tears. "I thought you were the best thing that ever happened to me because you loved me and you took me away from my parents. And maybe at first that was all true, but by the end, I was completely broken down. I'm doing better than ever now, and I'm not willing to risk that."

"But you're my person," Jay said, and for the first time in all the time she'd known him, he sounded small.

She shook her head. "No, I'm not. I'm not your person, or my parents' person, or anyone else's. I'm *my* person."

"Tessa—"

"Can I get you folks any dessert?" They both started at the server's cheery voice, but Tessa wasn't one to look a gift horse in the mouth.

She grabbed her purse. "Actually, I was just leaving. Thank you for lunch."

She stood, but Jay reached out and grabbed her wrist, his grip tight. "I'm not going to stop trying to get you back."

"Let go of me. Please." She hated how her voice wavered, but it worked. She held her arm to her chest. "Jay, we're done. I mean it. Please, for once, respect that."

CHAPTER EIGHTEEN

Tessa

She fled before he had the chance to grab her again, through the restaurant full of rubberneckers and into the throng of photographers outside. She hardly breathed until she was safely in a cab.

"Brooklyn," she said, when the driver asked her where to, rattling off Aaron's address without a second thought. She didn't even know if they were home, but she couldn't face River and Cass yet. She knew she had to talk to them, but her thoughts were far too muddled.

The sky was a brilliant orange by the time she jumped out of the cab and knocked on Aaron's door. She breathed a sigh of relief at the sound of thundering footsteps.

"Hey, T." Aaron's smile was full of sympathy as they bundled her out of the frosty night and into their apartment.

"I'm sorry I didn't call, I just… I just needed to talk."

"You don't need to call. We're friends," Aaron replied

with a shrug, as if it was the most natural thing in the world. "Come on, I'll make tea."

They didn't speak again until they settled on Aaron's cushy bean bags with steaming mugs of chamomile tea in hand.

"Probably a stupid question, but are you okay?"

Tessa sighed, but nodded, drawing her knees up to her chest. "Yeah, I am. A little shaken, but fine." She sipped at the scalding tea. "He says he's sober, six months. He went to rehab apparently."

Aaron nodded appreciatively. "Good for him." They tilted their head, a sandy curl falling across their forehead. "Do you believe him?"

Tessa groaned, rubbing her face. "I don't know. I want to," she replied. "But it doesn't matter anyway. It's not enough."

"No. It's not."

"Everyone knew, right? How he treated me?" she asked, the question spilling out before she could decide if she really wanted to know.

Aaron said nothing for a moment, the rush of Brooklyn traffic the only sound. "Yeah," they said, finally. "Everyone knew. We all knew."

Tessa sucked in a breath that sounded more like a sob.

"It's my biggest regret, you know," Aaron continued. "Not calling him out on it. I knew you wouldn't talk to me about it, knew the best I could help you was by helping you get it out in your songs, but Jay… I spent so much time in the studio with him. I should have said something. You deserved someone in your corner. I'm sorry."

Tessa's voice felt stuck in her throat. She swallowed, tears threatening her eyes again. "He would have ruined you. All it would have taken would have been one phone call and your career would have been over. He had, *has*, so much power." Aaron was only a few years older than she was, still in the early years of their career and not long out as non-binary. They had everything to lose.

Only once had someone stepped in to defend her from his vicious drunken rants. One of Jay's drivers, an older man named George, had literally stepped between them one night when Jay was drunkenly brandishing an empty bottle at her. He'd taken her to the staff apartment, where Jay's security stayed, and made her hot chocolate.

The next day, Jay had fired him without any kind of severance pay. Tessa had squeezed his address out of one of the other drivers and written him a check herself. It wasn't enough—he would never work as a driver again—but it was something. Jay found out what she'd done the morning of the Grammys and accused her of cheating on him. That night was the first time he hit her.

So she understood why no one else had stepped in, but it still stung.

"I don't blame you," she assured Aaron. "I'm just so mad at myself for staying for so long. Besides, you've always been there when I needed you to be." Aaron had been there for every late night, every early morning, since long before Jay was in the picture. On the nights they'd let her stay with them because she'd known what would happen if she went home; the mornings after when she couldn't focus enough to write, when she could still feel her dad's hands, still hear her mom telling her to be quiet, and Aaron didn't question her, just let her sit with them and stare into space until she was ready.

And with Jay, when Tessa had needed to get out of the penthouse and write her feelings down, Aaron's door had been open. She'd even stayed with them for three months when she was twenty-three, after finding out Jay had been cheating on her for a second time and calling it quits. Of course, Jay hadn't had to try too hard to win her back, and Aaron hadn't once made her feel like shit for going back to him.

And then there was the abortion. She and Aaron had never talked about it, but they'd shown up without hesitation when Tessa had been doubled over in pain with no one else to call. They hadn't judged her, just held her hand and read through the side effects of the pill, assuring her it was normal and would pass soon. They'd kept her secret, and to this day, Jay had no idea that they'd almost been a family of three. But Tessa had been the child of an addict, flinching every time she heard footsteps nearing her bedroom door late at night. She refused to repeat the cycle.

Aaron nudged her with a slipper- covered foot. "He made himself your whole world. I know your family was just as bad, but he took you away from them and instead of getting you help and encouraging you to build a new support network, he kept you completely isolated.

"You know, I tried to come over after Rhys went to the press. A few times. I figured that, even if you didn't want to talk, it might help to write with someone you were used to writing personal shit with. Jay said no, every time. He said you weren't ready. And maybe he genuinely thought he was doing what was best for you, but I didn't see you for eight months after you moved in with him, and by the time I did, it was like you'd turned off any bit of yourself that might be used against you."

Tessa frowned, trying to think back to those months, but they were foggy. She'd been distraught over what Rhys had done, but so determined not to show it, she'd made herself cold. "I don't remember that," she admitted. "But for so long I just trusted he would always do what was best for me."

"You deserve that," Aaron told her, a knowing smile on their face. "And there are people who will always do what's best for you, so maybe let them in, yeah?"

"Oh, it's not like that—"

"Really?" Aaron drawled. "You're telling me the sudden surge of sexy love songs you've been writing is just a coincidence?"

Tessa laughed. "You have me there. It doesn't matter, though. It's not… we can't."

"Why not? They're pretty amazing, T. And clearly crazy about you."

"I—they?" Tessa asked, blinking at Aaron in confusion. "I mean, yeah, there's something between River and me." She had no reason not to tell Aaron that she and River were sleeping together; they weren't shy about sex. She and Aaron had traded plenty of hook up stories over the years. Hell, Aaron had joined Tessa and Jay in bed for more than one drunken night before things with Jay had gone south and he'd grown jealous of how close the two of them were. But this thing with River, whatever it was, felt too fragile to put out into the open; she just wanted to keep it to herself for a little while longer.

"Yeah, obviously there's something between you and River, but I have eyes. I can see how you look at Cass," Aaron pointed out, rolling their eyes.

"I don't look at Cass as anything more than a friend," she protested, but it sounded weak even to Tessa's ears.

"We've been friends for ten years," Aaron said. "And you've never looked at me like you look at either of them. You look at them like…"

"Like what?"

"Like you used to look at Jay before he turned into such a dick."

That was fucking dangerous. Things between the three of them were so new; so delicate. If Aaron had noticed her looking at them both like that, had River and Cass? She had to get a handle on her feelings before she fucked this up and lost them.

"They're good people," Aaron interrupted her racing thoughts. "They're not like Jay."

"I didn't know Jay was like Jay at first either," Tessa pointed out. "He was perfect at the beginning."

"Jay was a forty-three-year-old rockstar who could have had anyone he wanted when you met, and he fell in love with a vulnerable nineteen-year-old desperate to get away from her family. Jay was *always* like Jay," Aaron said gently, and Tessa's heart clenched painfully. "I'm not saying he didn't love you—I know he did—but he was never a good guy. Not really."

Despite the distance, despite how they'd ended, Tessa couldn't wrap her head around it. She couldn't have been wrong about him the whole time. "I know what he did to me was wrong. I know how he treated me was… awful. So why can't I see it like you do? Why can't I hate him? Why am I still trying to defend him?"

Aaron considered her, opening and closing their mouth as if reconsidering their next words. They sighed, squaring their shoulders. "How old were you and Rhys when your parents started abusing you?"

Tessa flinched involuntarily at the word *abused*. She knew that's what it was—with Jay and her parents—but hearing it out loud… She'd never told Aaron about her parents; she'd never told anyone about her parents. If Jay knew or suspected, he'd never let on, but Tessa had long suspected Aaron had figured it out through her lyrics.

Six years had passed since she'd last seen her parents; they couldn't get to her anymore. She didn't want to talk about it, but Aaron already knew and they were still here. Confirming it wouldn't change anything.

"We were eight," she said eventually, squeezing her nails into her palms. "But it was just me. Never Rhys."

She watched the implications that went along with the knowledge that Tessa's parents had only abused their daughter sink into Aaron, watched them swallow it down as their face drained of color. They rubbed their eyes. "Fuck. Well, the first couple of years with Jay, after you stopped speaking to your family, that was probably the first time you'd felt safe in years, right?"

Tessa nodded. Though she'd moved out at eighteen, her parents had demanded a key. Even her apartment hadn't been a safe place, but Jay's penthouse had.

"There's probably a part of you that will always be grateful that he took you away from them," Aaron reasoned. "Even though you know how it turned out, he still gave you that."

"I guess," Tessa mumbled. She hadn't been looking for someone to save her from her parents, but Jay had given her a space to get away from them. She looked up at Aaron, her stomach in knots. "You told River and Cass that Jay…" She took a shaky breath. "That he hurt me?" She stumbled over the words, saying it out loud for the first time.

Guilt flashed across Aaron's face. "I'm sorry, I didn't mean to. I was talking about your parents and it just slipped out and—"

"It's okay," she assured them. "When did you tell them?"

"After the open mic."

Over a week. They'd known for over a week, and they hadn't treated her any differently. They weren't disgusted by her or ashamed of her. River hadn't treated her like some breakable, fragile thing in bed. Nothing had changed.

Tessa breathed a sigh of relief. "Thank you," she told Aaron, who blinked in surprise. "I don't think I would've been able to tell them myself, and I'm glad they know."

"It'll get easier to open up to them. Give yourself time, T." Aaron stood and held out a hand to pull her up. "Now go home and put them out of their misery. You know they're probably pacing, worried sick about you."

"True. Thank you," she said, pulling Aaron into a hug. "For everything. Even if you couldn't call Jay out, you were the closest thing to safe I had for a long time."

But now, she had more than just Aaron waiting for her at home.

CHAPTER NINETEEN

River

He was going to wear a hole in the fucking hardwood if she wasn't home soon. He needed a drink, and he needed to wrap his arms around Tessa and never let her go. Not in that order.

"Sit down, River. She'll be home soon."

He spun on Cass, almost toppling a miniature Christmas tree as he did. "How are you so calm about this?"

Cass sighed and held a hand out for him. He took it and allowed Cass to tug him onto the couch. "I'm not calm, not even a little, but she's an adult, and I trust her. She's in a public place and he won't touch her with the press looming over them. We have to trust that she knows what she's doing."

River ran his hands through his hair with a groan. "I do trust her. He's the problem."

"Yeah," Cass agreed with a weary sigh. "I wonder how this even—"

A key rattled in the door and River was on his feet in a flash as it swung open and Tessa appeared. He flicked his eyes over her quickly, settling on her face and breathing only when she appeared fine.

"I brought donuts," she said, holding up a tote bag, but he hardly heard her, enveloping her in a hug instead. "Whoa, picking me over sugar? How far we've come," she joked breathlessly.

"You're okay?"

She pulled away and nodded through a deep breath. "As I'm sure Cass has already told you, I'm *fine*," she grumbled, rolling her eyes. She moved past him, but he snagged her hand, threading their fingers together as she went, just so he was touching her. She glanced down at their clasped hands and squeezed.

What was wrong with him? Sure, he'd been worried about Tessa seeing Jay, but she was fine. He could see that she was fine, physically, and she didn't seem tense or sad or anything remotely worrying, so why couldn't he stop touching her?

She didn't seem to mind, at least, leaning into him when they sank into the couch beside Cass. He looped his arms around her, a hand resting on her ribs so he could feel the steady beat of her heart. The other settled on her thigh and he felt her heart racing at the touch.

She opened the box of donuts and Cass took one, but River declined, because that would involve removing his hands from her and he was, apparently, an unhinged fucking mess. She frowned at him, but set the donuts on the table.

They did smell fantastic, like brown sugar and cinnamon and chocolate.

"Okay," she began, leveling them each with a stare. "While I agree that I should have let you know before I went out with Jay, and I promise to keep you updated in the future, I need you to trust that I know how to keep myself safe. This," she said, gesturing to them, "can't happen again. I'm an independent adult, and I have been since I was eighteen. I love that you care so much, but this level of overprotectiveness might be a little much."

Cass nodded, dusting sugar from his jeans. "I'm sorry for showing up today, and for the… four phone calls. We trust you."

They both looked at River, who grunted in agreement. Tessa laughed, the sound sending the butterflies in his stomach wild. "I'll take it." She turned to Cass. "Why didn't you tell me you were a fan of Jay?"

Cass ran a hand over his head, a sheepish expression on his face. "I wasn't sure how. At first, I didn't want you to think I only wanted to be your friend because of him. But then when you told us what he was like…" Cass blew out a long breath. "It felt like it was too late to bring it up then."

Tessa said nothing for a moment, her face not betraying how she felt about Cass being such a big fan of Jay.

"I've never liked him, if it helps," River offered.

A smile flitted across Tessa's lips. "Don't be a kiss-ass." She sighed before relaxing. "It's fine, Cass. Really. I mean, it's really fucking wild that we almost had a three-some a few years ago—" River had forgotten about the time Cass was propositioned at a meet and greet until he'd mentioned it to Aaron. It hadn't even occurred to him that the *girlfriend* Jay had mentioned was Tessa. His mouth went dry as an image of Cass's lips brushing across Tessa's skin filled his head. "—but I can't be mad that you didn't tell me when I'm not exactly Miss Forthcoming. It's not like I told you I was going today," Tessa continued.

"How did this even come about? You haven't been talking to him, have you?" Cass asked, frowning.

She rolled her neck before answering Cass's question and River's eyes were drawn to the small marks, invisible if you didn't know to look for them, left behind by his teeth the day before. "He texted me a few days ago and asked if I'd meet him for lunch."

River's eyes snapped to hers. "And you just said yes?"

"Yes," she continued carefully. "He wanted to apologize for everything that went down and—"

"Like an apology is going to make up for him hurting you."

Tessa glared at him. "Can I finish a fucking sentence?"

He met her glare until Cass nudged them both and said, "Play nice."

River looked away first, knowing Tessa was too stubborn to do so. "Sorry," he grumbled.

She leaned closer into him. "He went to rehab. That's where he's been since we broke up. He's six months sober, he's doing well."

Cass whistled. "That's impressive. Makes sense that he'd want to make amends."

"Being drunk isn't an excuse for what he did to you."

River frowned at the thought of anyone laying a hand on her.

"No, it's not, of course it's not. But making amends is part of the process, and I owed him that."

Owed? She owed him nothing. "He *abused* you, princess."

She flinched at the word and fuck if that didn't make River see red. How many times had she flinched because of Jay?

She took a deep breath. "Yes. He did, and that was wrong. But I forgive him."

Cass's dropped jaw was the only reason River realized he hadn't misheard her. "You don't think forgiveness is a step too far?" Cass asked gently.

She shrugged. "Maybe, but I never forgive anyone and it's fucking exhausting. I'm tired. I'm so tired. I'm trying."

"*This* is when you choose to try forgiveness?"

"Yes," she said, simply.

"So what, that's it? You're getting back together?" The words left River's mouth before he could think them through and they sounded bitter, curdled, even to his own ears. Cass didn't even try to hide his raised brows.

Tessa's eyes flicked to his face, as if searching through the shadows that lived there. "No." She shifted. "He wants to. I don't. I made that very clear to him."

The relief that flooded him was… problematic. He leaned back and ran his gaze over her. There were smudges of purple below her wary eyes. She hadn't been sleeping well since her brother's letter arrived. If forgiving Jay brought her peace, that couldn't be a bad thing. Sure, he wanted to rip the asshole limb from limb but, considering he would likely never be in the same room as him, he could push it down.

"You're sure you're okay?" he asked, and she nodded.

"I went to Aaron's after I left Jay and talked everything through. It helped." She took a deep breath. "And I'm sorry that I lied and told you he never hurt me physically." Tessa stumbled over the words, her cheeks flushing. "It's just really fucking embarrassing to think about how long I stuck around after the first time; how many excuses I made for him. I was so delusional." Tessa rolled her eyes, as if she was more mad at herself than she was at Jay. River had to bite his tongue.

Aaron had been scant with the details of Jay's abuse, but they'd told River and Cass enough to form a devastating picture. So many people had failed her, and even after walking away, she still blamed herself.

"You're not the one who has anything to be embarrassed about," Cass said softly. Tessa opened her mouth to protest, but snapped it closed, frowning.

"Maybe not. I don't like to talk about it," Tessa admitted, shifting uncomfortably.

"This is progress, princess. Proud of you," Cass said, leaning in and pulling them both into a hug. "I'm going to jump in the shower and then we should do takeout and a movie."

"Sounds good."

Cass slipped into the hallway, closing the door softly behind him, and Tessa twisted around to look at River. He knew what was coming and couldn't meet her eyes. "River."

He said nothing. "River, look at me." She reached up to cup his jaw and looked at her, her amber eyes burning. "What's going on? Beyond the whole being worried about my safety thing, what's going on?"

He shrugged and said nothing, even though he knew exactly *what* was going on. The sex between them had been phenomenal. They were closer than ever, and it wasn't enough. He needed more of her, all of her.

"Are you... were you really worried Jay and I would get back together?" she asked softly. "Are you jealous? Is that what this is?"

He looked away, shame coursing through him. "I have no right to be jealous. I have no... no claim over you or whatever. And I don't want to be like him. We're just friends, I know that."

She was quiet for a moment, the air in the room thick with tension, clawing. "We're not just friends. I... I don't know what we are, but even if we weren't sleeping together, we wouldn't be just friends. We're best friends, right?" She stumbled over the words, her voice cracking, and River cursed himself for making her question it.

"Of course, princess. We are best friends, always will be," he assured her, holding her close to him. "That's not... that's not what I mean."

"No, I know," she said with a heavy breath. "Look, we agreed not to pretend the feelings aren't here, right? Well, they're here. And you have plenty of claim over me, you know. I'm not interested in anyone else, it's you and me, okay? We're doing whatever it is we're doing and I'm not just going to run off with someone else."

Tessa said everything with conviction; stubbornness lined every word out of her mouth, just daring you to contradict her. He hadn't realized how much he fucking loved that until she was talking about them, them as a *we*.

He lowered his lips to hers and finally kissed her. It felt like hours had passed since she'd walked through the door, but everything disappeared when he tasted her. Fuck the donuts; Tessa was all he needed. She smiled against his lips. "I take it that's okay with you, then?"

"Yeah," he breathed. It wasn't what they wanted, not really, but for now, it was everything they could have and he would relish in it. "And for the record, I'm not going to run off with someone else either."

"Of course you're not. Who else is going to bake for you as much as I do *and* volunteer to be your guinea pig for all the sex scenes you're writing?"

She squealed as he rolled her onto her back and straddled her hips, nibbling at her neck. He kissed her throat, her jaw, her lips, and pulled back enough to look into her face. "Tessa, you know how I care about you, right? I love what we're doing, but I don't want you to think this is *all* there is between us."

She nodded and answered, breathlessly, "I know. I care about you too." She brushed a thumb across his lip and he leaned down to kiss her.

"Good, because I'm crazy about you, princess." He ran a finger down her torso, brushing between her legs. Her thighs parted, her dress riding up, and she groaned.

"You're not like him, by the way."

"What?" He could hardly think with her below him.

"You said you didn't want to be like Jay. You're not. When he got jealous, it scared me. But when you're jealous… it's kind of hot." She gave him a wicked smile.

"Just kind of?" He hooked his thumbs in the waistband of her tights and she opened her eyes to watch him, her chest rising and falling. She bit her lip.

"Cass could come back in at any moment."

But she made no move to stop him as he pulled the tights down her legs and tossed them to the side. If anything, her breathing seemed to become shorter at the thought of him walking in.

River smiled against her calf as he littered kisses up her legs. He brushed a kiss over her underwear and she covered her mouth with her hand to stop herself from crying out.

He kneeled between her thighs and she looked up at him with dark eyes like molten gold. He rolled his hips against her and she bit her lip, her head falling back. "Tell me you don't want anyone else, princess."

"I don't… Fuck," she panted at the friction of his jeans against her underwear. "I don't want anyone else, only you."

He leaned down to lick her neck and smiled. "No one else?"

"No," she gasped.

"Not even Cass?"

"I—what?"

She looked at him with wide eyes, and he laughed. Her eyes fluttered, as if she could feel the vibrations. "I see how you look at him, princess, feel your heart race when he touches you."

He dragged his teeth across her throat, and she squirmed beneath him. "Oh my God, fuck…"

"Tell me, baby, what do you see in that beautiful imagination of yours? Do you imagine being between us, my hands, and his, roaming every inch of you?"

"Yes," she whispered, panting. "Fuck, yes."

He brushed his lips across hers. "Interesting," he murmured. "*Very* interesting."

Through Tessa's ragged breaths, he heard the soft creak of a door opening and released her hands, tugging her back to a seating position and pulling her dress down.

"What are you—" she began, blinking as he turned on the TV and began flicking through the channels. She trailed off as Cass walked through the door, wearing nothing but a towel around his hips.

River fought the urge to smile as she suddenly glued her eyes to the TV.

"Everything okay?" Cass asked, grabbing a drink from the fridge.

"Yeah, all good," River said, twining his fingers with Tessa's. "Right, princess?"

"All good," she said through gritted teeth, as Cass took a seat beside her.

"Great, what are we watching?"

He tossed the remote to Cass. "You choose." River couldn't help but smile as Tessa's eyes betrayed her and fell to Cass's chest.

CHAPTER TWENTY

Tessa

"We haven't even made it outside yet and you already look like Rudolph."

Tessa covered her scarlet nose with one hand—December in New York was no joke—and flipped Cass off with the other. He chuckled and tugged her bobble hat down while River shook his head at them, a fond smile playing on his lips.

"Cheer up, princess, it's Christmas eve," Cass teased.

"Remind me again why we're venturing out into tourist central, and not staying home and watching Christmas movies?"

"Because it's tradition." His dark eyes twinkled in the glittering elevator lights.

Neither River nor Cass had any religious affiliation with Christmas, but there was one thing they loved year round that the holidays made even more interesting: people watching. On one hand, Tessa understood. Living in arguably the busiest city in the world meant that there were always interesting people to watch. On the other hand, when River and Cass had told her about their yearly Christmas Eve tradition of planting themselves at the window seats of a coffee shop on Fifth Avenue to watch the last minute frenzy of Christmas shoppers, she'd questioned their sanity.

She reached up to straighten Cass's scarf and smiled. "Only for you two would I brave Fifth Avenue, you know."

Cass beamed and River pressed a kiss to her already-frozen cheek as the elevator chimed and the doors slid open. If Cass had noticed the increased touching between River and her, he hadn't mentioned it, and Tessa certainly wasn't complaining.

A thick layer of condensation covered the glass doors to their building, the metal handle icy cold. Tessa shivered and pushed her way out onto the street, straight into a large crowd of people who, upon seeing her, began screaming. Cameras flashed and Tessa stumbled backwards into River and Cass, her eyes wide. Strong arms immediately wrapped around her, trying to help her back towards the door, but the press had closed in, circling them.

White noise filled her ears, air escaping her lungs in ragged gasps. She could hardly make out what they were shouting, screaming, over the rushing of her blood, but she heard her name and Jay's, among things like *home wrecke*r, and "*Are you and Jay back together, Tessa?*"

She looked up straight into the lens of the cameraperson standing before her, focusing just enough to hear, "Who are your friends, Tessa? Are you cheating on Jay?"

She looked around at the greedy cameras focused on her

and, worse, River and Cass, and saw red. She reached out and pushed the camera in her face away with such force it slipped from the photographer's hand and they had to stumble to catch it.

"Get the fuck away from us," she growled. She stepped back into whoever was closest to her—River, if the smell of gingerbread was anything to go by—and he pulled her through the throng of people as Cass pushed at them, making a path.

They fell into the lobby, breathless. Thankfully, the elevator was still waiting, and they stumbled in. River immediately tilted her face to his, searching it. "You okay, princess?"

"No," she admitted, counting her breaths to calm them. "I'm fucking furious."

Cass reached out and tapped her nose, his eyes bright. "Fury looks good on you."

"It feels better than curling up in a ball and forgetting how to breathe." She leaned back against the mirrored wall with a sigh. "I'm sorry. I fucked up your Christmas Eve tradition."

"You didn't. Those vultures did," River assured her.

"Yeah, don't sweat it," Cass chimed in. "We'll have an even better day at home, promise. As long as we're together."

And fuck if Tessa's heart didn't soar.

As guilty as she felt for ruining their Christmas Eve, neither Cass nor River seemed particularly upset to be staying home. Tessa poured a bottle of mulled wine (surprisingly difficult to find stateside) into a saucepan to warm and just as she was reaching into the cabinet on her tiptoes, struggling to grasp the glasses, her phone rang shrilly.

"Hey," she answered. River squeezed in behind her and reached above her head for the glasses.

"Hey, are you okay?" Concern colored Aaron's voice. She didn't have to ask how they already knew the press had accosted her. Like Cass, Aaron had set up a google alert for her name years ago, just to keep an eye on what people were saying about her.

"Yeah, I'm—" She faltered as River's hands roamed over her hips, her ass. Shielded from Cass, who had already planted himself beneath a blanket on the couch and had the TV remote in hand, by the kitchen island, River tugged her skirt to the side and brushed the front of her underwear.

"T, are you there?"

She cleared her throat. "Yeah, sorry, the connection isn't great. It must be the weather. But yeah, I'm okay. Thank you for checking. We're just going to stay in." River took the word *in* literally, slipping his hand inside her underwear and pressing a finger lightly to her clit. She bit down on her lip, staring intently at the island.

"That's probably for the best," Aaron replied with a sigh. "This is shit, I'm sorry."

"It is, but it's fine," she replied, hoping she didn't actually sound as breathy as she thought she did.

"Do you think it might be worth looking into security? I still talk to some of Jay's team—I could speak to them and get a recommendation."

"I don't know," Tessa managed, trying to focus on Aaron. River flicked his finger, and she squirmed against him, electricity sparking through her veins. "I'm sure it'll die down. But if it doesn't, I'll think about it."

River withdrew his hand as they said their goodbyes and hung up.

"How does this look?" Cass called from the couch when she put her phone down, and they looked over to the screen, where he had some kind of Hallmark Christmas movie lined up.

"Looks good," she told him, knowing she wouldn't be able to concentrate anyway, thanks to River's fingers. "You're evil," she whisper-hissed, scowling at his shit-eating grin.

"Hmm, I like angry Tessa," he told her with a wink, squeezing her ass before taking the glasses with a clink and heading to the couch.

Tessa took a deep breath and turned away, rummaging around the cabinets for snacks. Her fingers closed on a box of dark chocolate and caramel edibles. She held them up for River and Cass. "Wine and weed: dangerous, or just what we need to make a wholesome Hallmark movie decidedly *less* wholesome?"

"Both," River and Cass said in perfect unison. Tessa laughed and let the cabinet close with a thunk. She tossed the box on the couch but didn't sit down as River patted the seat beside him.

"Wait," she said, crouching by the tree and pulling two matching gifts from the back. She dropped one in each of their laps and they raised their brows at her. "I was going to give you these when we got home tonight, but they're a must if we're having a movie day."

They tore into the packages and laughed as they pulled out the matching Christmas PJs. "These are amazing, princess," Cass told her, immediately pulling off his shirt to swap it for the soft red flannel with his name embroidered on the breast pocket. He stood to change his pants and she turned away, blowing out a breath.

Merry Christmas, indeed.

"I have a set too. I'm going to change," she said and escaped the living room as quickly as her legs would allow.

She discarded her dress and fell back onto the bed with a groan, rubbing her face and wondering how long she could realistically sneak off for during the movie. Just ten minutes alone with her vibrator while they were distracted with the movie would do the trick to get her through the rest of the night... Maybe she should just wait until the edibles kicked —Cass would probably nod off anyway.

The door opened, and soft footsteps padded across the floor. She peered through her fingers to see River, his new PJs slung over his arm. He sank to his knees before her, parting her thighs.

"I'd say I was sorry for teasing, but how about I just make it up to you instead?" he asked, tugging down her underwear and placing soft kisses on her inner thigh.

"But Cass—"

"His dad called, and you know how much he talks. You just have to stay quiet, baby. Can you do that?"

She was quite sure she couldn't do that, but she nodded anyway.

"Or maybe," he continued, sliding a finger inside her and curling it so that her hips jumped off the bed and she had to bite down on her own tongue. "Maybe you want him to hear—to wonder what's going on through here." He added a second finger, massaging the spot that made her see stars. "I bet he'd come to check on us, see what was taking us so long."

Tessa whimpered, and his fingers stilled. He gave her a warning look, his eyes black. She shivered, covering her mouth with her hand, and he curled his fingers again.

"I just know he wouldn't be able to resist tasting you, princess," he murmured before bending his head and circling her clit with his tongue. Tessa bit down on her hand, panting and thrashing beneath him. God, it should be illegal for something to feel this good.

River devoured her like she was his last meal, pulling back only once to growl, "*So fucking sweet.*"

He slid a third finger inside of her and she shattered, tightening around him and shaking. He stroked her gently until she stopped trembling and withdrew his fingers. He kissed her clit, her hip, between her breasts, her throat, branding her, and finally paused at her lips. "Better, baby?"

She hummed in answer, and he laughed. He parted her lips with his tongue, kissing her deeply. "See how good you taste?"

She pushed lightly on his chest until he pulled back and gave him a wicked smile, before bringing his fingers to her mouth and licking each one clean. He groaned, his eyes becoming heavy.

"Not a tease, a promise," she told him. "You can cash in when Cass inevitably falls asleep."

"Don't think I won't," he answered, his voice husky and full of exactly the kind of danger that made her toes curl.

"I'm counting on it." She stretched and stood, winking at him as she strode for the closet.

"You know you're top of the naughty list, right?" River called after her.

Cass was saying his goodbyes by the time they made it back to the living room, and if she looked disheveled, he didn't notice. He tossed his phone carelessly to the side, while River poured the warm wine and pressed a glass into her hand.

"To new traditions," Cass said, holding up his glass. They clinked glasses and Tessa took a long draw of the deep, spicy wine. She grabbed a chocolate from the offered box of edibles, and popped it in her mouth as she sat down, letting it melt on her tongue as she snuggled close to River and propped her feet up on Cass's lap.

Snow fell past the window like powdered sugar, before the woman from the big city had even made it to the same kitschy small town all Hallmark movies seemed to feature. Tessa let the high take her slowly, her head falling onto River's chest, and watched the snowflakes fall.

She wondered if the press were still waiting outside, sacrificing the perfect Christmas Eve with their families for the chance at the perfect picture. Well, as perfect as a picture intended for the front page of a tabloid could be. She almost felt sorry for them in her little blissful bubble.

She looked up, her eyes hazy, and found River watching her instead of the movie. She smiled at him and he brushed her hair out of her face. She felt it fall against her neck, every touch heightened by the alcohol and weed.

Her gaze moved to Cass, who was watching them both with a fond smile. There was no air of suspicion in his eyes that perhaps she and River were closer than they should be, just pure, unadulterated care and love for his best friends.

"C'mere," she said, beckoning him closer. He gently lifted her legs from him and snuggled into her back, throwing an arm around her waist and pulling a blanket over the three of them. As if on autopilot, he reached for Tessa's hand, which was lying on River's chest, feeling his heart beat.

River followed the movement with his eyes and reached up to lay his hand over both of theirs, and Tessa wondered if they could feel the way her heart skipped in her chest.

CHAPTER TWENTY-ONE

Tessa

"Wake up, princess. Santa came."

"I hope he at least took you to dinner first," she grumbled, burrowing further into whoever she was lying face-first on. She opened one eye and squinted at the Black, inkless chest. She was draped over Cass, and River was nestled against her back, his face hidden in the crook of her neck.

His lips brushed her skin, out of sight of Cass, who was practically vibrating with Christmas excitement. She blinked up at Cass's grinning face and chuckled. "This might be the first time I've ever seen you as a morning person."

"Don't let him kid you," River said, pulling away and stretching with a yawn. "It's after ten, and I woke up first."

"But I woke up more festive," Cass added, winking at Tessa and standing up, tugging her from the bed and patting her on the ass before running to the living room, humming jingle bells.

She looked from her ass to River, who was fighting a smile. "I know my experience with friends is pretty limited, but he is more… grabby than friends usually are, right?"

"Oh, yeah," River agreed, beckoning her over and wrapping his arms around her. "But you're also just so fucking grabbable." He proved his point by grabbing her hips and pulling her close. "Merry Christmas, princess."

"Merry Christmas," she murmured, trailing off as his lips touched hers.

"Let's go put Cass out of his misery or he'll start opening presents without us."

Since River and Cass didn't spend Christmas with their parents, they usually spent the day eating takeout and lazing around. Well, Cass did. River usually spent it tapping away at his computer, unable to give himself so much as a single day off for writing. This year was the first day they'd had a real Christmas dinner since Cass's parents moved back to Senegal, and Tessa had gone all out. The UK wasn't well known for their food, but you couldn't beat a British Christmas dinner.

"What was Christmas like for you growing up?" Cass asked later that afternoon, when the wrapping paper had long been ripped from the piles of presents and they were recovering from a mountain of trifle with freshly whipped cream (River had given her the gorgeous sage green mixer she'd been lusting over for weeks, and she had thanked him with extra dessert, which was, of course, his motivation for gifting it.)

"When I was a kid, we usually went to stay with my grandparents in Caerphilly. It was nice, quiet." She shrugged. "That's how I learned to bake—my grandma taught me over the holidays."

"I love your grandma," River said, earnestly, rubbing his belly. He'd not only eaten three servings of trifle, but both he and Cass had eaten two full plates of the roast dinner. She'd never had anyone appreciate her cooking quite so much.

"She was great. My grandparents passed before we moved to the UK, though, so I didn't get to spend as much time with them as I'd have liked. Just holidays. Rhys and I would sing carols at a local nursing home every year. Well, until, you know." He would play piano, she would sing, and the elderly folk would sway in their chairs or waltz in the lights of the Christmas tree.

"I bet Christmas with Jay was a culture shock, huh?" Cass said with a smirk and she laughed, shaking her head.

"You have no idea. Picture twenty-year-old Tessa hiding in the corner at Elton John's Christmas party playing with an old dog who looked about as done with people as I was." It would have been a funnier memory if she hadn't been photographed. The press had branded her antisocial, ungrateful, and had printed several choice words about how women with her body type should avoid wearing such bold colors.

She and Jay had turned the offending articles into confetti and sprinkled them in the fire a few days later.

Cass's phone rang and Tessa took a breath, shaking the cobwebs of nostalgia from her head. Thinking about her past was like forcing herself through a thorny rosebush, leaving behind scratches that lasted for days.

"Princess, come say hey to my parents."

She started and looked up to see River and Cass squeezing into the camera frame, Cass's parents on the other end of a video call.

She tucked herself between them. "Merry Christmas, Mr. and Mrs. King."

"Merry Christmas, darling. And please, it's Melanie and Kurtis," Cass's mom answered with a warm smile. Though Cass was his dad's double, his smile was the mirror image of his mom's, full of sunshine.

Melanie and Kurtis began regaling them with tales of their Christmas day, spent mostly at the hospital Melanie worked at, and Tessa leaned back into River, grateful that Cass, at least, had parents who loved him.

River nudged her with his foot. She looked up, and he mouthed, "*Are you okay?*"

She nodded, however unconvincing it may be, and gathered their empty glasses. She could use another drink. "I'm going to get started on the washing up. It was lovely to see you guys. Merry Christmas." She waved goodbye to Cass's parents and stepped into the kitchen.

She stacked the dishes littering the counter into the dishwasher and poured the dregs of yesterday's mulled wine into a pot to warm. While she waited, she leaned back against the counter, flicking through her phone.

It buzzed with a text from Aaron, who was back in England with their parents:

Emailed you a new draft of Curse Breaker.
I think this is the one.

She rolled her eyes and replied, *Why are you working on Christmas?* Before opening her emails.

Aaron had, indeed, sent her the new draft of the song they were working on for an up-and-coming indie pop duo, but that's not what caught her eye.

(1) Rhys Reid
No Subject
Hey Tessa, Merry Christmas. I don't know if you got my lett...

Tessa locked her phone and dropped it face down on the island, her heart a knot in her stomach. She turned off the burner and set the wine aside, standing on her tiptoes to reach the bottle of whiskey. She took a swig from the bottle, then another, before pouring the wine into River and Cass's cups and taking another mouthful of the amber liquor. It burned as she swallowed, a steady fire in her chest.

When she set the bottle down, River and Cass were staring at her, the video call over. She blew out a breath and carried their glasses to them, pressing them into their hands.

"I..." she began, stumbling over the words. "Rhys emailed me again."

Worry shone on their faces. "Does your family usually reach out over the holidays?" She shook her head at Cass's question.

"Tess—"

"I'm okay," she interrupted River. She was lying, of course, and she knew they knew that, but she didn't want to ruin Christmas. "It's just, fuck, it's been a week, you know? I'm going to go jump in the shower."

She spun on her heels and fled the room before the tears threatening her eyes joined the errant ribbons and pieces of tinsel littering the hardwood.

The burning shower soothed her muscles, hitting each knot in her shoulders, her chest, until her body relaxed. She turned off the water and lathered her body in snickerdoodle scented body lotion, purely because she knew it would drive River crazy.

She let her hair fall from her messy bun and stared at herself in the foggy mirror. Her parents were written all over her face, from the smattering of freckles on her pale skin, to the slight upturn of her nose and full lips, but the stubborn fire that lived in her eyes was all Tessa. She took a deep breath, gripping the counter.

She had made it. She was twenty-six, fiercely independent, with the career she'd always dreamed of… mostly. She had River and Cass and a home to call her own in them. Her family could go fuck themselves, as far as she was concerned. They had no hold on her anymore. She owed them nothing, and she wanted nothing from them. She couldn't, wouldn't, let them smother her flames.

Resolved not to let them ruin the day, she pulled on another soft, oversized, Christmas flannel pajama shirt and matching shorts and sat on the bed to tug matching fluffy knee-high socks over her legs. It *was* Christmas, after all, as if she needed an excuse to luxuriate in the coziness.

River and Cass were speaking softly when she walked into the living room, but they went quiet at the sight of her, twinkling Christmas music echoing quietly around the room from the speakers.

"You okay?" River asked, and she nodded.

"Yeah, I'm good. I'm sorry for... you know."

She turned towards the kitchen, but River's hand closed around her wrist and he tugged her gently until she landed on his lap. She sucked in a breath as she felt him hard beneath her. God, would she ever get enough of him? His dark eyes were full of mischief and hers widened, darting quickly to Cass and back. River wasn't even trying to be subtle. So much for keeping quiet. "Don't apologize, it's okay. We've been talking, princess, and we want to make you feel better."

Tessa opened her mouth before her brain fully processed, and then paused as the words sunk in, her heart going still in her chest. "We?" she asked, with a shaky breath.

She almost jumped out of her skin as Cass placed his hand on her bare knee like a brand. "If you want that."

Fucking hell, she wanted that. As if she hadn't been fighting filthy thoughts of Cass for weeks, feeling greedy for wanting both of her best friends in exactly the way she shouldn't. And maybe it was a terrible idea, but she'd had the week from hell and she'd be damned if she was going to turn down the chance to have her hands all over both of them.

"Yes, um, I, ah, please." She tripped over the words and River chuckled, his breath warm against her neck as he pressed his lips to her skin. Her head fell back, and she groaned at his touch. Cass's grip on her knee tightened and her eyes snapped to his, dark and hazy, with an edge of danger she'd never seen before. One she very much wanted to learn more about.

River turned her so her back was pressed to his chest. While he trailed his lips across her shoulders and down her arm, Cass leaned in and tilted her chin up, gripping it lightly, and she swore she stopped breathing. He stroked his thumb along her jawline and every nerve ending in her body seemed to sit up and take notice.

Her gaze was glued to his full lips, her tongue begging for a taste.

"Princess," he said, commanding her to look up at him. His voice was still soft, still *Cass*, but with an edge she had never been privy to. She'd imagined him to be dominant, though perhaps not as much as River, but it sent a thrill through her bones.

"Yeah?"

"Breathe."

Before she even had time to consider a response, he leaned in and pressed his lips to hers. They didn't bother taking it slow; Tessa's mouth parted and his tongue swept inside, eliciting a moan from her that was lost to the blood rushing in her ears.

If River's kiss was his namesake, full of wild abandon, Cass kissed like the ocean. Deep and dark, like Tessa's tongue was full of secrets and he wanted to devour them one by one.

River's hands stilled at the sounds spilling from her lips

and she vaguely heard him curse as he withdrew from her, as if he had pulled away to watch them.

Cass's hand tangled itself in her hair, and she felt his other reaching out. She realized, through her kiss-drunken haze, a moment later than he was reaching for River as she felt their joint hands settling on her lap.

Tessa had no time to think about how that made her heart flutter, because River stood, gripping her hips and lifting her until her legs were wrapped around Cass's waist. She gasped. Thank fuck for Christmas pajamas, because she could feel *everything* through the thin fabric.

Cass walked backwards into the hallway, holding tight to Tessa's ass with firm hands, kissing her jaw. From her back, River's hands snuck between them, unbuttoning the flannel enough to slip his hand inside and stroke his thumb across her nipple. She groaned his name, and Cass looked up at the two of them, licking his lips.

He kicked the bedroom door open, and they stumbled into the room. River lifted Tessa from Cass as he sat down on the bed, staring up at her with glittering eyes, and reached for the buttons on her flannel, shredding through them like they were made of paper.

"Fuck," he whispered, as River slid the flannel from her shoulders and he took her in. He hadn't seen her in anything less than a tank top, had never seen the tattoos that wound themselves across her torso. He ran a gentle finger across the ink before palming her breasts and closing his eyes, leaning forward to kiss the spot above her belly button.

River's hand slipped inside her shorts and he hummed as he found her drenched and ready for him. He circled her clit with one finger as Cass took her nipple into his mouth with a groan, and Tessa's knees buckled. They felt so fucking *good*. She spiraled faster than she ever had before; the orgasm storming her.

River stepped back a little, and she sank to her knees between Cass's thighs. If she didn't taste him soon, she thought she might explode. She pulled down his pants and her mouth dropped open.

"Fucking hell," she breathed. She'd seen him in sweats enough to know he would be big, but she wasn't expecting the piercing. Somehow, for Cass, it made perfect sense, and she was desperate to feel the gold bar inside her.

She closed her fist around his cock and drew it up the shaft. Expletives tumbled from Cass's lips and he gripped the comforter for dear life as she bent her head and took him in her mouth. She had to stretch to accommodate him and she hummed as she took him in as far as she could, the metal bar cold against the back of her throat.

She opened her eyes to find Cass watching her, his eyes hazy and black. She sat up a little and tugged at his t-shirt until he pulled it over his head.

Tessa had imagined Cass naked more times than she could count, but she hadn't done him justice. She'd seen marble statues less fucking sculpted, and certainly less beautiful.

She twisted to look up at River, who was watching the two of them, his chest rising and falling heavily. She beckoned him closer and pushed down his pajama pants. He'd already discarded his shirt somewhere along the way. She fisted his cock in one hand, Cass's in the other, and sighed contentedly. She leaned her head back into River's hand, licking her lips to make her intentions clear. "I want you to make me," she said, and he smiled her favorite wicked grin, knotting his hand in her hair.

"Your wish is my command, princess," he murmured. "Slap Cass's knee if you need to stop."

She nodded and flashed Cass a smile before taking him in her mouth again. He reached for River's free hand and held it tight as River pushed Tessa's head down, forcing her to take every inch of Cass she could, testing her. When she had reached her limit, he dragged her back slowly by her hair, before pushing her back down on Cass's cock. Curses filled the room. Cass reached for her and she slipped her fingers between his. He squeezed and fuck if she didn't want those fingers around her throat.

With Cass's cock in her mouth, and River's in her hand, this was almost certainly the best Christmas Tessa had ever had.

"Fuck, Tessa," Cass cried as he came, shuddering, his face falling slack. He was so fucking beautiful. She swallowed before River pulled her back, tilting her face up to him and devouring her in a fierce kiss.

When they pulled apart, Cass beckoned them closer, panting, and pulled Tessa to him. She straddled his hips and groaned as his length slid along her; the piercing grazing her clit so perfectly. He pressed a kiss to her lips before looking over her shoulder at River, who moved closer, bending to kiss Cass. He nipped at Cass's lower lip, and he groaned, gripping Tessa's hips so much she thought he might leave bruises behind. She hoped he would.

"Condom?" he asked breathlessly.

Tessa shook her head, perhaps a little *too* enthusiastically. "I'm on birth control."

"Sure?"

"Mhmm," she replied, rolling her hips against him. He cursed and gently smacked her ass while River teased her nipples with one hand, his other stroking her throat. Tessa moaned, spurring Cass on. He lifted her hips, positioning them, and she cried out as he pushed into her.

As big as he was, he was the perfect fit. She fought the urge to roll her hips—she could tell he wanted the control, and she loved it. His hands firmly on her ass, he moved her hips, rising to meet her, hitting her so deep she saw stars with every thrust.

"Fuck, princess, you look so good on my cock," Cass gasped, slapping her ass. His words were her undoing, and she tightened around him, flames burning every inch of her, calling his name. He groaned. "God, your pussy feels amazing."

She was pretty sure she could die happy now that she'd heard Cass say pussy.

River held tight to her throat, his other hand sneaking between them to massage her clit. She let her head fall back against him and sobbed as the sparks of pleasure overtook her.

As she came down from yet another orgasm, she opened her eyes and looked up into River's face. His jaw was slack, his eyes blazing as he watched his best friends. "Please," she begged, and he chuckled, letting go of her and walking to the nightstand.

Cass's movements didn't falter when River walked away, or when he returned with the bottle of lube in hand. For a moment, Tessa saw what looked like a puzzle piecing together in Cass's dark eyes, but the press of River's cock to her ass made her forget how to think.

Cass slowed as River pushed into her, oh so fucking slowly, and they both stilled inside of her, catching their breaths. River leaned over her, taking Cass's hand and pressing a breathy kiss to her neck.

"Okay, baby?"

Okay wasn't even in her wheelhouse anymore. She had never felt so full, literally and figuratively, as she did with them both inside her, with them holding hands. Together like, perhaps, they were always meant to be.

Tessa nodded, and River chuckled. "Words, princess. Tell us you're okay."

"I…" she panted. "More than okay. Fuck."

Cass's lips lifted, and she felt River smile against her shoulder. As if in sync, they moved in perfect harmony. Tessa braced herself, her hands on Cass's chest. They were better than any liquor, any drug, she'd ever tried, a high that kept giving as she stumbled from orgasm to orgasm, the wave cresting so high that she thought she might drown when it finally came crashing down.

But time seemed to still when it began to fall, everything disappearing except the two men wrapped around her, their ragged breaths, Tessa's name falling from River's lips and Cass's shouted curse as the wave crashed over the three of them.

Tessa collapsed on Cass's chest, trembling, and he

stroked a tender hand through her hair while River pressed soft kisses to her spine.

"Come on, princess," he said, pulling her to her feet. Her legs were like jello, so he swept her into his arms and held another out for Cass.

They didn't even turn the bathroom lights on as they stepped into the steaming shower, the glow from the bedroom illuminating the room just enough for them to lather each other in cookie-scented soap. Cass worked his fingers into Tessa's neck, massaging the knots away, while she soaped River up, and by the time they were clean and dry, she could barely keep her eyes open.

They fell into bed together, as they did most nights. Tessa didn't know when the right side of the bed had become Cass's, the left River's, but she had never felt safer, happier, than she did in the middle.

CHAPTER TWENTY-TWO

Cass

Cassian King was a fucking idiot. *When had he become so oblivious?*

There wasn't a shred of awkwardness at the breakfast table that morning, but there wouldn't be, would there? Though he knew that River and Tessa had hooked up before they'd met officially, they'd clearly been sleeping together again for a while. He hadn't missed the signs; he just hadn't realized what they meant.

He and River had slept together only once since Tessa had moved in, yet River had been calm as ever and Cass couldn't remember the last time he seemed so... light. He'd assumed River was just happy to have Tessa in their lives.

Tessa was harder to read; Cass still wasn't sure how many of her smiles were genuine and how many were simply armor. She seemed happier and more comfortable with them than she had been when they'd met, at least. She was having fewer nightmares and was, occasionally, opening up to them about her past.

However things had happened between her and River, it seemed to be working well in both of their favors. They were perfectly relaxed at the table; Tessa with tea in one hand, a book in the other, and a sleepy smile on her face at whatever was happening between the pages. River's eyes were bright and glued to his phone, his lips silently mouthing the article he was reading. And Cass was... confused.

He couldn't deny that he felt lighter, less on edge, than he had lately. Sure, good sex did that, but last night... He'd had a lot of sex in his life, several threesomes—even some with River—and nothing had ever come close. There was no awkwardness, no fumbling, just three people who fit together perfectly. The energy had been nothing short of golden and he had been struck with the notion to grasp onto them and never let go. It was fucking terrifying.

Tessa had fallen asleep in their arms, River had taken his hand and done the same, and Cass had lain awake for hours, his heart racing, wondering what the hell was happening to him. It wasn't something he was willing to deep dive into right now.

Besides, he had questions. He cleared his throat. "I have a question."

"Hmm?"

"How long have you two been sleeping together?"

River's eyes snapped to his, wide and somewhat panicked. Tessa looked up slowly, her face giving nothing away.

"Well, it's a—" she began, but River interrupted.

"Why would you… What are you even… Fuck." He choked on the words and Tessa turned to stare at him, confusion on her face.

"What the fuck?"

He covered his face with his hands. "Yeah, I'm shit at lying."

Tessa laughed, throwing her hair back. "Why are you trying to lie? We agreed to tell him when he figured it out."

"I don't know. I panicked."

She shook her head and rolled her eyes at him before turning back to Cass. "We're sorry we didn't tell you. I was… scared, I guess, that it would change things. But we were always going to explain when you figured it out. Or at least, we agreed to." She frowned at River, who was hiding beside his coffee.

"Hey, it's okay, princess," Cass told her earnestly. He couldn't imagine how terrifying it must be to be confronted with feelings for someone after getting out of such a toxic relationship. "So, this whole time?"

"Since you went to LA," Tessa clarified.

"Are you just sleeping together, or…" He trailed off as River looked away and Tessa stared at her lap. He'd clearly touched a nerve.

"It's complicated, you know," Tessa said finally, and River nodded in agreement. "I'm just… it's soon."

"Yeah, we have feelings and we're not ignoring them. We're just figuring things out as we go." Shadows fell across River's face, but he shook them away before Tessa could notice. "How did *you* figure it out?"

He raised an eyebrow at his best friend. "You mean besides the fact that you knew where to look for lube?"

"That'd do it," Tessa said with a laugh, leaning her face on her hand. "You're sure you're okay with it? We don't want anything to be weird."

"Hey, I'm happy if you're happy," he assured her, reaching across to tap her nose.

She smiled between the two of them. "I'm pretty happy," she confirmed. "Last night was… I mean, what the fuck, right? That was unreal."

He nodded in agreement as River said, "The rule of three."

She looked at them blankly.

"The idea that everything is better in threes," Cass chimed in. "That's why you so often see trios in books."

"I wrote my thesis on the effectiveness of the rule of three in modern literature," River told her. "Good concept, terrible execution." He wrinkled his nose.

"In your defense, you wrote the whole thing in two weeks high as a fucking kite. It's a miracle you wrote it at all."

"True." He shrugged nonchalantly. "But that's probably why we work so well together," he told Tessa. "Well, that and our outstanding chemistry."

"Can't forget that."

He leaned forward and tucked her hair behind her ear, a wicked gleam in his eyes. Cass's stomach fluttered at the easy way he touched her. *What was wrong with him?*

"So it lived up to the fantasy then, princess?"

"Eclipsed it," she replied.

"What fantasy?" Cass asked, dragging his gaze from their smiles and fighting the urge to reach for them. Jesus, he'd slept with them once and suddenly they were like magnets. He was jealous, he realized; jealous of the way they could reach for each other without questioning their feelings.

"You've been driving Tessa crazy with all the casual touches," River told him. "She's been dying to get her hands on you. Or your hands on her."

"Happy to oblige anytime," he said, winking at Tessa and trying not to show how much he liked that she'd been thinking of him like that.

He'd long since accepted that he was drawn to River as more than a friend—though never quite in the right way—but he had been grappling with wanting Tessa since he laid eyes on her. She'd just come out of a shitty situation, and then she was theirs. Their best friend, and he never wanted to fuck that up.

"You better mean that, because I'm definitely taking you up on it." Tessa's eyes were molten, flashing the devilish side of her he was very much looking forward to getting to know better.

"Next time, you shouldn't hold back," River told him, smirking. Tessa raised a brow.

"That was you holding back?"

Cass shrugged, sipping his coffee before saying, "I didn't want to scare you." Like River, he'd always liked things a little more intense in the bedroom. With River, they'd traded off on who was dominant, depending on who needed it more. But with Tessa...

Her eyes widened, not in trepidation, but in excitement. "Jesus. Please scare me, I would very much like that." She leaned forward on her elbows and River brushed a hand down her back. God, he could so easily lose himself in both of them.

He stood, gathering their cups to give himself something to do with his hands. "I'm about to see a whole new side of you, aren't I?"

And perhaps, he realized, *he was about to see a whole new side of himself.*

Tessa

"It's going to be super casual. Just you and me for an hour. It's basically like a long open mic. Please, T."

Tessa was only half paying attention to Aaron. She had her phone on loudspeaker, sitting on her chest, while Cass stroked her inner thighs and shot her a warning glare whenever she stopped paying attention to the call. He'd hardly stopped touching her since the day after Christmas, like he couldn't quite keep his hands to himself, and she certainly wasn't complaining.

"T?"

"Sorry," she said, squeezing her thighs together and, regretfully, pushing Cass's hand away. She sat up. "It's not a long open mic. You're trying to talk me into doing a show," Tessa countered. "No one is going to pay for a ticket to come and see a show where I'm half of the lineup." Tessa had done several open mics since River's birthday and, though the reception towards her songs had been largely positive, there were still whispers and sneers.

"You don't know that," Aaron tried. "Maybe now that you and Jay are over—"

"Aaron, I'd only do more harm than good. I'm happy for you to play our songs, and you know I'll be there in the crowd."

Aaron was quiet for a moment, and she could practically see their eyebrows draw together as they tried to think of another way to convince her. "Do it as an early birthday present?"

"Your birthday is in July."

"*Please*, Tessa. If not for me, do it out of spite. If people show up just because they want to hate you, you can prove them all wrong."

Tessa hummed. Now Aaron was speaking her language. "You have me there. I *do* like being petty."

"Perfect, you're in! I'm going to call the bar. Okay, love you, bye." Aaron hung up over Tessa's spluttering. She looked at Cass, who was watching her with an amused expression. "I don't think I said yes. Did I say yes?"

He beckoned her closer. "I don't think it matters. It sounds like you're in whether you like it or not."

She climbed onto his offered lap and slung her arms around his neck with a sigh. "Looks like I'm doing a show, then."

"It'll be good, princess," Cass assured her.

"I suppose I could be sick that day," she said, with a

small, very fake cough, her mind already whirring with ideas on getting out of the show.

"Counter offer." Cass ran a finger along her jaw and pulled her closer. "You do the show and then River and I spend the rest of the weekend showing you just how proud of you we are." He gave her a teaser with a fierce kiss and she melted into his lips, reveling in the simple act of being able to touch him like this.

"You drive a hard bargain," she murmured as she pulled away, breathing hard. "Fine, I'm in."

"In what?" River joined them, fresh out of the shower with dripping hair, and sank down onto the couch beside them.

"Tessa and Aaron are doing their show," Cass explained, along with the bargain they'd struck for the weekend after.

"Already proud of you, princess," River said, tugging her down and kissing her lightly, his hand entwined with Cass's. Her heart clenched.

She stood and started towards the kitchen, taking a deep breath.

"Where are you going?"

She looked back at them, and her steps faltered. Cass's head was nestled on River's shoulder, their hands clasped on his chest. They looked perfect, sitting there together. "Muffins," she forced out, somehow managing not to sound like her heart was twisting uncomfortably. "I'm going to make muffins."

She could have sworn River's eyes darkened at the mere suggestion of baked goods. "That sounds like a great idea," he said, licking his lips, and she forced a laugh and an eye roll.

She crouched down behind the island, rummaging through the cabinet for the muffin pan and, out of sight of River and Cass, took a moment to sit back and breathe. The way seeing the two of them together made her feel... It was too much, too soon, too strong. She was slipping, falling into something she had no business falling into.

It was never going to work. Even if she and River did have feelings for each other, they were never going to have more than this. She wasn't going to risk her friendship with him and Cass for the chance at a relationship that would almost certainly end in tears. River had already had his heart shattered by one best friend. She wouldn't let it happen again.

And Cass... well, she was setting herself up for disappointment by even thinking of him beyond her best friend. She *knew* that. And yet, her heart still raced when he touched her, with the audacity to hope that maybe they could all work it out.

Sure, and maybe hell would freeze over too.

It was just new to her, that was all, she told herself, over and over. She wasn't used to having people in her life that she felt truly herself with, nor was she used to sex so good she might actually be addicted. It was only normal for things to become foggy. She would get used to it. Or, at least, she would get used to lying to herself about it.

She knew they couldn't do this forever. She wanted to settle down one day, start a family, and she couldn't exactly do that while sleeping with her best friends. But the thought of giving them up… well, she didn't have to think about it for a while, at least. Not that she could seem to stop. Falling felt pretty good until the impact, after all.

"Princess?"

She looked up from her spot on the floor, her knees pulled to her chest, into River's concerned face. "Yeah?"

"What's wrong?"

"Nothing," she said, too quickly, too quietly. Panic was clawing its way through her chest. He rounded the island and sat down beside her, offering his arm.

Tessa hesitated, but shook her head, her eyes glued to her feet. Touching him was the last thing she needed, even if it was the first thing she wanted.

"What do you need?"

"I… I don't know," she mumbled. *But you do know,* she thought, *you know exactly what you need—who you need.*

She let loose a shuddering breath and reached out to grab his hand. A sense of calm washed over her instantly as the warmth of his skin sunk into her. "Can we just sit for a bit?"

"Of course."

River brought her hand to his chest and laid it flat against his heart. It beat steady as a stone, like she could reach out and anchor herself to him if she needed to. She slowly matched her breathing to the rise and fall of his chest, her racing heart calming with every breath.

Finally, she sat up straighter, the knot of panic unraveling.

"Better?" River asked, stroking his thumb across the top of her hand.

"Yeah. Thank you," she croaked.

"Good." He brought her palm to his lips and pressed a gentle kiss to her skin. She waited for the question, the push to get her to talk. But River just said, "Do you still want to bake?" She nodded. She needed the structure, the methodical measuring of the ingredients. River smiled and stood, offering her his hand and pulling her to her feet. "Perfect. Can I help?"

CHAPTER TWENTY-THREE

River

Something was wrong with Tessa. She looked fine, dropping yet another blanket in the overflowing IKEA cart, but something about her painted-on smile was off.

"What else is on the list?" Cass asked, stepping behind her and wrapping his arms around her, trapping her to the cart. Her cheeks glowed red, and her smile softened.

With Cass joining their arrangement, things between the three of them were closer to what River wanted than ever before. And he could no longer pretend he wasn't hoping for more, even if it was a fool's hope.

"Just the big things: a bed and a couch."

The three of them had been sleeping in her queen-sized bed for months now. It wasn't the *most* comfortable fit, but it was fine for just sleeping. River and Cass were cuddlers and snuggled so far into Tessa that they could probably fit in a twin bed. It wasn't nearly big enough for everything else they were getting up to these days, though. Tessa had finally relented the day before when, mid-orgasm and post-spank, she had slipped right off the edge of the bed and fallen to the floor, banging her head.

Considering the sheer amount of sex they were having, she was far from calm. She'd been on edge since he'd found her sitting on the kitchen floor, on the verge of a panic attack, but she hadn't talked to either of them about it, and he wasn't going to push when she wasn't ready. It had been a wild year for her, and, with Jay showing up and her brother reaching out again, December had been especially tough.

But River didn't think that was the problem. His theory lay in the moments she thought he wasn't looking, when he spotted her staring at Cass, frowning in concentration like she did when she was stuck on a melody. And the moments he felt her gaze linger on him and looked up, that same expression disappearing as soon as he caught her eye.

It wasn't that she wasn't subtle—he wasn't sure she even realized she was doing it—but she was trying to piece together a puzzle of feelings with only mis-matched pieces. They'd still been trying to figure out how to navigate what they felt for each other when they'd added Cass to the mix, and while he was glad they had—and he knew she was too—it had opened old wounds for him, and brand new ones for Tessa it seemed. River knew that, like him, she felt everything with so much weight it could have buried her, but she was too stubborn to let it.

And too stubborn to talk it out. For now, she was just trying not to be a deer in headlights in what was widely known to be the most domestic store in the world.

"What do you think?"

Tessa jolted River from his reverie, drawing his attention to a hanging duvet cover, light green with dark green leaves embroidered, similar to her tattoos. He smiled. "It reminds me of you, so I love it." The words slipped out before he thought them through, and a split second of panic appeared on Tessa's face before she recovered, her forced smile showing up once more.

"Well then, we'll have to get it."

She dropped the biggest size into the cart and turned away from him, but she reached her hand back for his as she did so, shivers spreading across River's skin as she twined their fingers.

"Excuse me," Cass asked a passing employee, Brandon, according to his name tag, as they followed the arrows into the bed section. "Can we test the beds?"

Brandon looked between the three of them warily. "Test them how?"

"Um, you know, just lie on them. To check the size."

He blew out a relieved breath. "Yeah, that's totally fine. Just… please keep your clothes on."

Tessa's brows shot up. "Does that happen a lot?"

He shook his head, thoroughly dejected. "You have no idea."

Brandon wandered off, and Tessa gave River a mischievous smile.

"Absolutely not. Did you see how traumatized poor Brandon was?"

She laughed. "I was going to suggest you put it in the

book you're planning at the moment, but if it wasn't for Brandon…"

It wasn't a bad idea (using the setting for his latest project, not scarring Brandon further.) But despite a plethora of inspiration, courtesy of his two best friends, he had been struggling to find the motivation to write lately. It was hard to put so much work in and not be entirely happy with the name on his covers. Publishers were still reaching out, but if he took one of them up on it, he had to out himself. Male romance authors were rare enough, let alone those with prison records, and he wasn't ready for the backlash.

"This is nice," Tessa said as they passed a bed with a velvet headboard. Cass scrunched his nose. "You don't like it?"

He ran a finger across the blush pink fabric and shrugged. "It would be pretty hard to tie you to this, but we could make it work."

Blood rushed to Tessa's cheeks and her eyes turned molten. "We should keep looking."

River chuckled and pulled her into his chest, spinning her and pointing to another bed. "What about that one?"

It had a simple iron frame with a large, plush linen pillow attached to the headboard frame. Tessa whistled. "I like that." She wrapped her hand around the iron frame and tugged. "Sturdy too. Let's try it."

Tessa shimmied into the middle of the bed, and he and Cass lay on either side of her. The three of them lay flat on their backs, staring up at the fluorescents and steel beams. She sat up to peer at the space on either side of them before flopping back down and taking their hands. "It's big. By New York standards, at least."

Cass wiggled around and let out a satisfied sigh. "This mattress is *nice*." It toed the perfect line between too-soft and too-firm. Even Goldilocks would approve.

"It is," Tessa agreed. "Do you like it?" She turned to River, and he pushed her hair behind her ear.

"Of course I do. You're in it."

She gave him a glowing smile that made his heart race. He was so unbelievably gone over her. "You're being extra sweet today. Unusually so," she told him.

"It's all that extra sugar you've been giving me lately." He smirked, and her jaw dropped. She prodded at his chest, laughing.

"You're terrible."

"I was talking about the muffins," he said with a wink, reaching behind her to grab Cass's hand and tug him closer. He slung his arm around Tessa, nestling into her back.

"Sure you were," Cass interjected, laughing. Tessa leaned in to brush a kiss to River's lips and turned to do the same to Cass. Over Cass's shoulder, River spotted Brandon hovering warily.

"We're still completely clothed," he called, and watched relief spread across his face.

"Thank you," he muttered, darting away.

The three of them stood, and Tessa noted down the product number for the bed and mattress.

"Couch time. What are you two thinking?" she asked them as they strode away.

Cass shrugged and bumped her hip with his. "It is *your* apartment, princess."

"On paper, sure, but when was the last time you were in your apartment for longer than it took to pick something up?"

It was true, he and Cass hadn't slept or eaten a meal in their apartment in… at least a month. They'd just settled into a routine with Tessa, and he couldn't imagine sleeping in his own bed.

"Is this your way of telling us you want some space?" Cass asked. His tone was light, a smile on his face, but River knew him well enough to know he was worried she would say yes.

But Tessa just glared at him and said, "Don't even suggest such a thing, you're not going anywhere."

"We *are* doing the whole domestic IKEA playing house thing. Can't go back from that," Cass said with a laugh, visibly relieved.

"Nope. You're both stuck with me now." Tessa shrugged like it was no big deal. Like it wasn't the best damn thing River had ever heard.

R iver leaned his forehead on the glass and closed his eyes, letting the hot water stream down his aching muscles. He hadn't done so much physical activity since prison, where there wasn't much to do aside from work out. He much preferred waking up with Cass and Tessa than any of his old cellmates, though.

He turned off the shower and yawned as he wrapped a towel around his hips. He was going to need a nap or some strong ass coffee if he was going to make his word count goal for the day.

Tessa was sitting on the bed, scrawling away in a notebook, when he exited the bathroom. She was still in her nightshirt, her golden hair in a messy, slept-in braid down her back. She looked up as he walked in and smiled, but it didn't come close to reaching her beautiful eyes.

"Hey, baby," he murmured, perching beside her and extending his arm. She tossed her notebook to the side and nestled into him.

"Hey."

"Are you okay?"

She shrugged, strumming her fingers on her thigh. Not in the off-hand way he did when he was anxious; the movements were precise, as if she was subconsciously playing a melody on her thigh. "Can I… I wanted to talk to you about something."

"Anything," he told her, shifting so he could pull the blanket over her goosebump covered legs. She gave him a grateful smile and took a deep breath.

"It's about Cass. Well, it's about *you* and Cass, actually."

"Yeah?"

She paused for a moment before saying, "How do you do it? How have you managed all these years, wanting him so desperately and knowing that you can't have him in the way you want?" Her voice splintered and his heart ache, desperate to soothe her at all costs.

He stroked the back of her head and let loose a breath. "I can't pretend it was easy. Or even bearable, most of the time. It's taken me years to get to a place of semi-acceptance, and I still struggle with it sometimes.

"I… I get really mad sometimes. Not at Cass, God, never at him, but at the universe for putting someone so perfect right at my fingertips but keeping him just out of reach. Don't get me wrong, I'm so fucking grateful to have him in my life at all, but I'll always want more, and he'll always know that." And then, in a cruel twist of fate, the universe had done it again.

You would think, after so many years of pining after Cass, that he would have been more prepared for Tessa, or even that wanting her might take away some of the constant ache for Cass. But now his heart just longed twice as hard, not split between them, but bigger and more desperate.

"I feel… so guilty," she admitted, sniffing, and he realized her eyes were wet. "I'm so lucky to have you both, to have *friends,* let alone best friends. It should be enough. It is enough," she added quickly, shaking her head. "I just… I don't know how to make sense of the feelings."

"Princess, if you need a break, some space—"

"No," she interrupted, looking up at him with watery eyes. "I don't want a break. I don't know what I want, but I know it's not that. I just can't make sense of the feelings."

"Have you tried writing it out?" River asked. Writing was the only thing, aside from Cass, that had gotten him through his worst years. He wouldn't have survived prison or rehab without writing out his feelings. He had learned to put every shred of guilt, regret, and pain down in ink until he could make sense of them.

River wiped away an errant tear and she scrunched her nose. "Putting it into words means I have to actually confront it."

"It doesn't have to be for anyone but you," he told her, nodding to the notebook. "Write it down and lock it away, if that's what you need to do."

"I guess it couldn't hurt to try," she relented.

River kissed her on the forehead, lingering a little longer than usual. "You know I'm unbelievably proud of you, right?"

She frowned at him. "For what?"

He stood and pulled his towel off, running it through his wet hair. "You've gone from sneaking away in the middle of the night because you were too scared to let anyone close to you, to not only letting Cass and I in but also talking to Aaron more, *and* forgiving someone for the first time. That's pretty huge."

She shook her head, letting loose a watery chuckle. "I guess I did do that. I'm a completely different person than I was when we met."

"Not completely different," River assured her. "You're still stubborn as hell, still full of that amazing fire I can't get enough of, still the most beautiful person I've ever laid eyes on." He emphasized each point with a kiss, but she pulled away at the last.

"Well, now I know you're lying. We both know Cass is the most beautiful person either of us has ever laid eyes on, possibly the most beautiful in the world," she said, fighting a smile.

"That's true. Second, then, but pretty damn close," he said, pulling her into a deep kiss. When they pulled away, they were panting, and Tessa's eyes were full of bad ideas. He stood up, laughing at her pout.

"I'm not going to hit my word count in here with you looking at me like that, so I'm going to go work at that new coffee place around the corner. Do you want to come?"

Tessa shook her head, picking up her notebook and getting to her feet. "I think I'll give this a go." She held her writing notebook up. "I don't want to start the new year in emotional turmoil."

"Sensible." He pulled her into a hug and kissed her once more. "Crazy about you, princess," he said. It's not what he wanted to say. They both knew that. The line they were trying so desperately not to cross was creeping closer and closer every day.

"Crazy about you too," she answered, her amber eyes bright with pining.

He let her go, struggling with every inch he stepped away from her, and pasted a smile on his face. "Go write a masterpiece."

Tessa dragged her fingers across the cold keys as she sat

down at the piano. She had written hundreds of songs sitting on the hard stool, so why did this one feel like climbing a mountain?

She had a process for every song that began with feeling out the notes, finding the chords that best fit with the story she was trying to tell. She took a deep breath and pressed on the keys, playing with different combinations, before finally playing the progression that had been stuck in her mind for months.

B F# G#m E

Tessa saw sounds around people like some saw colors. Every person, every thing, could be broken down into pieces of music, and, though she couldn't explain it, those four notes were River and Cass; were how River and Cass made her feel. The notes weren't joyful; they weren't melancholic; they were somewhere in between. Somewhere full of longing and aching and want.

She let the notes spiral around her, her hands playing in perfect harmony, like she, River, and Cass did too. She let them pull her away, out of her head; from a place of fear, of panic, and crumbling walls.

Tessa opened her mouth and let the words spill.

She finally pushed away from the piano, just in time to hear a key turn in the front door. She gathered up her notebook and walked away from the piano, three songs heavier, but so much lighter. River had been right. She'd found the closest thing to peace she could; somewhere between the melody and the lyrics; somewhere between River and Cass.

CHAPTER TWENTY-FOUR

Tessa

"Why the fuck did I agree to this?" Tessa grumbled, smoothing down her hair, her skirt, her fucking nerves.

"Because you love me?" Aaron replied with a shit-eating grin.

Tessa rolled her eyes. "I do, it's true."

The show had snuck up on them faster than Tessa had realized. She'd already been regretting agreeing to it (not that she *had* agreed to it), but walking into the bar and seeing her name front and center on the advertisements alongside Aaron's had almost made her throw up. Aaron had pleaded ignorance, as if they hadn't been the one to design the posters and give the details to the venue.

The showcase had sold out and panic had spread through Tessa's chest, the voices in her head cruelly telling her that anyone who had been enticed to the show by her name was probably just there to watch her stumble and fall.

Well, not everyone; River and Cass were sitting in the crowded bar, a promise of her reward.

Aaron pulled a pen from behind their ear and made a few scribbled amendments to their planned set list before handing it to her to look over. "Does that look okay?"

Tessa blanched. "We can't do *Fingertips*." They'd recorded a rough demo of the song she had written the week before about not being able to have River and Cass and Tessa couldn't deny it had turned out beautifully, but she couldn't *share* it.

"We're doing *Fingertips*."

"But—"

"Tessa." Aaron gave her a determined look. "That is the best damn song you've ever written. We're doing it. Besides, didn't you say you were trying to open up about your own life a bit more?"

She frowned. "I'm almost certain I didn't say that."

Aaron shrugged. "Maybe that was just a dream I had. Either way, we're doing it, and it's showtime. Let's do this." Aaron grabbed her arm and dragged her onto the small stage at the back of the bar.

Heads turned and Tessa gulped as every eye in the room turned to face them. She didn't get stage fright, but she also rarely performed ticketed shows. There was a big difference between an open mic and a sold out show.

There was a smattering of applause as Aaron took their seat behind the equipment they'd brought. Aaron didn't travel light; Tessa swore they'd packed half of their studio onto the little stage. Tessa had brought her keyboard, an acoustic guitar, and a whole puddle of nerves.

She shuffled into place behind her mic, relieved to be cast in shadow. Until Aaron nodded to the bartender and a spotlight lit them up. *It was nice while it lasted.*

The crowd tittered, and the knots in Tessa's stomach tightened. From her spot on the stage, she could see several people side-eyeing her, and some even outright glaring.

"Look at her trying to claw back her joke of a career." Perhaps the blonde in the front row had intended Tessa to hear her. She certainly hadn't tried to be quiet, but her words landed. Tessa looked at the ground, leaning back from the microphone so that the crowd wouldn't hear her anxious breathing.

Tessa glanced at the set list. They were starting with *Unmarked Grave*, and she knew Aaron was supposed to play the keyboard, but she needed to feel the keys beneath her fingers. She looked up at Aaron and nodded towards her keyboard. Understanding, Aaron nodded and picked up their guitar. They'd experimented with adding a little guitar to the track, so it wouldn't be far off.

Tessa took a deep breath as she stood behind the keyboard and let her fingers rest on the keys.

"Ready?" Aaron asked, and Tessa ignored every one of her screaming nerves and nodded.

"Yeah."

"Hey everyone, my name is Aaron Peters, and this is my good friend, Tessa Reid."

Cass

He couldn't take his eyes off her. Tessa moved around music like she could see it, like she was spinning silk with her fingertips and turning it to gold with her tongue. She was incredible.

And every time she looked over at them and smiled, he almost came undone. *What the hell was wrong with him?*

She had relaxed considerably once the music had started, losing herself in the beat. While Tessa sang, River reached almost absentmindedly and took his hand. Warmth spread through him, his heart racing, his stomach doing somersaults. He leaned into him and watched River's lips lift in a smile.

Cass was struggling to pretend these days that something inside him hadn't shifted. Or maybe it hadn't— perhaps it had been lying dormant, waiting. He was fucking terrified.

"You're thinking awfully loudly over there," River murmured as Tessa and Aaron swapped their instruments for the next song, like a well-oiled machine. He looked up and met River's dark eyes, sparkling in the dim lights of the bar. "You okay?"

Cass nodded. "Yeah, sorry, my head's just hazy right now, a lot going on, you know?"

"Yeah. You can talk to me. I'm here."

Cass squeezed his hand and murmured his thanks. He

couldn't talk to River about this. Nor, he supposed, could he talk to Tessa. When River and Tessa got stuck, they wrote, but whenever Cass had been stuck on his feelings before, he'd spoken to River.

What could he say? *"Hey, River, I know I broke your heart and contributed to your life spiraling out of control, but my feelings for you and Tessa have become kind of conflicted, and I think maybe I made the wrong decision to end things between us?"*

Yeah, probably not. River was healing, *really* healing, now that he'd opened his heart to Tessa. Cass wouldn't come between them. Hell, he didn't want to come between them. He wanted... he didn't know what he wanted, but he knew, whatever it was, he couldn't have it.

It was moments like this when he missed his parents most; phone and video calls were great, but sometimes he just needed a hug from his mom and a glass of his dad's ataya.

Aaron cleared their throat from the stage, and Cass looked up, tearing his attention from River. "Tessa brought me this song a couple of days ago and I haven't stopped thinking about it since. It's pretty rough, we haven't worked on it much, but this is the best thing Tessa has ever written, if you ask me. This is called *Fingertips*. Tessa, do you want to tell everyone what it's about?"

Tessa, who was tapping her foot nervously on the scuffed stage, leaned towards the microphone and said, "Absolutely not, thank you."

Aaron chuckled and there were even a few smiles across

the room, as if they could no longer quite hate Tessa for the scathing headlines she'd never deserved.

Aaron began the intro, and Tessa glanced up at River and Cass, chewing her lip, before looking away quickly and taking a deep breath.

River

"*I was untethered until you put my roots in the ground...*"

Tessa's voice shook for the first time that night, her golden hair falling across her face and casting it in shadow. She was nervous. Not of the crowd's reaction, he realized, as he slowly pieced together the lyrics. Of them, him and Cass.

This was the song, the one she had written to work through her feelings. This wasn't some story from one of the many romance novels on her shelf with a guaranteed happy ending; this was their story, with no such guarantees. And as painful as that was, Aaron hadn't been lying when they'd said it was some of Tessa's best work.

Perhaps he was biased, recognizing himself and Cass between the melancholic lines, but Tessa seemed to transform as she sang it too. There was so much heart in her voice. Pain danced around the edges, pain that made him ache, but, mostly, love lay there. He knew she loved them both, perhaps romantically, perhaps not, but she had made magic from those conflicting feelings.

"With you, I gladly would drown…"

She looked up at him as she sang. Her amber eyes sparkling across the room, catching the light and every inch of his heart, as she sang and swayed. River's heart swelled with the music, racing so much he thought it might jump out of his chest.

She had perfectly captured the years of longing, of wanting someone who was right at his fingertips but still so out of reach. He still couldn't believe it had happened again with Tessa, and he hated that she felt the same.

"It's like the end of the world,
And we're on a sinking ship,
This can't end well,
With you at my fingertips…"

Tessa brought the song to a close and looked down, her cheeks rosy red as the room went wild. Aaron smiled at the whistles and applause, waving as they exited the stage into the back room. Tessa left the stage with a backwards glance that could have killed, a final reminder to the room that they should have known better than to talk shit about her.

Fuck, he loved her.

Of course he did. He had been fighting it since the second she had walked out of her apartment and found him in the hallway, and he couldn't do it anymore.

"Hey." Cass pulled him from his reverie, standing and holding a hand out to him. He let him pull him to his feet and didn't have to ask where they were going.

Cass knocked on the door to the side room and pushed it open as Aaron called, "*Come in.*"

Tessa had kicked her shoes off and had her bare feet kicked up on a couch, sipping gingerly at a steaming cup of tea. His heart raced just at the sight of her.

She stood up, smiling, as they walked over.

"You did good, princess." Cass picked her up and spun her, her dress flying around and falling like snow. Her squeals echoed around the room, but she was smiling widely. "You too, Aaron," he called over his shoulder, grinning.

"Thanks, man. I don't get a spin?"

Cass set Tessa down in front of River, laughing, and pulled Aaron into an equally tight hug.

River was more gentle as he stepped closer to Tessa, wrapping her in his arms and buried his face in the crook of her neck. He was conscious of Aaron standing a few feet away, but he no longer cared. "I'm so fucking proud of you, baby," he murmured, and Tessa seemed to melt in his arms.

"I'm going to head out before I see something I don't want to," Aaron drawled, winking at them as they picked up their beer.

Tessa spun around, whipping River in the face with her hair. It smelled like sugar; he wasn't complaining. "What? How did you…" she trailed off and Aaron laughed.

"I have eyes and ears. Besides, I know you well enough to read between your lyrics."

They started for the door but paused as a knock sounded and it opened.

River saw red.

Tessa stepped in front of, putting a hand out as if to shield him from Jay as he stepped fully into the room (or perhaps to shield Jay from him.)

Jay's eyes immediately zeroed in on how close they were.

"What are you doing here?" Tessa asked, not bothering with introductions. Her entire body tensed.

"I need to talk to you about how we left things the other week." Jay's voice was softer than River had expected—it was hard to imagine jagged words in the smooth Australian accent.

"I have nothing more to say," Tessa answered, her voice wobbling a little.

"Please, sweetheart." Jay stepped towards her and, as if instinctually, Aaron, River, and Cass did too, closing around her until everyone stilled. "I just want to talk."

Tessa took a deep breath and said, "I don't want to talk."

"Jay, you should go," Aaron said, but Jay ignored them, turning his attention to River and Cass as Tessa stepped closer to them. River saw the change in his eyes; the moment soft blue turned vicious as anger flashed across Jay's face. And as Jay moved closer, River smelled the whiskey. *So much for rehab.*

He could tell that Tessa smelled it too, that she'd clocked the change in Jay's body language. He could practically feel her shrinking, trying to make herself smaller for her ex-fiancé.

"Which one of them are you fucking?" Jay all but growled. Tessa flinched but said nothing, and it took every shred of self control River had not to push her safely behind him and break Jay Hutchison's fucking nose.

"Both of us," Cass answered smoothly beside him. "And if you ever fucking speak to her like that again, you'll have all three of us to deal with." He gestured towards Aaron, who nodded in agreement.

"I'm going to say it again, Jay—you should go." Aaron put a hand on his shoulder and pushed him towards the door. Jay shrugged them off, but finally walked away.

"This isn't over," he said before leaving, the door banging behind him.

"Thank you," Tessa said to Aaron. Aaron gave her a quick hug and said their goodbyes.

Tessa burrowed into River's chest and held a hand out behind her for Cass. He closed in behind her, resting his chin on her head.

"You want to talk about it?"

"No, I'm okay. Promise." Tessa tilted her face up and River leaned to press a kiss to her red lips, groaning as she slipped her tongue into his mouth. She tilted her head slightly, and he felt Cass's head bow to nestle in and, based on her gasp, bite down. "Let's go home."

"You don't want to go celebrate your show?"

She stepped away with a mischievous smile. "That's exactly what I want to do, at home, with you two, and our new bed."

Home. Our bed. River almost stopped breathing.

They packed up in a hurry, the promise of testing out the bed that had finally been delivered that morning, lighting a fire under them.

They made it home in record time, the New York traffic favoring them for a change. Cass unlocked the door and pushed it open, not giving them time to follow him before turning and picking Tessa up.

She'd protested exactly once that she was too heavy to be carried, and River and Cass had spent the most blissful hour making those protests die on her tongue; River holding her up against the bookshelves, Cass against the window that looked down on Cornelia Street.

She hadn't objected since, and she certainly didn't when Cass dropped her gently on the bed and the two of them slowly pulled her dress off—slowly because they kept pausing to kiss her, and each other.

Tessa whimpered on the bed, her nails dragging along their arms as she grasped for them while they finally removed the scraps of gold fabric that looked far better on the floor.

Cass tutted, bringing her hand to his lips. "We can't be having that, princess."

Tessa watched, her lips parted, as Cass crossed the room and pulled a length of red cord from a drawer. He held it up in question, eyes twinkling, and she nodded.

"Sit up, baby," he murmured, climbing onto the bed behind her.

Tessa's eyes were wide as River tilted her chin up. "Safe word?"

"Red," she replied, her voice breathy.

Cass pulled her hands behind her back and wrapped the cord around her wrists with expert precision. "Can you snap your fingers?" he asked when the rope was tight around her wrists and wound around her torso.

Tessa frowned in confusion, but snapped her fingers. "Why—"

"Because," River said, closing the distance between them and catching her bottom lip in his teeth. "You might want to tap out when your mouth is otherwise occupied. If you do, you snap. Promise us."

"I promise," she all but whispered as Cass dragged his lips down the curve of her shoulder.

"How gentle do you want us to be, princess?"

"Not even a little bit."

Cass grinned River's favorite, unhinged grin and tugged on the rope until Tessa's back was pressed against him. "God, I want to do the most depraved things to you," he breathed, almost to himself.

Tessa's face relaxed, her head falling back against his chest. "Please," she begged.

He pushed her forward, trailing a finger down her spine. "Undo River's jeans, princess."

He and Cass had always been dominant in the bedroom, and River loved watching Cass call the shots as much as he loved holding the reins.

He expected Tessa to blink, to look around in confusion, but she did nothing of the sort, leaning forward and using her teeth to wrestle with the front of his jeans. Her face grazed his cock, and he groaned. She looked up at him through dark lashes, licking her lips.

River looked at Cass, watching them with fire in his eyes. At his nod, River pushed his jeans and underwear down, before stepping out of them and stripping off his shirt.

Tessa's eyes glazed as she took him in, trying to lean forward against Cass's bonds. He tutted and tugged her back, wrapping an arm across her front roughly. "Are you that desperate for River's cock in your mouth?"

Tessa didn't have the chance to reply before his fingers slipped between her legs and she cried out, squirming. "*Yes*," she cried, and Cass chuckled, releasing her.

"Since you asked so nicely." He pushed her forward, so she was on her hands and knees. "Open those pretty lips." Like a puppet master pulling her strings, he lowered her mouth onto River's cock.

River shuddered, every nerve in his body standing up and taking notice. He wanted to tangle his hands in her hair and fuck her mouth, but he knew Cass was in control here.

Cass brought his hand down on her ass, before parting her thighs and pressing into her. Tessa moaned around River's cock, the vibrations making him shudder. He fought his eyes, so desperate to close. He didn't want to miss a second of this.

Cass gripped the ropes around her wrists with one hand and her hair with the other. And as he fucked her, he pushed her head down and pulled it back, using River's cock to fuck her mouth too.

It was like something out of River's deepest, darkest fantasies; Tessa's golden hair wrapped tightly around Cass's hand, tears pooling at the corners of her eyes, trailing mascara lines down her cheeks as they fell, a look of bliss on both of their faces.

"We're going to fucking ruin you, princess," Cass growled, smacking her ass so hard her whole body seemed to shake. "This perfect pussy and that mouth, so that no one else, no other cocks, will ever feel this good."

His cock muted Tessa's moans, but she still cried out as she came, before looking up at River, her expression saying exactly what he was thinking: *I'm already ruined.*

CHAPTER TWENTY-FIVE

Tessa

"What's the damage?"

River shook his head at his phone, his brows knit together. "There are a lot of positive comments, but the press is being pretty brutal."

Tessa sipped her coffee and tried not to panic. She didn't blame the bar for live-streaming the show, but, if she'd known, she'd never have played *Fingertips*. So, naturally, it had gone viral. There was no point in pretending it wasn't her best work yet. She knew it was, but that didn't mean she wanted the whole world hearing it.

"It'll die down, princess," Cass said from the driver's seat, squeezing her knee. She'd never seen him drive before —he had no need in the city—and had been skeptical of the shiny pickup he'd rented for the drive up to River's parents, but the three-person bench had its perks. And Cass driving, in a grey t-shirt and sunglasses, with an arm resting on the open window, was almost enough to distract her from the fact that her name was, once again, all over the internet.

"I know, it always does. I just… Of all the personal songs, that's the last one I would want to go viral."

"It's a damn good song, baby." River had been watching the video on repeat with headphones all morning, humming along without even noticing. It had been too fucking cute for her to complain about, even if it drove the butterflies in her stomach wild.

"Yeah, it is. My best, probably," she replied, resting her head on his shoulder. But it was *theirs*. It didn't feel right to share it with everyone else.

The shrill ring of her phone made her jump, and she groaned as she glanced at the screen. *Empire Records.* They'd been calling all morning.

"You should answer it. Get it out of the way."

Tessa grumbled, but held the phone to her ear anyway. "Hello."

"Tessa, it's so great to hear your voice." Henry Carver, the head of Empire Records, was an asshole. He had been as long as Tessa had known him, but he'd believed in her enough to give her a songwriting contract when she was sixteen, so she kind of owed him.

"Hey, Henry. How are you?"

"Good, good," he said quickly, dismissively. "Listen, Tessa, *Fingertips*? Amazing. Your best work yet."

"Um, thanks—"

"We've had so many calls. There are at least a dozen artists who want to buy it."

She frowned, letting the words sink in. "You… you want me to sell it?"

"Why wouldn't you want to sell it? That song is going to make us a fortune." By *us*, Henry meant Empire, not Tessa. She didn't do badly with royalties, but that was down to the sheer number of songs she had written and sold. Her percentage was below the industry standard, thanks to the ten-year contract signed when she was sixteen.

"I'm not selling it," she said firmly. "If anyone is going to record Fingertips, it's going to be me."

Henry sighed, and she could picture him running his fingers through his perfectly gelled blonde hair. "We've talked about this, Tessa. You know we can't offer you a recording contract."

"I know," she said, simply. "But I'm sure there are plenty of labels out there that would be interested, especially since my writing contract is up for renewal in March." The threat slipped out before she knew it was coming. Tessa had hardly thought about her renewal, and hadn't really considered leaving Empire. Both River and Cass's heads swiveled towards her.

"You're seriously threatening to go elsewhere if we don't let you perform? I made you, Tessa. Besides, no other label is going to take a chance on someone with your reputation."

She rolled her eyes at the way his tone had suddenly turned aggressive. "Half of your artists only have decent songs because of me. I made myself, and you can go to hell if you think otherwise. Goodbye."

She hung up before he could respond, groaning and

clenching her phone. She was over seeing other artists' names on her hard work, tired of them being praised while she was slandered. Hopefully, Henry would take her threat seriously and would consider letting her record. Starting over with a new label would be terrifying. Though she wasn't attached to Empire, was Henry right about other labels fearing her reputation?

"That was…" Cass trailed off.

"Unexpected?" River offered.

"I was going to say fucking sexy, but that too."

Tessa turned her phone off and dropped it in her bag before she could do anything else she might regret later. She blew out a breath. "I have no idea where that came from. It felt pretty good, though."

"Would you do it? Leave Empire?" River asked.

"Honestly? I don't know. I haven't thought about it before, but I suppose there's nothing keeping me there." She would never have considered leaving when she was with Jay. Though Tessa wrote for artists at different labels, working with Jay was much easier since they were both signed under Empire. Tessa had written or co-written all but six of the songs on his past three records. She'd more or less single-handedly revived his career with her songs. Maybe one day in the future she'd be ready to write for him again, but it wouldn't be anytime soon. She could leave Empire and never look back.

"It's something to think about, princess." She snuggled into River, her mind racing as fast as the highway flying by.

Tessa would have rather walked straight into a crowd of paparazzi than sit through another second of dinner with River's family. Sandwiched between River, who was more on edge than she'd ever seen him, and his uncle, Kevin, who was absolutely brushing her knee with his on fucking purpose, she understood why River needed the moral support. She was going to scream.

She couldn't even hold River's hand to help calm him, though she and Cass had spent most of the meal trading glances and searching River's face to make sure he was okay.

Esme and Jonathan Sage sat opposite them, flanked by Jonathan's parents.

There was nothing of Jonathon in River. Looks-wise, he was all his mom; her warm brown skin, the slight wave to her black hair, the soft curve of her nose. She was beautiful. His parents were dressed expensively, polished and poised, like they were attending a political gala and not a family dinner. Esme had glanced at Tessa, who had never felt so underdressed in her life, and recoiled a little as she'd taken in her pale blue dress. She could only imagine how they'd reacted when they'd first seen River's face tattoos.

Tessa had seen pictures of them, but nothing had prepared her for the way their faces tightened when their gazes passed over their son. She couldn't imagine River growing up in a house like this.

House didn't seem enough. It had looked big from the outside, but she'd been taken aback by the sheer grandness of just the foyer. Spanish-style tiles covered the floor, and a curved, sweeping staircase with a wrought iron banister led upstairs. Above the staircase was a domed ceiling with an honest-to-God chandelier.

Tessa had grown up firmly working class, and though she'd lived with one of the richest musicians in the world, there was a big difference between a penthouse in London, and a mansion in upstate New York.

They were discussing some colleague of Jonathan's divorce when River's grandfather asked River, "Are you seeing anyone?" as he took a plate of mashed potatoes from him.

River had been quiet since they'd arrived, letting Cass fill the evening with chatter. Though River's parents didn't approve of Cass, or his relationship with their son, he seemed unfazed.

River cleared his throat and looked his grandfather straight in the eye as he replied, "Yes. I am, actually."

The table went silent; Cass froze, Esme's mouth settled into a thin line, and Tessa was torn between being turned on by River's sheer pettiness in saying it straight to their faces, and mild panic. Sure, she could pretend to be his girlfriend for his parents. Hell, if he wanted to piss them off, he couldn't have picked a better person to present to them. Still, some warning might have been nice.

His dad recovered first, his of surprise transforming into a somewhat forced smile. "How nice. What's she like?"

Tessa fought the urge to roll her eyes at the heteronormative question. It wasn't as if his family didn't know he was bi—he was sitting beside his ex-boyfriend, for crying out loud.

"*They* are great," River said, emphasizing the lack of

gender. Tessa moved firmly from mildly panicked to turned on. Apparently River being petty did it for her. "It's new, so we're still figuring it out, but it's going well. We're happy."

He brushed her leg with his under the table, and she squeezed his knee. That wasn't so bad.

"Then we're happy for you," his mom said, her smiling almost frighteningly pasted on.

"What about you, Tessa? Are you taken?"

Tessa turned to face Kevin's sleazy smile. "I'm working on me right now," she said firmly. "And you?"

His cheeks turned pink, and he cleared his throat. "That's good. I'm married. Last year, actually."

She raised a brow. "Congratulations, how lovely for you both."

Tessa turned away and met Cass's eye before he ducked his head, fighting a laugh.

Cass

When the plates had been cleared away and drinks had been served, Cass wanted nothing more than to disappear with River and Tessa. Thank God they only had to sit through this once a year. River's dad had spent the entire dessert course grilling Tessa on her opinions on everything from the British Monarchy to whether she put jam or cream on her scones first (she didn't even like jam, so it was a moot point.)

They'd settled around the marble fireplace, and it was River's uncle's turn to be grilled, though his questions were mostly centered on his new wife, who was noticeably absent. Aside from his grandfather's question, River had been asked nothing, as if his parents were scared to find out the answers.

Exhaustion lingered in Cass's bones as he sat in the firelight and tried not to yawn every two seconds. They'd stayed up past three after they'd gotten to the lodge last night, their bodies worn out and orgasms long faded, just talking.

Talking about a future in which Tessa got to perform her music with no strings attached, a future in which River's own name was stamped across his writing. Cass didn't have a plan for the future, not really. He wouldn't model forever, nor did he want to. He was growing weary of the toxic industry, wearier of the regular trips away from River and Tessa.

Once upon a time, he had wanted marriage and kids, but that dream had died when he'd broken River's heart.

As long as River and Tessa were in it, he would be content with whatever future he had. Hell, maybe the two of them would figure their shit out, have kids, and he could be the cool uncle, at least. He knew River wanted to be a dad, and Tessa seemed like she'd be a good mom.

He yawned and leaned closer to her. "Do you want kids?"

She peered at him from over her untouched wine glass. Tessa hated white wine, but she had been too polite to decline the glass as Esme had all but forced it into her hand. "What?"

"You know, long-term, do you want to be a mom?"

She shrugged. "I'd like to, if I get the chance. I've always wanted a big family. Why?"

"Just curious," he said, turning away and trying his damndest to block the barrage of images that flashed through his mind of the three of them surrounded by a gaggle of toddlers, and the subsequent butterflies that fluttered around his belly.

"Do you?"

He turned to Tessa's curious face and just said, "Yeah."

"I bet you'd be a good dad. Super chilled. You'd be like the good cop and River would be the bad cop."

It didn't escape his notice that Tessa defaulted to thinking of him and River parenting together. He wondered if she also pictured a family where some kids had River's coloring, some his, and all of them had Tessa's amber eyes.

He was pulled back into the conversation as River said, "It's been good, thank you. Sales are still pretty steady."

His dad's nostrils flared. "I just don't understand why you can't write something more... respectable. If you did, you could use your real name."

"I've been considering transitioning to my real name anyway," River said steadily. Cass and Tessa exchanged a surprised glance. River had mentioned wanting his name on his books the night before, but not that he was actually considering it.

His mom blanched and grabbed her husband's hand.

"But you can't. You can't have our name associated with that fil—with those things you write."

"Besides, do you really want everyone to be able to look you up and find out you're an addict? A criminal?"

River folded in on himself, his shoulders slumping, his face falling. "That's not who I am anymore."

"Oh River, you know what we mean," his mom said, waving him away. "We're sure you're better now, but that's who you'll always be. You can't outrun your past."

It was the absolute worst thing she could have said.

River stilled. Then he stood, turned on his heel, and walked straight out of the patio doors and into the yard.

"I don't know what's gotten into him." His mom shook her head, returning to her wine like nothing had happened.

Cass set his drink down, readying to check on River. "It's nothing, it's not you—"

"Bullshit."

He closed his mouth at Tessa's proclamation. Her eyes were livid as she stared at Esme. "Tessa…" he began, but she held up a hand.

"No, this is ridiculous. Esme, Jonathan, it *is* you. Well, it's all of you, actually. He made a mistake over a decade ago and has spent every day since trying to prove himself. Which, for the record, he shouldn't have to do at all. You should be proving yourselves to him, considering you just gave up on him."

"Now, Tessa, you don't know what it was like," Jonathan spluttered, and Cass wasn't surprised that River's dad was shocked. He wasn't sure he'd ever heard anyone stand up to River's parents. River certainly never had. The rest of the group was silent, eyes wide.

"I don't care what it was like. I care that River has spent the last ten years feeling like a burden, and like the only person he had in the world who truly loved him, was Cass." She fixed his parents with a glare that made them blanch. "None of you deserve him."

She stood up, her dress flying behind her as she stormed after River.

Esme turned to Cass, tears in her eyes. "Is that true? Does he really think we don't love him?"

Cass stood slowly, taking his drink with him. "Yeah. Everything Tessa said was true."

He didn't give them a chance to respond before walking out, leaving them to talk amongst themselves, to make excuses and somehow put it all back on River. He strode outside, but didn't follow Tessa across the lawn into the trees where River was pacing.

He sat down on a creaky wooden bench, his heart thundering as he recalled Tessa defending their best friend, and took a deep breath. He could no longer deny it, no longer pretend it wasn't happening.

Cass had been wrong, so wrong, when he ended things with River.

He was in love with his best friends. Both of them.

CHAPTER TWENTY-SIX

River

He was fucking through with all of them. Ten years of trying, ten years of snide remarks, he was done. Why did he even bother dragging himself upstate once a year for these dinners? All they did was make him feel like shit.

River leaned against the trunk of an old pine, closed his eyes, and took a deep, steadying breath. He had Cass and Tessa; the rest of the world could burn as far as he was concerned.

"Hey." He opened his eyes to find Tessa, red-cheeked and panting slightly, as if she'd run across the yard. "You okay?"

He nodded, pushing off the tree to close the distance between them. "Yeah. Fuck them."

The corners of her mouth lifted, flames he hadn't noticed before dying down in her eyes. "I agree. And I'm pretty sure I just told them as much, so we might have to leave."

His heart thumped in his chest as he stepped closer, closing his arms around her. "You told my family to go fuck themselves?"

"Not in those words, but I think they got the sentiment," she replied, holding him tightly. "What, you thought I wouldn't go to the mat for you?"

She had defended him, knowing who he was and what he'd done. He looked down into her perfect face, every freckle standing to attention on her pale skin, her cheeks glowing in the cold air. He swallowed. "I can't do this anymore."

Tessa went completely still for a moment before her eyes widened and she stepped back. "Oh. Okay, yeah, that's… yeah, cool," she said, nodding too quickly and turning away from him.

Fuck, he was an idiot. He reached for her, snagging her arm. "No, princess, I didn't mean… Okay, I fucked that up. Let me try again."

"Okay," she answered shakily, staring resolutely past him into the trees beyond.

"I mean, I don't want to do *just* this anymore. Just sex, if that's even all it's been. Fuck, Tessa, I want us to be together, *really* together." A weight lifted from his shoulders as the words tumbled out.

Tessa closed her eyes, taking several steadying breaths, the silence dragging on and knotting his stomach. Finally, she met his gaze and said, "River, I… We can't." Her voice broke, and he wanted nothing more than to reach for her, hold her, kiss away the tears forming in her eyes. But he was already struggling to keep a clear head.

Tessa stepped back, tears streaming freely down her face. "You and Cass are the best thing that's ever happened to me. I've never felt more myself than when I'm with you, and I can't risk that."

He moved towards her, but she continued moving backwards. "You're not going to lose us, Tessa. We're not going anywhere."

"You can't know that," she cried, her voice rising until she was shouting. Over her shoulder, he saw Cass approaching, concern on his face. "What happens when this thing goes to hell and we can't stand to be around each other? I lose Cass because you two have so much history, and I lose you, and I'm all alone again."

His heart broke in two at the anguish on her face. "That's not going to happen. We can make this work."

"How can you be so sure?"

"Because I fucking *love* you, Tessa."

The words slipped out before he could stop them. Tessa stilled, panic shining in her eyes, an expression on her face like she'd been punched in the stomach. Even Cass stopped on his way across the lawn.

"Don't say that, please don't say that," Tessa whispered.

River stepped forward, stopping right in front of her. "But I do. I love you so much I can't breathe sometimes."

She swallowed. "You shouldn't. Please," she begged.

"Why? Why is it such a bad thing?" River asked, stepping back, frustration leaking into his tone, as hard as he tried to fight it.

Tessa covered her face with her hands, sobs wracking her body. "Because," she cried, wiping away her tears. "Everyone who has ever claimed to love me has betrayed me. My friends, my family, Jay. I can't go through that again, and I don't think I could survive losing the two of you."

Every part of him ached for her, his fingers itching to reach out and brush every shred of hurt from her face. But he could do nothing for the pain that had been burrowing its way beneath the surface, hidden by Tessa's sheer stubbornness. He felt tears pricking his own eyes.

"We aren't them, princess. We're not going to hurt you," he said softly, calmly.

Tessa took a deep breath and shook her head. "I can't… I need to be by myself. I'm sorry." She turned and fled, leaving him standing amongst the trees with tears slipping down his cheeks.

Cass called to her, but she ran past him. He stopped in front of River. "I'm sorry, she'll come around. This is just scary for her. Give her time."

"Yeah," he replied, blowing out a shaky breath.

Cass seemed to hesitate for a moment before shaking his head and stepping forward, pulling River into his arms. They clung tightly to each other, Cass laying his head on River's shoulder.

"She's been hurt so much," he said, his voice thick. "She's so young, and she's been hurt so much."

"Too much," River agreed, wiping his face. "And she's weathered it all alone."

"She doesn't have to anymore. We'll make sure she

knows it."

They walked, hand in hand, to the deck and sat down on a bench. River wasn't yet ready to face his family.

"What happened?" he asked. "Tessa said she talked to my family."

Cass let out a watery chuckle. "Fuck, it was amazing. She really let it all go, told them exactly what she thought of how they've treated you." He shook his head, a pensive look on his face. "She did what I should have done years ago. I'm sorry I didn't."

River waved him away. "It's different. You grew up with my family; you weren't ready to say anything for the same reasons as I was. They were all we had."

Cass threaded their fingers together. "Not *all* we had. And if they're not willing to treat you fairly, we don't need them at all. You, me, and Tessa; we're our own family."

"Yeah, we are." River smiled. Tessa would come around. A lot had happened in a short space of time. It was enough to overwhelm anyone. "Should we... do you think we could check on her?"

Cass stood and held a hand out to him. "Let's go make sure she's okay."

His family was deep in conversation when they walked into the house. They went quiet upon spotting him, and his parents jumped to their feet.

"River," his mom said, reaching for him but dropping her hand. "Can we talk about this? Please."

Her dark eyes, the spitting image of his, were devastated. Beside her, his dad looked shell-shocked.

River glanced at Cass, who was watching them all with

a stoic expression. "Actually, no, I don't think we can. I think I'm done here." Perhaps one day he would be ready to repair what had been so broken for so long, but he couldn't do this anymore. "Where's Tessa?"

His parents exchanged a look. "Tessa left."

His stomach dropped. "What?"

"Fifteen minutes ago, she said she had to rush back to the city for work and called for a car. She didn't tell you?"

He met Cass's wide eyes, dread settling in his stomach.

The two of them rushed back to the lodge and burst into their room. All of Tessa's things were gone. It wouldn't have taken her long—they hadn't bothered to unpack the night before. All she'd left was a folded piece of notepaper on the bed with their names.

Cass picked it and offered it to him, but River shook his head. Cass opened it, scanning it quickly. He sat down on the bed and rubbed his jaw. "She left."

River frowned at him. "Yeah, clearly."

Cass looked up at him. "No, she *left* left."

He pressed the note into River's hand. He opened it slowly.

> I'm going back to the UK.
> I'll let you know when I land.
> I just need to get away for a while.
> I'm sorry.
> - T x

River sank down beside Cass and closed the note,

holding it to his chest as his heart shattered.

Tessa

Tessa hardly remembered the drive. She'd spent the two hours from Heathrow to her cottage in South Wales in an exhausted daze, music blaring to drown out her own thoughts.

She'd cried through most of the flight; at first because she'd made such a mess of things with River, and then because she was stupid for fleeing the fucking country solely because someone dared confront her with her own damn feelings. It was a little dramatic, even for her.

Tessa was a pro at running away, but, for the first time, she wanted to run back.

She'd considered booking a flight straight back to New York when the plane landed, but perhaps it would do her some good to spend some time alone, to figure out what she really wanted, needed. And what she would allow herself to have.

She'd sent a message to River and Cass letting them know she'd arrived safely, another to Aaron, telling them she was going off grid for a few days, and turned her phone off. Already she felt the absence of River and Cass like a fissure, but Tessa was nothing if not stubborn, and she would see this through.

She drove through the frosty fog, over the rickety bridge

and onto the gravel driveway of her cottage in the early hours of the morning. She'd considered selling the forest cottage several times since moving to New York—the village of Coed-y-paen was hardly an easy trip from the other side of the Atlantic—but as she parked the rental car and the headlights lit up the white stone, she was glad she hadn't.

Set in a valley a five-minute walk from a reservoir, the cottage was a little slice of peace that she'd been sorely missing in the city. She stepped out of the car, the ice covered ground crunching beneath her feet, and breathed in the countryside air. Her head felt clearer than it had in weeks.

Since she was so rarely here, she occasionally rented the place out for holiday makers and paid someone local to keep the place clean and stocked with basics. Tessa turned on the lights in the kitchen and groaned in relief when she confirmed *the basics* included coffee. She dropped her bags on the floor and made a pot before settling on the couch.

She didn't light the fire, just wrapped a blanket around herself and stared around the room, gripping her coffee. It was so quiet, so empty.

Tessa was used to being alone. For years, she had relished escaping London to the cottage. Though Jay would occasionally join her, more often than not she made the trip by herself, locking herself away for a few days with a couple of good books and the old piano in the corner. She liked the solitude and enjoyed walking along the reservoir's edge alone with her morning coffee. Sure, she struggled to sleep alone, but she could sacrifice a little rest for a few days of calm. It had been the perfect escape when London or Jay had overwhelmed her.

But now… she missed them. She missed Cass humming to himself as he scrolled through his phone or flipped through a book, missed River's furious typing and the constant rustling packaging of whatever sweet treat he'd managed to get his hands on. She missed being sandwiched between them on their couch—still too small, even after sizing up—and sipping her morning coffee felt wrong, alone, three-thousand miles away, instead of opposite them at their tiny dining table, watching Cass struggle to keep his eyes open.

She turned on some music to cut through the silence and lay back on the couch, staring up at the ceiling.

What did she want?

She wanted River and Cass, in whatever capacity they wanted her, that much she was sure of. She wanted to let herself have them.

No, she *needed* to let herself have them. She needed to trust them and herself. She needed to believe herself when she told herself it wasn't her fault, what had happened with her friends, her parents, Jay.

She sighed. She needed therapy, most likely. She'd stopped going years ago, after being photographed leaving her therapist's office by the press.

For now, though, she needed time. She would stay in Wales, give herself a week to think everything over. There was a conversation coming with River and Cass; Tessa owed them that after running away, regardless of what she decided to do.

CHAPTER TWENTY-SEVEN

Cass

"**F**uck this."

Cass started, his eyes snapping opening and his coffee cup sliding precariously near the edge of the table. He squinted at River, who was staring out of the window like he was considering razing the city to the ground. "What?"

River pushed away from the table and began pacing. Pacing was becoming somewhat of a daily activity in the King-Reid-Sage household, for the Sage and King parts of it anyway. They'd passed the five days since Tessa had left by pacing, guzzling coffee, thanks to their absolute lack of sleep, and staring at their phones, hoping she might call.

It might have been funny if they weren't the ones living it, consumed by panic and loss, as if Tessa had gone for years and not days.

Cass had never felt so empty. He had spent his whole life searching for the missing piece in his relationship with

River; he'd grown up with an empty space. But now he knew what it felt like to have someone fit so perfectly in it, and the worry that Tessa wouldn't come back to them had left a chasm.

"She could be hurt, something could have happened, and we would have no clue," River ranted.

Cass hummed his agreement. It was the same conversation, three times a day. They traded off who began the conversation, and Cass had started it over dinner last night, so it was River's turn. "I know, but I'm sure she's fine." He rubbed his eyes.

"We should go get her."

"She would have—what?" Cass blinked at him. *That* was new. They'd agreed to give her a week and had hated every second thus far. "River, we don't even know where the hell she is. How are we supposed to go get her?"

"We could call her?"

Cass sighed and drained his coffee. "Her phone is off," he mumbled and River narrowed his eyes.

"How do you know that?" Cass didn't reply, just raised a brow at him and River's mouth popped open. "You tried to call her? When?"

"This morning," Cass admitted. "And also yesterday. And maybe the night before that."

River sat down, dejected. "I miss her," he said, his voice small.

Cass reached across the table to take his hand. "Me too."

A loud knocking sounded at the door, and Cass's heart raced. The two of them were up and at the door in a split second, moving faster than he thought was possible after no sleep. River wrenched the door open and Cass's heart sank at the sight of Aaron.

"Um, hi," they said, looking them both over, alarmed. "Oh no. This is a little sad."

River held the door open and groaned as Aaron walked into the apartment. They took one look around the room, at the empty coffeepot on the table, the half empty takeout containers stacked on the island, and the various empty bottles of liquor and nodded. "Yikes." They turned to them. "I see you're handling Tessa running away well, then."

Cass and River exchanged a long look.

"Are you saying this is a *thing* she does?" Cass asked, his voice mirroring the disbelief on River's face.

"It's been known to happen," they assured them with a sympathetic smile. "Were there feelings involved?"

River dropped onto the couch and nodded. "I told her I loved her."

"Ah." Aaron took a seat on the couch. "That would do it. She used to leave a lot when she got overwhelmed. She'd go away for a few days to clear her head." Cass supposed they should have known that, given how she had snuck out on River the night they met. "It's not that she doesn't trust your feelings, it's that she doesn't think she deserves them," Aaron added with a frown. "I imagine everything with Jay made that significantly worse."

"What do we do?" Cass asked, well aware of how desperate he sounded. "Do we go find her? Leave her alone?"

Aaron tilted their head, considering. "A year ago, I would always have said to leave her alone. Tessa has been fighting for herself for so long. She's never let anyone else fight for her. But now… I think she might let you fight for her."

Cass already knew he and River would fight for her for as long as she would let him.

"I don't suppose you know *where* she might have gone?"

Aaron smiled. "There's only one place."

Tessa

Tessa had written nine songs, read three books, drank at least a dozen pots of coffee, and slept for all of six hours in five days. She wasn't just exhausted; she was bored out of her mind.

She hovered by the front door at least once a day, considering giving up on her one-week promise and driving back to Heathrow, but Tessa Reid didn't give up on anything.

Late-January was really too cold to enjoy the Welsh countryside. The windows were thick with frost, and Tessa hadn't packed for a Welsh winter. Hell, she hadn't packed for Wales at all. She'd brought a scarf and found a holey pair of gloves in the back of a drawer, but the one pair of ballet flats she had packed to take to River's parents weren't ideal for trekking through rain and sleet.

The doorbell rang, and she shot up. Thank fuck for

books with next day shipping; she had run through the three she'd brought. Tessa was shitty company for herself when she had nothing to do.

"Two seconds," she shouted through the door, hurriedly pulling her rattiest cardigan on over her tank top and underwear. The fire left the cottage sweltering, but she didn't want to give the delivery person too much of an eyeful.

She ran to the door and wrenched it open, her mouth dropping open and her heart stilling as she took in the sight before her.

"Hi, princess."

Nothing had ever looked better than River looked standing before her. Peace settled into her bones, one of her missing pieces clicking into place. "Hi."

River stepped forward tentatively. "Can I…" He held his arms out and Tessa flew into them, burrowing herself against him. The tears came thick and fast, blurring her vision. "Hey, it's okay, I'm here baby."

He walked her gently backwards, closing the door, and never letting go of her.

"I'm sorry," she sobbed, shaking. "I'm so fucking sorry for running." She pulled back enough to look up into his face, his perfect face.

"It's okay, there was a lot going on and you weren't ready and—"

"No, it wasn't okay," she interrupted, shaking her head. She took a deep breath, her heart racing. But not from fear; from anticipation. She had held back, from him and from herself, for too long. No more.

"River, I am so unbelievably in love with you."

River

She loved him. She really, truly loved him.

River wiped the tears from her cheeks and leaned closer, pressing a kiss to her freckles. "You love me."

Tessa let out a watery laugh. "So fucking much."

Grinning from ear to ear, he picked her up and spun her around. Tessa squealed and smiled. He'd been dreaming of that for days.

"I love you, baby, so much." He set her down and pressed his forehead to hers. "I know you're scared out of your mind about this, but we can talk about it, okay? We'll figure it out."

Tessa nodded, taking a deep, relieved breath. "I'd like that." She brushed the purple bruises below his eyes and frowned. "I'll make coffee."

"Wait," he said, pulling her back to him. "Forgot something."

Tessa smiled and stood on her tiptoes to kiss him, sighing contently as their lips touched. His whole body seemed to relax into her, as if saying *home*.

She was smiling as she walked into the kitchen to make the coffee. "Is Cass okay?" she asked, pulling cups from the cabinets while River removed the three million layers he was wearing. Wales wasn't colder than New York, but fucking hell, it was wet.

"Yeah, he's here. He dropped me off and went for a

drive to give us some time. I'll text him."

Tessa nodded, toying with his hands. "I'm sorry for not calling. I didn't mean to worry you. I just… I didn't know what to say."

River crossed the room and wrapped his arms around her. "You don't need to apologize." She, too, had dark circles under her eyes. He brushed them with his thumb. "I think it's been a rough week for all of us. But we're together now, and Cass will be here soon too."

"I've missed you both so much," she said, resting her head on his chest.

"We've missed you too, princess." More than he could even put into words.

They settled on the couch, coffee in hand, and threw a blanket over themselves. "How did you know where I was?" Tessa asked.

"Aaron came to check on us and make sure we were holding it together. We weren't in the slightest, but they knew where you'd be."

She wrinkled her nose. "I can't believe I've become predictable. I'm glad you came, though."

Flames danced in the fireplace as Tessa turned her face to peer up at him and swallowed. "I'm ready to talk, I think."

River tapped her nose. "We're just talking. No need to look like someone died."

"I'm not good at this bit. The feelings, I mean."

He brought her fingers to his lips. "Then we'll break it down into smaller pieces. Take Cass and I out of the picture." She frowned. "Long-term, what do you want in life?"

"I've thought about it a lot this week," she admitted. "I want to record my music. I'm going to follow through on the ultimatum I gave Empire if they're not willing to work with me."

She took a deep breath, sitting up and holding the blanket tight to herself as if hiding behind it. "I want a family. I want to get married and have kids and fuck…" She looked up at him, tears lining her eyes. "I can't take you and Cass out of the picture, because I want you there for all of it. And I know that things are complicated with Cass and he wants none of that, but if you do…"

"I do." He didn't even have to consider it. He wanted all that and more with her. With both of them, if he was being honest. He reached for her and, after a moment's hesitation, she let him pull her onto his lap. "I can't promise that it's all going to be easy. I can't promise to get it right all the time." She shook her head but smiled, and the sight sent a wave of calm through him. "But I promise to try, and I really think we can do it."

"I want to try."

River's heart soared. Tessa's face was a familiar sight of stubborn determination. If she'd decided that she wanted to make it work with him, he had no doubt in his mind she would make it work. *They* would make it work. "You have no idea how happy that makes me," he breathed, his cheeks aching from smiling so widely.

She cupped his face. "I suppose you *could* show me."

Heat flooded him as he brushed his lips against her.

Fuck, he'd missed this. He laid her back on the couch and nudged her knees apart, her cardigan parting and taking his breath with it. "Done with talking, princess?" He dragged his lips across her throat and she groaned, her head falling back.

"I—wait." Her eyes snapped open. River sat back. "What about Cass?" she asked quietly, and he sighed.

He loved Cass, he would never stop loving Cass, and he didn't want to give up what they had, but it had been tearing Tessa apart. He'd had almost two decades to get used to the fact that Cass would never love him in the same way; for Tessa, it had only been a few months.

"Do you want to stop? With him, I mean."

"No," she said, slowly. "I mean…" She blew out a breath, looking away from him, her eyes sad. He took her hand and gripped it. "I love him too, obviously. I don't understand how you made it this far without completely shattering, but you did, so I will too."

"He's always going to be with us," he assured her. "And I'll be here to help you navigate the feelings."

She chewed her lip. "I bet your family hates me now. They're probably not going to be happy that we're together."

River leaned down, hovering over her with a smile. "They don't hate you, and, even if they did, I once again don't give a fuck. I'm done with them. It's just you, me, and Cass, and everything else is white noise."

Tessa's heart raced beneath him. "Don't ask me to explain why, but that might be the hottest thing I've ever heard you say."

He chuckled and looped his thumb in the strap of her tank top, tugging it down. "I'll need to try hard to top it, then."

A soft knock sounded at the door and Tessa sat up so quickly she almost toppled him from the couch. He chuckled and stood, holding a hand out to her. "I might be mad about that if it wasn't so cute how much you've missed him."

She practically ran to the door, shouting behind her, "I'm going to be really pissed if it's the delivery person with my books."

It wasn't. Cass stood in the doorway, a smile like sunshine on his perfect face as Tessa launched herself into his arms. River's heart melted enough to warm the frigid January evening.

"I missed you," Tessa said, her voice muffled against Cass's puffy coat.

"Missed you like crazy." He pulled back and looked between the two of them. "Are we good?"

They both nodded. "Yeah, we're good."

Relief flooded Cass's face. "Good. I have a bone to pick with you, princess." He wrapped his arms around her, walking her backwards until she was pressed against the island, then lifted her on to it, so they were closer to eye level. He hovered not an inch from her lips, Tessa's eyes wide and bright.

"We don't run from each other. If you need time or space, that's fine and we'll make it work, but we don't run."

She nodded, silver lining golden eyes. "I'm sorry."

"Hey." He brushed his thumb across her jaw. "You don't

need to apologize. I know this is all hard on you, but we'll get through it together, okay?"

"Yeah."

"Where's the bedroom?" River asked, grabbing their discarded phones and bags.

"Up the stairs, first on the left," Tessa said with a yawn, resting her head on Cass's chest.

"Let's get you to sleep," he said, and she looked up, frowning at them both.

"I don't want to sleep."

"But you need to. Besides," River reached for her chin, leaning across Cass's shoulder to kiss her. "You're going to need your energy for tomorrow. We have catching up to do."

CHAPTER TWENTY-EIGHT

Tessa

F rosty grass crunched beneath three pairs of boots as they walked along the water's edge. River and Cass had had the foresight to bring Tessa some proper winter clothes, though their overprotective nature had caused them to go somewhat overboard. Besides her winter boots, Tessa was bundled up in a puffy coat, thermals, fuzzy socks, a scarf, and gloves. She'd been forced to de-robe before getting behind the wheel of the rental car for a drive to the grocery store, concerned she wouldn't actually fit in the driver's seat.

When she complained she felt like a marshmallow, River had simply kissed her, bitten her lip, and said, "Delicious."

She was no longer complaining, though, holding River and Cass's hands, strolling along in the biting chill.

Though Tessa loved lying by the water in the summer,

letting the sun tickle her skin and paint her freckles darker, there was something magical about the iced over water. It sparkled in the morning sun like a looking glass right out of a fairytale.

They settled on a bench overlooking the frozen peaks. Tessa hardly felt the chill of the metal on her ass, thanks to the many layers.

"We should come here again when it's warmer. It's incredible."

Cass lit up at her suggestion. "I'd love that. We spend too much time stuck in the city. We should get out more."

It was true they could all do with more fresh air. "It's a plan," River said, stretching his arm across her shoulders.

"We should do more of that too, making plans. As much as we love spending all of our free time curled up reading or watching movies, we should… I don't know, go out, do things."

River and Cass exchanged an amused glance at Tessa's stammered suggestion. "Who are you, and what have you done with Tessa?"

She rolled her eyes and pushed Cass's arm. "It's called character development." Truthfully, it was called realizing she was no longer stuck under the rule of an overbearing rockstar and could do whatever the fuck she wanted.

"Speaking of character development," River began, scraping the toe of his boot along the ice. "I got another offer from that publisher. I'm going to meet them, I think. See what they have to say. Either way, though, I think I'm going to put my name on my books."

Pride flooded through Tessa at the kindling of hope in his eyes. "River, that's amazing," she squealed as Cass said, "It's about damn time."

He shrugged, a blush spreading across his cheeks. "You know, when I started writing, I was so scared of anyone finding out who I am. But I like who I am now. I'm happy."

Years of making music and nothing had ever sounded sweeter to Tessa's ears. But it was Cass she watched, tears of pride springing to his eyes as he turned away so quickly she wasn't sure River had even noticed.

"Besides," River continued. "I figure if Tessa can stand up to Henry fucking Carver, I can manage this."

Tessa frowned, a new worry winding its way through her bones. "You know, if people find out we're together, it might not be great for your image. Publishers might hesitate. Maybe we should keep this—"

"No," River said, simply. "We're not hiding this because you've been made to feel like shit about yourself by the press for no reason. Besides, it goes both ways; if you want to start performing more, my past isn't going to reflect well on you either."

"That's a valid point," she grumbled.

"You could just say I'm right," River said, clearly fighting a laugh. Cass didn't even try, chuckling and shaking his head.

"I definitely couldn't." She could admit to being wrong in her head, but out loud? The world would stop turning.

"Speaking of you performing," Cass cut in, taking pity on her. "What's your plan for that?"

Tessa wrinkled her nose. She drummed her nails against the coffee cup. She always kept them short, but she'd bitten them to hell and back this past week and they hardly dinged against the metal. "I'm going to email my manager, let her know I'm giving Henry an ultimatum. Maybe if it comes through her, he'll be more inclined to listen. If he's not, fuck him. I'll look for representation elsewhere and if no one else wants to sign me because of my reputation, I'll just... figure it out, I guess."

"That won't happen," Cass assured her. "Even if every other label in the world said no to you, Aaron's going to keep writing with you. And writers work without labels all the time these days, right?"

"Right," she agreed, though the thought of doing it on her own was terrifying.

He pulled her into his side and kissed her forehead. "You're going to be fine. We all are."

"So what now?" she asked. The last thing Tessa wanted was to return to the real world. She wished the three of them could stay in the valley forever. Going back had always been Tessa's least favorite part of running away but at least this time, she wasn't going back alone.

"I reckon we can hide out here for a little while before we have to go back."

It didn't feel like hiding, though. Whispering *I love you* in River's ear while he gave her a piggyback along a slushy stretch of road; brushing snowflakes from the shadow of stubble on Cass's jaw with her fingers, then her lips; walking into a cafe with held hands and wide smiles; Tessa felt fully, truly seen for who she was, and who she wanted to be.

And for the first time in a long time, she didn't mind.

Cass

Cassian King was happy for his best friends.

No, really, he was.

But panic clawed at him. He loved Tessa; he loved River. *Had* loved River all along, that much was obvious. What wasn't obvious was how he'd fucked it all up so thoroughly, how it had taken him almost twenty years to realize that the feelings he had for River were, in fact, romantic.

He couldn't have figured it out at a worse time. River had finally found someone, finally allowed himself to love again. Cass wouldn't, couldn't, fuck it up for him.

He stared out the window, watching sleet rain down and smear the glass. Tessa and River were in the kitchen, Tessa teaching River to make some kind of Welsh fruit bread. Mostly, she was hovering around him, trying not to take over.

Soft music played from River's laptop on the coffee table, the open plan living room and kitchen bathed in the orange glow of the fire and the blue light from the open refrigerator.

Cass looked up at the sound of Tessa's laugh to see River spinning her around, dancing in the refrigerator light.

His heart clenched in his chest, wanting. He looked away, picking up the beat-up paperback he'd stashed on the arm of the couch, opening it, and staring at the page without reading until the words blurred before his eyes.

If time passed, he didn't notice until he felt the couch shift and looked up to see Tessa sitting down beside him. She held out a steaming mug of tea that smelled remarkably like whiskey. "You okay?"

Cass nodded, closing the book without bothering with a bookmark. He would have to start over anyway. "Mhmm. Thanks, princess."

He patted his lap, and she lifted her bare legs onto him. Tessa's inability to dress for the cold weather was a fucking hazard. He and River had more or less convinced her she had to layer up before going outside. Inside, though, she still refused to wear pants, and Cass didn't mind in the slightest as he ran his hand up her soft calf. "Where's River?"

"He went upstairs to take a shower. I wanted to talk to you about something."

"Yeah?"

Tessa reached out to take his hand, her skin warm against his. "I know things are changing between River and I. Well—" she wrinkled her nose, "—the label is changing anyway. But everything else is going to stay the same. And… we want things between *us* to stay the same too."

Cass swallowed, his mouth suddenly as dry as sandpaper. "I don't want to come between the two of you."

"What? Why would you come between us?"

He shrugged, sipping his tea—which was, in fact,

incredibly boozy—before answering. "You're a couple now."

Tessa frowned, her brows pinching together. "Yeah, but that changes nothing about our relationship with you. I mean, if you don't want to do this anymore, we totally get it," she said quickly and Cass shook his head.

"No, no, I do."

Tessa breathed a sigh of relief. "Well, good. Because we don't want things to change." She stood and held out a hand to him. "Come on, let's go see if we can squeeze into the shower with River and inevitably make a mess of the bathroom."

Cass let her pull him to his feet, let her hold his hand on the way to the bathroom, but worry burrowed into his bones. Things would change, whether they wanted them to or not. He couldn't be a third wheel for the rest of their lives. If all went to plan, at some point, River and Tessa would get married, start a family, and where would that leave him?

He would stand with a smile and watch his friends walk down the aisle and walk away bonded by law, and he would be happy for them. He would help them build cribs and love their kids like they were his own, and he would be happy for them.

But for now, while they hid away in the Welsh countryside, he would believe Tessa, and he would let himself pretend that what they had now could last forever.

River was already in the shower, running his soapy hands across his inked chest, when the two of them made it up the stairs.

"It's about time," he said, a grin splitting his face as they walked into the room. Cass hadn't seen River smile so openly, so often, since they were teenagers. "Get in here."

Tessa eyed the shower warily.

"Come on," River coaxed. "If we don't all fit, we'll at least all be naked, and think of the fun we can have with that."

Cass snorted and quickly shed his clothes. Tessa, who had started undressing, paused, her eyes roaming him. He beckoned her close, and she licked her lips.

Cass undid the rest of the buttons holding her shirt together and pushed it down her arms until it fell to the floor. She had forgone a bra, and he brushed his fingers across her nipples, then down her stomach, before pushing her underwear down. She shivered, pouting as he stepped away towards the shower.

River's eyes flicked between them, darker than the night sky peeping through the bathroom window.

Cass groaned as he stepped into the warm water.

Tessa pulled a scrunchie from her bag on the counter and tied her hair in a messy bun on top of her head. "This is going to end badly," she said, stepping into space between them. "See? I told you we would all fit," River pointed out, smugly.

"It *is* nice," Tessa relented.

Cass ran his fingers lightly across her shoulders before massaging firmly. Tessa moaned, her hand flying up to grip River's bicep. His hand disappeared between them and she cursed, her eyes falling closed. Cass couldn't see what was happening, but Tessa's shaking legs and the rise and fall of her chest filled in the gaps.

River's other hand palmed her breast, and his name tumbled from her lips. Tessa's eyes were hazy gold when she opened them and licked her lips.

"We need to hurry with the showering part. It's too small in here for the three of us." The water streamed down their bodies, reflecting the light, so his best friends looked like something straight out of one of the fantasy stories they adored.

Cass met River's wicked smile. They weren't making it to the bedroom. River looped an arm around Tessa's waist and she squealed as he backed against the wall, gripping her ass. He lifted her and she wrapped her legs around his waist, whimpering as he dragged his teeth across her throat.

Cass pressed in behind her, trapping them against the wall.

"Please," she begged, and River cursed as he pushed into her slowly. She tightened her hold around his neck, crying out, and Cass backed away enough to smack her ass. The sound was lost to Tessa's moan, so sweet that he couldn't help but do it again. "Cass," she whimpered, and he reached out of the shower, into the medicine bag for the lube, desperate to be inside her.

Cass gently pulled the scrunchie out of her hair, and watched it tumble down her back in perfect, golden waves. He wrapped it around his fist and tugged her head back until her throat was exposed. He dragged his lips up the curve of her neck before claiming her mouth, tasting sugar and liquor on her tongue, as she bounced on River's cock.

He positioned the head of his cock against her ass and teased her until she was begging. He pushed into her, groaning as she so perfectly hugged his cock. "This ass is ours, princess, isn't that right?" He palmed her ass and squeezed.

"Yes, God, yes," she gasped.

River's hips had stilled, and Cass leaned forward over Tessa's shoulder to kiss him, his wet hair curling around his jaw. If he hadn't been inside Tessa, Cass's knees might have buckled as River bit down on his lower lip. He cursed and pulled back, panting as River's bright eyes sending a shiver down his spine.

He bit down on Tessa's neck and she cursed. "Hair or throat, baby?"

"Huh?" she said, panting.

"Do you want me to hold your hair or your throat?"

Tessa whimpered and leaned her head back further. "My throat."

"That's our girl." Cass gently kissed her cheek as he wrapped his fingers around her throat and squeezed.

Fuck, she felt like heaven.

He and River moved in unison. He could feel River's cock inside her as they fucked Tessa like their lives depended on it until all three of them were trembling, water coursing over them. Tessa was close, her moans turning to cries and her body trembling.

"No," he gasped, holding tighter to her throat. "We come together."

Tessa whimpered and he wound his free hand beneath

her to cup River's balls, gently brushing his thumb across the taut skin.

"Fucking hell," River said, his head falling back against the tiles.

The moment the three of them crossed some invisible line, the world around him stilled and all that he felt, all that mattered, were River and Tessa. Light flared behind his eyelids as he came, incoherent words slipping from his tongue.

They came down in a wave of panting breaths and buckling knees. Cass pulled out of Tessa and gently lifted her from River, who all but slumped against the wall, panting.

Cass spun Tessa slowly and pressed soft kisses across her face before kissing her throat in the spots he had been holding. "You okay, baby?"

"Yeah," she croaked, a sated smile on her lips. River turned off the shower and enclosed her in his arms. Cass stepped out and rummaged around in the medicine bag on the counter for the bruise-prevention lotion they'd bought after learning that Tessa bruised like a peach. *"But I like having your marks on me,"* she'd grumbled when he'd brought it home, until he reminded her that she was regularly photographed by the press.

He rubbed the lotion onto her neck with tender fingers while River kissed the top of her head. This part—when the high leveled out and all they wanted to do was hold each other close and never let go—might be his favorite part of being like this with River and Tessa.

They fell into bed and wrapped themselves around each other. Tessa and River drifted off slowly, but Cass fought sleep, watching the moonlight filtering through the blinds, lighting them up in shards of silver.

And when he finally fell asleep, he dreamed of weddings and honeymoons, cribs and babies. But they weren't just River and Tessa's.

Even in sleep, Cass knew it was reckless to dream of such things, but it wasn't nearly as dangerous as the single flame of hope that bloomed in his heart.

CHAPTER TWENTY-NINE

Tessa

Tessa smoothed down her skirt for the millionth time since leaving the apartment. She wished River and Cass were with her, but then she always wished they were with her and *that* was called codependency, which wasn't something she wanted to add to her long resume of things that had fucked her up.

There had been no frost on the ground when they landed in New York, but the city still felt colder than the cottage had. She already missed being bundled up by the fire with a cup of tea in one hand, Cass's hand in the other, and her head resting on River's shoulder.

Her manager, Rebecca, had come through. She'd taken Tessa's ultimatum to Empire Records, to Henry Carver himself, and set up a meeting with Tessa and the label executives. They'd been in New York anyway for some major music awards and had booked a meeting room in their Fifth Avenue hotel. She didn't know if she was going into a contract termination or a job offer, but Aaron was by her side, ready for either outcome.

Rebecca met them in the hotel lobby, the raven-haired woman smiling widely. "Tessa, Aaron, it's good to see you." She opened her arms and gave Tessa a polite hug before saying, "Shall we head up?"

Tessa turned to Aaron, and they nodded, an *everything's going to be okay* kind of smile on their face. "You've got this, T."

She followed Rebecca through the lobby, forcing her hands to still.

Tessa and Rebecca had never been close. Many of the musicians she had met over the years, Jay and Aaron included, were friends with their managers, but, although they'd been working together since Tessa was sixteen, the two of them had never really clicked. She didn't do much, in Tessa's opinion. Sure, she filtered emails and collaboration requests, sent her contracts to lawyers, and sent Tessa periodic updates on her royalties, but she'd never championed Tessa's career in the way she'd seen other managers do.

Rebecca turned to her as the elevator doors slid open on their floor. "Just hear them out, Tessa. You don't have to decide anything today."

"Yeah, sure."

Rebecca knocked on the door and pushed it open when a familiar voice called, "Come in."

Henry Carver sat at the head of the large meeting table, a glass of what looked like whiskey grasped in his hand. His black suit was impeccably pressed, not a single one of his peppered grey hairs was out of place, and, already, a smirk dripping condescension lined his lips.

Tessa hated him.

Flanking him were the six white men that made up Empire's oh-so-diverse board of executives, and Tessa's arch-nemesis; Empire's head of publicity, Candy Langham.

"Rebecca, Tessa, welcome. Take a seat. Drinks?" Henry gestured to the seats closest to the door, opposite the board, and Tessa sat down.

"No, thank you," she said. The sooner she could get out of here, the better. As if he could see right through her, Henry's smile grew.

"Well, let's crack on, shall we?"

They began by droning on about Tessa's achievements, or rather *Empire's* achievements, by proxy of her hard work.

It was impressive to see it all laid out, she could admit. In the decade she had been with Empire, she'd sold well over a hundred songs, more than half of which had charted. Nineteen had gone number one, and eight had won her Grammys before she'd even turned twenty-five. And sure, Empire's name had been stamped on the credits, but it had been her hard work that had won the awards. Not enough, apparently, for them to give her the one thing she'd been asking for since she was a teenager.

"Now, Tessa, we know you're looking for a recording and performance contract, so let's talk about that?" Henry turned to Candy. "Candy, you had some questions for Tessa?"

"I sure did." Candy's smile was saccharine. "As you know, your reputation has been far from... stellar since you signed with Empire. What with your friends and family going to the press and your relationship with Jay." She tutted and Tessa bit the inside of her cheek in an effort to stay quiet. "Your public image has improved since your show with Aaron Peters, but we have some concerns."

"Go on."

"Well, first, your demeanor isn't the most… marketable, you know? In past interviews, you haven't always been particularly… warm, if you will."

Tessa fought the urge to roll her eyes. "I don't really know how you expected me to react when the so-called journalists alluded to me being a gold-digging home wrecker, Candy."

She pursed her lips condescendingly. "Well, we do have media training for that very purpose. I know you've been against it in the past, but if you were to represent Empire by performing, that would be essential."

Tessa shrugged. It was a small compromise. "I could do that."

Candy smiled widely. "Excellent. Now, onto the other concern we have. You were recently photographed with Cassian King and River Sage."

"Yes," Tessa replied, tightly.

Candy peered down at her tablet screen through her gold-rimmed glasses. "Cassian King, thirty-eight, is a model," she told the board. "And well liked, I must say. None of my research showed anything negative about him at all. River Sage, on the other hand…" She frowned at Tessa. "Are you aware that he's done prison time?"

"I am."

"And you're friends with this man?"

Tessa took a deep breath, ignoring the scandalized glances. "River and Cassian are my best friends, and River and I are dating. And before any of you have anything to say about that," she said, bitingly. "I should remind you that two people sitting in this room have been convicted of tax-fraud, and one of your wives did thirty days for driving under the influence. So let's not throw stones."

She had expected them to bring up River's past the moment they were photographed together; she'd done her research.

Candy's face fell, but she recovered quickly. "It's something to keep in mind. I'm sure, if needed, we could spin it in a positive light."

Tessa returned her pandering smile tenfold. "If anyone could, Candy, I'm sure it would be you."

Henry clasped his hands on the table and cleared his throat. Considering it was his wife who had done time, she could only imagine he wanted to move on. "Well, with that out of the way. Tessa, we don't want to lose you a songwriter. You've done great work for us and, admittedly, the reception to your show with Aaron has impressed us. We're willing to offer you a recording and performance contract, so long as you're willing to meet our conditions."

Tessa reserved her excitement. "I'm listening."

Henry smiled. "It's important to us that you also remain a songwriter for our other artists. We understand that working on your own music will take up more of your time, but we would still want you to be working with other artists, even if only at a quarter of the volume you are now."

Tessa nodded; she had no intention of giving that up. She liked writing for other people. "That's doable."

"Like Candy said," Henry continued, "we would require you to undergo some extensive media training, and have a publicity team on hand to handle any… issues. Now, we would look for you to have a record out within the year. I assume you have enough material for that?"

"Yeah, I have plenty. I've been working a lot with Aaron, and we have demos ready to go," Tessa told him with a nod. "Anything else?"

"One more thing." Henry's smirk grew. "While working on your public image is important to Empire, your physical image is too. We would require you to drop to a size four to six within six months."

And there it was. Tessa almost laughed. "Are you serious?"

"Quite."

"Even if I was willing to do that, which I assure you I'm not, I'm a size fourteen now. I couldn't possibly lose that much weight healthily."

Henry's eyes flicked to Rebecca, who reached out to pat Tessa's arm. Of course, she must have known ahead of time exactly how this would go. "It's doable, Tessa. We can get you a nutritionist, a personal trainer. Surgery is always an option…" She trailed off at Tessa's glare.

"You have to understand, Tessa, we don't want to be seen to be promoting an unhealthy image," Candy chimed in and Tessa laughed, fire brewing in her belly.

"That's rich," she said, shaking her head. "Half of your male artists are photographed with drugs every other weekend, and no one bats an eye. You don't give a fuck about anyone's health. Let's call it what it is: my body makes you uncomfortable." She shrugged. "I'm not here to make you comfortable. I'm here to make music."

"It's not personal—"

"Bullshit, Henry," she spat. "It's absolutely personal. And it's absolutely your loss. I like my body, not that it should matter, and I have no intention of changing it for anyone. I'm not interested." She stood up, shouldering her bag. "When my contract ends in March, I'm out. Oh, and don't bother trying to get any more songs out of me in the meantime."

Rebecca stood and reached for her as she moved towards the door, but Tessa stared her down. "If it wasn't obvious, Rebecca, you're fired. And you can all go fuck yourselves."

In a move that even she could admit was a little too petty, she flipped them all off and slammed the door in Rebecca's face.

As the elevator descended to the lobby, she slumped against the mirrored wall. She had either made the best or worst decision professionally, but personally? She'd never felt better.

So her body took up a little more space than some; so what? She wasn't going to apologize for it. She looked in the mirror and saw a successful woman who looked damn good, and, frankly, she didn't give a fuck what anyone else thought when they looked at her.

She took a deep breath as she stepped out of the elevator, high on the buzz of standing up for herself.

Aaron stood up and looked her over. "I'm going to go with congrats?"

"I quit. And I fired Rebecca." she said, too quickly, and Aaron was silent for a moment while she chewed her nails.

"Whoa," Aaron said, holding a hand out to her and pulling her from the lobby onto the busy street. "I mean, good fucking riddance, but what happened?"

They jumped into a cab and they listened as Tessa spilled, interrupting only to curse everyone associated with Empire Records at various points. She was well aware of their cab driver listening too, as his eyebrows seemed to rise with every layer of the story. As proud of herself as she was, anxiety was filtering in through the buzz. She had just quit the best job she'd ever had. Truthfully, the only job she'd ever had if you didn't count the multiple minimum wage jobs she'd juggled trying to help pay off her dad's gambling debts when she was a teenager. Empire was all she'd ever known.

"Jesus, Tessa, I'm so sorry," Aaron said when she'd finished. "I knew Henry was a dick, but that's ridiculous. You made the right call."

"You think?" she asked, nervously. "I don't know where to go from here. What if no other label or manager wants me because of my reputation?"

"Your reputation isn't nearly as much of a problem as Empire made it out to be, T," Aaron said gently. "Do you have any idea how many industry folks have asked me when your contract is up over the years?"

"Seriously?"

"Yeah. Rebecca never told you? I know tons of people who reached out to her."

Tessa growled, cursing her manager. Ex-manager, she supposed. "No, she didn't. She's been in Henry's pocket all along."

"Of course she didn't," Aaron said, shaking their head. "Let's put a demo together and I'll put the word out that you're leaving Empire in March. You're going to have people lining up to work with you."

Tessa cringed. "Oh, I don't know, I—"

"Tessa." She could hear the smile in their voice. "I'm not doing it because we're friends, though there would be nothing wrong with it if I was. I'm doing it for the same reason I wanted to work with you when you were seventeen; you're fucking talented."

"It feels like nepotism or something," she said, wrinkling her nose.

"All I'm doing is letting people know you're available and how to contact you. You've done the rest already by building a damn impressive resume."

Tessa sighed, wringing her hands. She would be an idiot not to let Aaron speak up for her, and she knew they were right; she'd done enough for her work to speak for itself. She just needed her name whispered in the right direction. "Okay," she relented. "Thank you."

"You're going to be just fine, don't you worry."

The cab pulled up on Aaron's street. She handed the driver a twenty and opened the door.

"Wait," he said, and her hand stilled on the handle.

"Yeah?"

"I think I saw your video online. The *Fingertips* song, right?"

Tessa blinked in surprise. "Yeah, that's me."

The driver smiled over his shoulder at her. "I really liked it. Can't wait to hear more."

"Thanks," she said, swallowing. She and Aaron stepped onto the sidewalk and watched him drive away with a smile.

She was going to prove to Henry, Rebecca, Candy, every asshole at Empire Records, that they'd lost the best thing to ever happen to them. More importantly, though, she was going to prove to herself that she had what it took to make it.

After all, she was too damn stubborn to let herself down.

CHAPTER THIRTY

Tessa

Quiet music played from the speakers as Aaron and Tessa poured over the list on Aaron's laptop. The number of demos they'd recorded together in the past year alone was in triple figures—narrowing them down to put together a demo of Tessa's best work was proving difficult. Though she couldn't sign with anyone else until her Empire contract ran out, it wouldn't hurt to reach out to people now. If she could at least have a writing contract lined up by then, she could figure the performing shit out later.

Tessa had come a long way from working multiple jobs to afford her shitty South London apartment while funding her dad's gambling addiction. She would have royalty payments coming in for the rest of her life and she could live comfortably on the royalties from her work with Jay alone, considering how much she'd written for him. But Tessa had been writing professionally for ten years; she couldn't imagine not doing it. A label was technically optional—there were plenty of independent songwriters around—but with Tessa's reputation and lack of manager, it would be tough. And given how things had ended with Jay… All he'd have to do was say the word and no one would work with her again. She'd seen it happen more times than she could count.

"*Fingertips* is a given," Aaron said, adding it to the list they'd started in an old notebook. "We'll need to record a more polished version, but I think we should still keep it pretty stripped back to emulate how it was at the show."

Tessa nodded her agreement. "We should avoid anything that's too obviously about Jay and me."

Aaron frowned, crossing out several songs on the list, but they didn't question her. Aaron knew as well as she did that the more she could do to distance herself from Jay, the better. She didn't want to be Tessa Reid, Jay Hutchison's ex-fiancée; she wanted to be just Tessa. If that meant ruling out some of her best songs, so be it. She could write more.

"At least we have some happy songs to choose for a change, since you're so disgustingly in love now," Aaron quipped. Tessa glared at them, though she couldn't disagree. Even in her happiest days with Jay, she'd leaned towards more negative songs, but since meeting River and Cass, there had been a shift.

"Not that one." Tessa leaned over, scratching out a song and ignoring Aaron's protesting groan. "You know Cass is going to want to send this to his parents and they don't need to hear me singing about going down on their son before they've actually met me in person." Even if they wouldn't know the song was about him, it was a little much.

"Ugh, fine. What about—" Aaron paused as Tessa's phone rang shrilly and they both looked up at it. Tessa's stomach flipped as Jay's face flashed on the screen.

She hadn't bothered changing his contact picture after the breakup, and her heart stung as she took his sleepy smile, his dark hair falling across his pillow-creased face. He'd sent the selfie to her the first time he'd gone on tour without her, just four months after they'd met. Two weeks they'd been apart, and it had felt like two decades. When he'd come home, they'd sequestered themselves in his bedroom for three days, shutting out the world.

"Are you going to answer?" Aaron asked, but Tessa just leaned forward and declined the call. "Okay then. So I was thinking—"

"For fuck's sake," Tessa cursed as the phone rang again. "He's just going to keep calling."

"You want me to get it?" Aaron offered, but she shook her head.

"I'll put it on speaker."

"I'll be quiet," Aaron said, dropping their pen on the notebook and sitting back.

Tessa took a deep, bracing breath and answered the call, turning on loud speaker. "What?"

"You answered." Surprise lit Jay's voice, and Tessa hated how quickly her heart raced at the sound. Despite everything, it still responded to him. Though, she supposed seven years of love didn't just disappear.

"You would have kept calling if I didn't."

Jay had the gall to answer with a laugh. "True."

Tessa leaned back, letting Aaron's couch envelope her. "What do you want? I'm busy."

"Henry called me." *Of course he did.* "You're not leaving Empire."

Aaron's head snapped towards the phone at Jay's commanding tone, anger flaring in their blue eyes.

"I don't remember asking for your opinion." Tessa didn't have to pretend to sound indifferent; she was so used to him using that tone with her, it didn't faze her anymore. It wasn't like he could hit her through the phone.

"Tessa." Jay's voice cracked, and she was surprised to hear what sounded like a note of worry. "Come on. I know Henry's a dick but Empire is the best of the best. You're not going to find a better label."

"It really isn't your problem," she told him, and he scoffed.

"Of course it is. Whether or not you believe me, I love you, Tessa."

The pain that lanced her heart was softer. "I don't think it's a case of me not believing you, but rather, a case of you doing a terrible job of showing it. But that's beside the point. Did Henry tell you why I quit?"

"He said you weren't happy with your contract renewal, but I can talk to him. We can work—"

"Jay," she interrupted. "I can't stress enough how much I don't want you butting into my professional life. I already have my work cut out for me trying to get people to see me as something other than your fiancée." Jay sucked in a breath and Tessa could picture his hurt expression perfectly.

She hadn't often bothered to fight back in the last couple of years—she hadn't even been scared of him by the end, just tired—but when she did, the same wounded look would fall over his face until she felt so guilty she apologized just to wipe it off.

"I want to record my music," she continued. "That's why I was meeting Henry today."

"Sweetheart, that's amazing," Jay said, and Tessa hated how instinctive it was to enjoy how proud he sounded. "I don't understand. Why wouldn't you want to stay on with Empire for that?"

Aaron snorted, then covered their mouth as if remembering loudspeaker worked both ways.

"Who is that?" Jay's voice was quieter, lower.

"It's me," Aaron said quickly. "You're on loudspeaker."

"Oh." Though he still sounded disgruntled, Jay's voice leveled considerably. Part of Tessa wished it had been River or Cass sitting with her, just to piss him off. *Maybe she could accidentally pocket dial him sometime when they were...* No. Definitely not. Tessa had no doubt that he'd looked into both River and Cass, the same as Candy had, and she didn't put it past him to find a way to use River's history against him or fuck up Cass's career.

"I did want to stay with Empire," she said, pulling the conversation back. "Initially anyway. But I'm not willing to meet their demands, so I quit."

"What demands?" Jay asked.

Tessa sighed. "They wanted me to lose weight. A lot of it."

Jay's silence was loud; Tessa could easily imagine

anger settling into the lines on his face, his fists balling. For as shitty as Jay had been to her, he didn't tolerate it from others—especially when it came to her weight. More than one journalist had lost their job over the years for writing fatphobic shit about her. He'd even had a top producer blacklisted after overhearing a comment at an awards show.

"That fucking—" Tessa tuned out his rant. She wasn't his to defend anymore, though she had no doubt he was going to do something about it anyway. She might feel sorry for Henry if he wasn't such an asshole.

Tessa tuned back in just in time to hear him say, "—kill that slimy fucking cunt." Aaron, who was as used to Jay's rants as she was, just shook their head and rolled their eyes.

"Right, well, as much as I appreciate that—" Tessa began before Jay could start ranting again, but he interrupted her.

"Fuck them, sweetheart. I mean it. You know any label would be lucky to have you exactly as you are. And after your song that went viral? *Fingertips*, right? It's fucking amazing. I can talk to some people, ask my team to set up meetings…"

Even Aaron looked surprised at the change of tone. Tessa sucked in a breath. It was easier to remember why she'd walked away when Jay was shouting.

"Thank you," she said softly. "But I have to do this on my own." Not exactly on her own—she had Aaron and River and Cass—but not with him.

"Tessa. Tell me we still have a chance here. Please." Jay's voice cracked, and Tessa had to close her eyes. *He hurt you*, she reminded herself. *It doesn't matter how nice he can be. He hurt you.*

"We don't," she replied, gently but firmly. "Leaving was the right decision for me. Besides—" Tessa took a deep breath. "—I'm with someone else now." He was going to find out at some point; she and River weren't exactly good at keeping their hands to themselves and there were cameras everywhere. It was better he found out from her.

"Is it serious?" Jay didn't sound surprised, just sad. He'd seen her with River and Cass.

"Yes."

"Do you love them?"

"Yeah, I do."

"More than you love—"

"Jay," she interrupted. "That's not fair. You know that's not why I left. I love you. I will *always* love you. But you were bad for me and I had to choose to love myself more than I love you."

Love, she had learned, was not a finite resource—nor did it make any fucking sense. She could love Jay, even if he'd hurt her and she'd moved on; she could love River even if it scared her, and she could love Cass even though she knew he would never feel the same in return.

And she could love herself, *would* love herself, even if she'd spent her whole life being told she wasn't worth it.

Jay was quiet for so long Tessa wondered if he'd hung up. But then he said, in barely a whisper, "Are you happy, sweetheart?"

"I am," she replied, and for the first time in a long time, she wasn't lying.

"Good. I know… I know I've done nothing to prove it, but that's all I want for you."

Tessa knew anyone would call her crazy for believing him, but she did. Because she remembered the days before his drinking had gotten bad; she would never forget what it was like to play second fiddle to a bottle, but she remembered what it was like to be the most important thing in his world. She could remember the good days, and still remember how it felt when he'd thrown her across the room. She could miss parts of him and fear the rest.

"I know you didn't go to rehab." She'd smelled the whiskey when he'd shown up after the show, and a quick google search had confirmed it. Jay had spent the six months after their breakup being photographed all over London. "Please get help. You're going to drink yourself to death. Go home—your mom wants to help, and she deserves to see you better before she's gone."

"Yeah," Jay agreed with a watery breath. "I think it might be time. You're right. I love you, Tessa. I always will. And I'm so sorry for everything."

"I love you too," Tessa replied and, as she ended the call, she knew it was the last time she would ever say those words to Jay.

CHAPTER THIRTY-ONE

Cass

Cass tried to lose himself in the book in his hand, but River kept drawing his attention. Watching him write was one of Cass's favorite things; the concentration on his face, how he traced the tattoos on his temple when he was stuck, when he pulled his lower lip between his teeth.

As if sensing Cass's eyes on him for the fifteenth time, River turned and caught Cass staring at him. "You okay?"

"Of course," Cass said quickly, and River's eyes narrowed. He was saved from further questions as their phones chimed. River grabbed his, holding it out so Cass could read Tessa's message to their group chat.

> Finished with the meeting. It was a complete shit show, but I'm okay, promise. I'll explain everything when I get home. Heading to Aaron's to get some work done. Miss you :)

"Can't say I'm totally buying the *I'm okay* part of that," River grumbled as he typed out a reply.

Cass nodded in agreement. "At least she's going to Aaron's and not running off." It was an improvement. Tessa was just as much of an emotional enigma as she had been before she and River made things official, but she was trying. "It's weird, right? To miss her when she's only been gone for a couple of hours."

River chuckled, his brown eyes shining. "Maybe, but I miss her too."

"Do you think it'll ever get easier?" Cass asked, though he already knew the answer.

"No. I still miss you when we're apart for five minutes, and we've known each other forever," River replied with a matter-of-fact shrug.

Cass's heart raced. "Yeah. Same."

He jumped as River's hand settled on his knee. "Are you sure you're okay?"

"Yeah, I'm fine." Cass could tell from River's raised eyebrow that he wasn't going to drop it. "It's just a lot of change lately. Good change!" he added quickly, when River's face fell. "But I worry about you, and I worry about Tessa." *And I worry about watching you grow old together and never getting to tell you how I feel.* It was probably best to keep that one to himself.

River's face softened, and he squeezed Cass's knee. "I'm okay, Cass. Seriously. For the first time in a long time, I can say that I am truly happy. I'm not naive enough to think it's all going to be smooth sailing from here, but I'm still going to therapy and I promise to talk to you if I get overwhelmed."

"Thank you." Cass would never tell him, but he still had nightmares about walking into the apartment they'd shared after college and finding River slumped over his desk, barely breathing. He hadn't been by River's side when he'd been forced to detox after being arrested, but Cass had seen enough in med school to have imagined the worst-case scenario, and the images still haunted him.

He hadn't slept through the night once in the thirteen months his best friend had been behind bars, terrified he was going to wake up to a phone call that something had happened to him. Cass was all too aware of how dangerous prison was for people of color, and he and River both knew how lucky River was to have made it out relatively unscathed.

It didn't matter that River had been drug-free for ten years; it was always in the back of Cass's mind and he still held his breath every time he walked in the door.

And now he had Tessa to worry about too. Between her running away, being surrounded by paparazzi every time she left the house, and going to lunch with Jay, Cass didn't know how *not* to worry about her.

He loved them both so much it was physically painful, and he couldn't do anything about it. It wasn't like he could tell River that's why he seemed off.

"You've seemed happier since you and Tessa have made it official," he said instead, and River's face lit up.

"I am. Are you? Happy, I mean," River asked, and Cass forced his face to mirror his best friend's joy.

"Of course I am. How could I not be?" he lied, and River leaned into him, resting his head on Cass's shoulder. The masochist that he was, Cass wound his arm around River and tucked him into his side.

The book in his hand continued to evade his attention as River tapped away on his laptop. He was working on an outline for a new project, and engrossed enough that he didn't notice how restless Cass was until he cleared his throat.

"I'm going to go jump in the shower," Cass said, untangling himself from River.

"Didn't you already shower today?"

Shit. "Yeah, but I worked out a little on the roof earlier when you were doing therapy," Cass lied. He'd spent the hour River had been in the office on a video call with his therapist sitting on the roof and glaring at the city.

"Fair enough. You want some company?" Mischief shone on River's face, and Cass was up and off the couch in seconds.

"Aren't you supposed to be finishing that outline today?" he asked, forcing his voice to stay light.

River pouted, and it took every ounce of Cass's self-control not to lean forward and capture River's lip between his teeth. "I'm almost done."

"Finish first. Play later," Cass said, turning away, his stomach doing somersaults. River sighed dramatically, but Cass heard him typing as he left the room and sped into the bathroom.

He showered in a daze, emotions threatening to overwhelm him as he tried his best to send them down the drain with the scalding water. How the fuck had River done this for so long? He was going to have to learn to live with the feelings of longing, the jealousy, the *need*.

It's only been a couple of months, he reminded himself. River had had to live for almost two decades knowing he couldn't be with the man he loved. Cass deserved to feel it too; he deserved to be riddled with guilt, to live knowing he would always be missing something.

Cass stepped out of the shower and wrapped a towel around his waist. He might not be able to have River and Tessa how he wanted them, but he was fucking lucky to have them at all.

River was in the kitchen, his laptop closed on the dining table, when Cass walked back into the living room. "You finished?" he asked, nodding to River's laptop.

"Yeah." River's voice was low, and Cass could see the desire etched all over his face.

Sure, he could deny his feelings, but this? Not a chance. Cass crossed the room and fisted his hand in River's hair, pulling him in and drinking down his moan as their lips touched. He could live a thousand lives and never tire of the taste of River's tongue—pure sugar and so perfectly like River that it tasted like home.

Cass nudged him towards the couch, breaking contact only to fill their lungs, before devouring each other over and over again. When the back of River's legs hit the couch, Cass pushed his sweatpants and boxers down while River pulled his t-shirt over his head. The towel had fallen off somewhere between the kitchen and the couch, and Cass pressed his naked body against River's. He trailed his finger over the swirls of ink on River's chest before placing his hand flat on River's heart. River's eyes fluttered closed, his forehead pressed against Cass's.

His beard was soft beneath Cass's fingers as he grasped River's chin, and tilted his head up to press a slow, gentle kiss on his lips. Then he pushed lightly on his chest until River sat on the couch, and Cass sank to his knees.

He started slowly, tracing the tattoos winding around River's cock with his tongue as River's hand grasped the back of his neck. When River's thighs were trembling, his hand shaking, Cass finally took his cock into his mouth, relaxing his throat to take him as deep as he could. He moaned as the head of River's cock brushed the back of this throat, swollen and demanding, all-consuming. Cass pulled back, dragging his tongue across River's velvety skin, and River's head fell back against the couch, his stomach muscles tightening.

"Fuck, Cass," he gasped, and Cass let the words spur him on, using River's cock to fuck his mouth. He relished in the tears that burned the corners of his eyes, the ache of his jaw as he pushed River closer to the edge, the rough hold of River's fingers on his neck.

Cass reached out, finding River's hand and threading their fingers together. River squeezed his hand, gripping him for dear life, and Cass's heart stuttered. *Dangerous*. He'd added a layer of intimacy by brushing his thumb across the back of River's hand, but he couldn't resist. *More*. He wanted more. He *needed* more.

River tugged on his neck, and Cass pulled away, looking up at his face. River's eyes were half-closed and desperate and Cass saw the word reflected on his face; *more*. He turned around to grab the lube stashed on the shelf under the coffee table—they'd taken to hiding it all over the apartment—and by the time he turned back, River was on his knees, waiting for him.

The click of the lube opening echoed loudly through the room as Cass kneeled behind him, and River groaned as Cass drizzled it over his ass and pressed his thumb into him. He leaned down to press a gentle kiss to River's lower back before pushing his cock slowly into him, his legs threatening to give way.

River shuddered, his body falling forward as Cass's name slipped from his tongue.

Cass gripped his hips, warming up with a few slow thrusts until River growled and pushed his ass back against him.

"Stop fucking teasing," he begged and Cass chuckled, tightening his hold and pulling all the way out before slamming back into River.

River clenched around him and electricity shot up his spine. "Better?" Cass asked, but River just pushed closer to him.

"*More.*"

Cass ground out a curse, fucking River furiously. He was sure his fingers would leave marks, and, *fuck*, he needed Tessa home so he could make the two of them match. His balls tightened—*fuck, he was close*—and he adjusted himself so he could reach around and fist River's cock.

He brushed his thumb over the tip and River cried out,

his hips faltering. He exploded all over Cass's hand, tightening around Cass's cock. What little control Cass had left snapped, his body moving mercilessly as fucked River, coming with a shuddering breath.

The room stopped spinning, and Cass sat back just in time to hear the click of a lock. He turned his head to see Tessa, her eyes hungry from across the room.

She licked her lips. "I brought dinner."

"We can reheat it," River panted.

Cass nudged River until he rolled onto his back. "Get over here, princess."

Tessa hummed, taking her sweet time to drop the takeout bags on the counter and shed her jacket. Every second felt like an hour as she stepped carefully out of her shoes, kicked off her tights, and tugged her sweater dress over her head. She finally stopped in front of them in only black satin underwear and Cass's breath caught in his chest.

Her golden eyes roamed the two of them, her pupils swallowing them. Before Cass could even reach for her, she knelt on the couch between them, her back pressed to him, and leaned over River.

"Fucking hell," River gasped. Cass assumed Tessa had taken his cock between her lips, but when his eyes zeroed in on her, his mouth went dry.

Tessa was licking every last drop of Cass's cum from River. *Fuck*, Cass couldn't wait any longer to get his hands on her. While River's fingers tangled in her hair, Cass wound his hand, sticky with River's cum, around her body and into her silky black underwear.

He circled her clit until her moans turned urgent, then

pressed two fingers into her pussy. Tessa gasped, pushing her ass into him, using his cum-covered fingers to fuck herself. He grasped her hips, fingers pressing hard against her, and Tessa spasmed around him, coming with a cry.

His fingers were dripping when he withdrew them. He lifted her until she was straddling River, lined up with his cock. Tessa sank down onto River, her head falling back against Cass. He trapped her to his body, holding her in place, running his lips up her neck, nipping at her jaw. She was so fucking sweet.

He brought his fingers to her lips. "Clean them off, princess."

Tessa moaned, opening her lips for him. She lapped greedily at the mix of their cum, wriggling desperately in his grip. River's breath caught with every one of her movements, but his eyes were glued to her mouth, shining with an expression that Cass could only interpret as *mine*.

And when River turned his expression on Cass, meeting his eyes like he owned him too… River had no fucking idea.

CHAPTER THIRTY-TWO

River

"Hey, it's time for me to leave."

River brushed a gentle hand through Tessa's hair and her eyes fluttered open. Cass, who was so thoroughly wrapped around her it would have been hard to tell them apart if not for their sheer difference in skin-color, opened one eye.

Tessa sat up and rubbed her face. "What time is it?"

He sat down beside her and enclosed her in his arms. "A little after three. My cab's going to be here in five."

Tessa leaned into him, pressing a kiss over his heart. "I wish we could come with you."

"I do too. Next time, though." He tilted her chin up and kissed her, relishing in her sweet taste. He was only going to be gone for four days, but he would miss this. "I love you."

"Love you," she murmured with one last kiss.

River hesitated for all of a moment before thinking *fuck it* and leaning across to give Cass a goodbye kiss too. Cass's hand reached up to cup his face, his thumb stroking lightly across his jaw, and River considered canceling his flight and climbing back into bed.

Somehow, he pulled away, his heart racing. He cleared his throat. "Take care of each other while I'm gone."

They nodded, and he tore himself away from their sleepy frowns and murmured goodbyes into the cold New York early morning.

The flight dragged without Tessa and Cass beside him, and when he landed in Heathrow nine hours later, all he wanted to do was get straight on a plane home. By the time he made it to his hotel, he was like a zombie, running on just a couple hours of sleep. He collapsed onto the squishy hotel bed and dozed fitfully until the sun rose over the London skyline.

It still didn't feel real as he dressed and jumped into a black cab. It'd all happened so quickly. One minute he'd sent an email agreeing to talk to the publisher who had been most enthusiastic about picking up his books over the years, the next he was standing in front of their main office in Camden. All it had taken was a five-minute call with the editor who had been emailing him for the past few years and she'd asked him to come to London to meet with her. And her boss.

He stopped at the reception desk and mustered a smile for the man seated there. "Hi, I have a meeting with Ramona Elgin and Charley Hale?"

The man checked a list. "River Sage?"

"Yeah."

"Great, you can grab a seat and I'll let them know you're here. Would you like a drink while you wait?"

"No, thank you." River's face felt frozen in that smile as he pushed away from the desk and sank into one of the plush leather chairs in the lobby.

His phone buzzed against his leg, and he pulled it out of his pocket, swiping it open. A genuine smile replaced the one he'd been forcing in an attempt to look calm as the picture loaded. Tessa and Cass in bed, bleary-eyed and frowning dramatically at his empty spot.

> Go blow their minds and come home to us. You've got this. I love you.

His heart warmed, calm settling into his bones. He tucked the phone away just as a cheery voice called his name and he stood up, swallowing.

He finally had the real life romance he'd always dreamed of—mostly anyway. Now for the career.

Tessa

Tessa cuddled further into Cass, tracing lazy lines across his chest as the movie credits rolled. River hadn't even been gone for forty-eight hours yet, and neither of them had any inclination to get out of bed. In their defense, both Tessa and Cass would happily laze in bed every day, if they could. River was the one luring them out of the mountain of blankets with the promise of coffee each morning.

"It's still good, no matter how many times I watch it," Cass said of his movie choice, *Stardust*.

Tessa hummed. "My grandparents took me and Rhys to see it at the theater. I miss them." And perhaps not just her grandparents.

Cass rubbed his hand on her back in soothing circles. "What were your grandparents like?"

"Grandma was an artist," she told him, smiling at the memories. "She painted landscapes. They were gorgeous. I always dreamed of having a gallery of her paintings when I moved out, but my parents kept them in a storage unit and it was seized when they stopped paying the fees." She had cried for hours upon learning her grandmother's life's work had been lost; her dad had barely blinked.

"Grandpa was the musical one. He taught my dad piano and the best thing my dad ever did was try to continue the tradition with us. Grandpa also loved astronomy." When Tessa and Rhys had visited their grandparents, their grandpa would sneak them out of bed late at night and into the back-yard to lie on a hand sewn picnic blanket and look up at the sky and teach them about the stars.

"I never forgot any of it," she told Cass. "I miss seeing the stars. That's one reason I love the cottage so much." She glared at the ceiling as if she could see right through to the starless New York City sky.

"Wait here, I have an idea." Cass slid gently from the bed and she rolled over to watch him walk away, the muscles in his back rippling. She heard the front door open and close and assumed he was getting something from his and River's apartment.

One of them dropped in every other day to make sure nothing disastrous had happened. Perhaps when River got home, they would talk about finding some use for it, instead of just using it to store the shit none of them wanted to sort through and throw away.

Cass's footsteps returned, and he called, "Close your eyes, princess," before pushing open the bedroom door. Tessa did as she was told, lying on her back and closing her eyes.

"What are you doing?"

She could practically see Cass rolling his eyes. "Have a little patience."

She could hear him tinkering around with outlets, typing on his computer, and a whirring electrical hum sounded. She heard the click of the lamp beside her as he presumably turned it off, and then he rounded the bed and lay down next to her, grasping her hand.

"Okay, open your eyes."

Tessa gasped, her free hand flying to her mouth, and tears springing to her eyes. "Oh my God, Cass."

He'd brought through his projector and set it up to shine the twinkling night sky on the ceiling. It was so realistic, Tessa could almost smell the sweet Welsh grass and her grandpa's menthols.

"This is what the stars would look like overhead right now, if we could see them," he said, watching her instead of the sky. She turned to face him.

"This is amazing. Thank you."

His answering smile was like a drug to her. "Tell me about them."

"The stars?" He nodded, and they both turned to face the ceiling. "That one there, that looks like an hourglass with arms, that's Orion—the hunter. And that one," she pointed beside Orion, "is Taurus."

"Like you," Cass murmured, squeezing her hand.

Tessa nodded, smiling. "Taurus was my grandpa's favorite. He was a Taurus too, and just as stubborn as I am. He told me that if anyone ever gave me shit for standing my ground, or tried to get me to change who I was, I could just blame it on the stars. And let me tell you, I've been given a lot of shit for being stubborn over the years." They laughed, watching the stars for a moment longer before Cass rolled onto his side.

"Tessa?"

She turned to face him, his dark eyes reflecting the stars. "Hmm?"

"I love how stubborn you are, you know. And I wouldn't change a thing about you, least of all that. You're perfect."

Tessa's heart went quiet in her chest, taking a backseat to soak in the moment, to treasure it. Cass reached for her, tucking her hair behind her ear. She held his hand against her cheek and swallowed.

"Thank you for this. For… well, for everything, really."

Her chest ached. Every day with Cass—every touch, every kiss, every moment he and River's eyes met and made her heart race—was an echo of how things could feel every day if they could be more. If Cass wanted more.

The longing in her heart was no less for the label on her

relationship with River. But she would learn to live with it, and Cass would never know how much she wanted him. The last thing she wanted was for him to feel any kind of guilt.

"Tauruses and Scorpios are pretty compatible, right?"

She blinked, his question chasing her from her thoughts. "What?"

"You and River," he clarified.

"Oh. Um, they're pretty compatible, yeah. They say that a Taurus and Scorpio together will be super intense, good or bad, you know? Both stubborn."

He gave her a wry smile. "That sounds like you two. What about Pisces?"

She swallowed. As if she hadn't checked their fucking star charts the moment she realized she had feelings for them. She was too much of a millennial not to. "Pisces and Tauruses are usually compatible. Pisces and Scorpio are a spot on match, actually. If you believe in astrology, you and River really were written in the stars."

"It's interesting that all three of our signs are so compatible," he mused, playing absentmindedly with the strand of her hair that wouldn't stay tucked behind her ear. "Do you? Believe in it, I mean."

The question, and his eyes, somehow felt weighted. "I don't know. It's nice to think that everything we are is part of something bigger. But do I think the three of us are compatible?" She nodded, biting her lip. "Yeah, I do. Whether the stars say so or not."

"Me too," he said, softly, and she had to remind herself

he didn't mean it in the same way she did. Cass leaned in to brush his lips against hers.

He was so soft, so slow, as if savoring the taste of her, and when his tongue slipped between her lips, meeting hers with gentle strokes, her heart flew into overdrive.

Cass rolled over her until he was kneeling between her legs, never once breaking their kiss. His hands clasped her face like she was made of something precious, the tender touch giving her heart all kinds of dangerous ideas.

She sat up and pulled the baggy t-shirt she was wearing over her head, anything to distract from the feelings coursing through her.

Cass trailed a finger from her throat, between her breasts, down her belly, pausing at the edge of her under-wear. "Beautiful," he whispered, before hooking his thumbs in the band of her underwear and tugging it off. His boxers landed on top of them on the floor with a soft thud and he nudged her legs apart with his knees, hovering over her.

He brushed his cock against her, the metal bar grazing her clit, and she arched her back, gasping. God knows she was already wet for him as he sank into her. She always was. Cass groaned her name, leaning over her to grasp her hands and kiss her.

And it was… different. Like something had changed in the stars dotted across the ceiling. Cass moved slowly, moving his hips in time with the rise and fall of their chests, their ragged breaths. When his lips left hers, it was to kiss her jaw, her cheeks, her forehead, never breaking contact entirely.

There were no hands around throats, just fingers gripping for dear life as wave after wave of pleasure, and feelings, and things Tessa should know better than to hope for, crashed over the two of them.

Tessa peaked as Cass whispered her name in her ear, shaking and shuddering above her, and she bit her lip to stop the words she was so desperate to say from tumbling from her lips. Cass came with his forehead pressed against hers, his eyes squeezed closed.

And when he opened them, right into Tessa's, he looked like he'd seen a ghost. He recovered quickly, shaking the shadows from his eyes, and leaned down to kiss her before lying down beside her.

The room was silent save for their uneven breaths and the soft whirring of the projector, but Tessa wouldn't have been surprised if the beating of her heart was audible.

She turned at the rustle of blankets as Cass pulled the covers over him, his eyes glued to the ceiling.

"Are you okay?" She hadn't meant to whisper, but it still felt too loud.

Cass took a deep breath. "Yeah, I'm just tired. You wore me out, princess." He laughed, but Tessa knew his laugh by heart and this one was forced. Her stomach flipped. "Are you okay?"

"Of course. I'm just going to go get ready for bed."

"Sounds good."

Tessa rolled off the bed, grabbing her t-shirt from the floor as she went. She got ready in a daze. Every time she told herself she was okay with loving Cass and not being loved back—romantically, anyway—he just had to look at her and she was gone.

She didn't understand how River had survived this.

By the time she made it back to bed, Cass was facing the wall. She turned the projector off at the outlet and climbed into bed beside him. His breaths were even, *too* even, his back too stiff. But Tessa let him pretend to be asleep, even if she didn't know why. She wanted to reach into his mind and find out what was going on, find out what she had done. Had she come on too strong? She didn't dare ask.

Sleep didn't come easily to either of them. Cass lay stiff as a board for what felt like hours, and Tessa could barely stand to breathe in the tense atmosphere. She burrowed into River's pillow, the spicy scent of him doing nothing to calm her nerves.

The clock on the nightstand flashed two when she gave up and turned to face Cass. She shuffled closer to him, pressed against his back. He didn't flinch at the touch, as if he had been expecting her all along. She slipped her arm over his chest and he clutched her hand, bringing it to his lips to kiss.

Tessa laid her cheek against Cass's warm skin and, within minutes, she was fast asleep.

CHAPTER THIRTY-THREE

Tessa

I f River could fly to London for one meeting and walk away with a three book deal from a major publisher, Tessa could get on stage and sing for a bunch of industry folk and find someone to work with her when her Empire contract ended. Or at least that's what she told herself as she touched up her lipstick in the mirror while Aaron tuned their guitar.

Proud didn't even begin to cover it. Tessa had cried like a baby and even Cass had been blinking back tears when River had called with the good news. Now they just needed him home to *really* celebrate.

She wished he could have been there for the last-minute show Aaron had talked her into. They'd pulled it together in record time, determined to cash in on the virality of *Fingertips*.

When Aaron slid her the set list, having taken the choice out of her hands once again, knowing she would shy away from choosing to play her personal songs, it was full of Tessa's newer tracks. She'd opened the floodgates with *Fingertips* and now she couldn't stop writing about River and Cass. Even if she sounded like a lovesick teenager, the songs were some of her best.

"Anything you want to change?" Aaron asked, shouldering their guitar and stuffing a handful of picks in the pocket of their leather pants.

Tessa chewed her lip, scanning the list. "I wrote something new this morning and I really love it. Do you think we could squeeze it in? Maybe close with it?"

"Sure, scribble it down."

Tessa took the pen from Aaron and slotted her new song on the list: *I'm Your Stars*. It was late enough in the set list that, if all went to plan, Cass would be several drinks in and wouldn't read too closely between the lines. Hopefully.

She followed Aaron out onto the stage and the spotlight induced butterflies in her belly were laced with excitement this time around. She flashed Cass a smile at the back of the room and, though he smiled back, his shoulders were stiff, his grip on the bottle in his hand tight. She wished she could go back to the night before and ask him what was wrong. Today, they were both firmly pretending nothing happened. Perhaps he just missed River; she certainly did.

But there was no time to dwell on it as the crowd hushed and she stepped up to the microphone. It went against her every instinct, but Aaron had made it clear that this was Tessa's show to run. She was trying to sell herself to the label executives and managers who were filling most of the seats in the room, after all.

She took a deep breath. "Hi everyone, thank you for coming out tonight. My name's Tessa, and this is Aaron." She smiled over her shoulder at Aaron, waving cheerily from the piano. "And we have some stories to play for you tonight. This first song is probably the reason you're all here. This is *Fingertips*."

She stepped behind the keyboard and lost herself in the music.

It was hard to gauge the crowd's reaction as the show progressed. They applauded when they were supposed to, sure, but Tessa couldn't see much of their reactions, the longer she spent blinded by the spotlight. It was better that way, she thought; she was too busy feeling the music to worry about what they were thinking.

She ran her fingers through her hair, breathing hard as she and Aaron closed on the penultimate song and applause echoed. Her skin was burning beneath the lights, sweat glistening on her bare arms. "Thank you," she said, pushing away from the keyboard and picking up her acoustic. She slung the strap over her shoulder and leaned into the mic. "We have one more for you tonight, and then we'll let you get on your way. I'm sure you're all just dying to get out into that stormy night." You can take the girl out of England, but you can't make her stop talking about the weather. Tessa strummed the opening chords. "This is a new song, so I can't promise I'm not going to completely forget the lyrics and wing it at some point. This one's called *I'm Your Stars*."

The night before played through her head like a movie

as she played; stars and short breaths, bright eyes and sleepless hours. She took a deep breath.

"*Shadows, memories,*
White lies, don't speak,
Slow burn, let me in, my love,
I've been looking so long for you…"

Everything but Cass faded to black. Tessa could feel his gaze like a brand, but she didn't meet it. She was vaguely aware of Aaron playing some soft piano chords behind her as she flowed into the second verse, but Tessa passed through the rest of the song in a daze.

When she finished, the room was so silent you could hear a pin drop. And as suddenly as the silence had hit, riotous applause sounded, and the crowd surged to their feet.

Tessa blinked in surprise at the noise, glancing back to Aaron, who had the widest smile on their face.

She stood and set her guitar on the stand, holding a hand out to Aaron, who joined her at the mic to bow. "Thank you all for coming out to hear us play tonight. We had a—" She paused as Cass stood and strode for the door, out into the dark night. She swallowed. "We had a great night, thank you," she finished, before switching off the mic and whispering to Aaron, "I have to go check on Cass. I'll be back."

She ran down the stage steps, into the crowd, her eyes fixed on the doors. Several hands reached out to brush her, congratulate her, and she murmured thanks as she went.

She finally burst through the door. Rain battered the sidewalk, splashing up and soaking through her tights to her skin. Tessa squinted through her hair as the wind whipped it around her face, looking for Cass. He was almost at the end of the block by the time she spotted him.

She cursed, wrapping her arms around herself. "Cass! Wait up," she shouted and his steps faltered. He stopped and turned to face her as she jogged up to him. His face was completely and utterly blank. "Hey, what's wrong? Where are you going?"

He looked away; the rain streaming down his face. "I, uh, I'm just going to head out for a bit. I'll be home later. I just need to be on my own."

Tessa's teeth chattered, a lump forming in her throat. "What? Were you seriously just going to leave and not say anything?" Cass said nothing, staring at the ground, his face inscrutable. Tessa sniffed and wiped the rain from her face. "You said we don't run from each other, remember?"

She hated how her voice broke and, for a split second, she swore pain flashed in Cass's eyes before they turned stony once more.

"I'll be home later. Aaron will make sure you get back safe." He turned and walked away before she could say anything. Tessa stood and watched him fade into the night, swallowed by the crowd, before moving.

She dragged her feet on the way back to the venue, hugging her arms to her chest like she could hold her heart in.

Her phone buzzed in her pocket as she approached the door, and she ducked into an alcove to answer it.

"Hey, princess, how was the show?"

The sound of River's voice almost made her knees buckle. She tried to answer, but all that came out was a choked sound. "What's wrong?" River asked immediately, worry sounding down the phone.

"Something's up with Cass," she managed. "He left at the end of the show and I caught up with him and… Fuck, River, I've never seen him like that. He was cold. Vacant. He said he needed to be alone but didn't tell me where he was going and he just left."

Logically, Tessa knew Cass was a strong thirty-eight-year-old man who had lived in the city for half of his life, but logic had checked out and left anxiety in its wake. For as long as the three of them had been friends, and more, she had always known where they were, when they would be home.

If this is how it felt when Cass was still in the city… a fresh wave of guilt crashed over her for fleeing the damn country.

"That's definitely not like him." She could hear the concern in River's voice. "But he'll be fine. Did something happen?"

"He's been acting weird since last night," she told him, giving him a brief rundown of their evening. When she'd finished telling him about her closing song, she sighed. "I shouldn't have fucking played it."

"Hey, no. You should have. Never feel bad for writing about your feelings," River said, and she could almost feel his soothing hand rubbing over her back. "Fuck, I have to board, but I'll be home around four and I'm sure Cass will be home in a couple of hours. We'll talk it out, it'll be okay. For now, go back in, rub shoulders with everyone. Your future label might be in there, you know."

"Yeah, you're right." Tessa sniffed. "I love you. Have a safe flight."

"I love you."

Tessa ducked into the bathrooms by the door to do damage control before heading back into the crowd; she wiped away smears of mascara, rung out her hair (and subsequently gave up, throwing it on top of her hair in a bun) and took deep steadying breaths. She would go out there and secure the contract she had wanted for years, and then she would go home and wait for Cass to come home.

And things would be okay between them. They had to be.

Cass

Cass skipped the elevator and took the stairs, the burn in his calves preferable to the burning in his chest. Every step towards the apartment felt like dragging his feet through mud, even as his heart pulled him desperately towards home. Well, half of home at least.

River wouldn't land for a few hours yet, and Cass had stayed out late enough that Tessa would be asleep, so he wouldn't have to see the hurt that had been written on her face when he walked away from her. He knew that flash of pain in her golden eyes would haunt him when he finally slept. How the hell was he supposed to forgive himself for walking away from her? They'd promised.

He reached the door and hesitated. Maybe he should go to the other apartment, leave her to sleep in peace. After how he'd acted, she probably didn't want to be anywhere near him.

Cass rummaged around in his pockets, but he only had keys for Tessa's. He would just run in, grab the keys, and leave her to sleep, then.

But when Cass stepped into the dimly lit apartment, Tessa was waiting on the couch, a blanket wrapped around her shoulders and a coffee cup in her hand. She sprung to her feet, the blanket slipping away.

"You're soaked," she said, worry etched in the lines around her eyes. "Let me get you a towel."

He hadn't noticed, but he was dripping rain on the welcome mat. He should move, take off some of the soaking layers, but he stood still until Tessa walked back in, a pile of towels in her arms. She handed him one, and he ran it over his head. It was warm.

He must have looked confused, because she said, "I put them on the towel warmer earlier. I figured you'd be pretty cold and wet when you got in."

He was fine until she added a tentative smile, and then he crumbled. Tears filled his eyes, and he made to turn away, but Tessa stopped him, a hand on his shoulder.

"Hey, talk to me, Cass. Please," she begged, anguish on her face. "Tell me how to fix this. What did I do?"

Alarm shook him. She thought this was her fault? He was the one being selfish, wanting things he shouldn't want. Sobs wracked his body. "It's not… You haven't done anything," he choked out and Tessa stood for a heartbeat before cursing and standing on her tiptoes to wrap her arms around him. "You're going to get soaked," he protested.

"I don't care."

He breathed her in, sugar and everything sweet, but these days, Tessa also smelled like River, spicy and warm, and Cass's lemon sandalwood soap. Like they were embedded in her.

"Please talk to me."

Cass took a deep breath. His feelings were a monster in his chest, trying to claw their way out, and he didn't think he could keep them in any longer. He stepped out of Tessa's arms, crossing the room with his back to her. He couldn't focus with her so close.

"Okay," he said, his voice small. He took his time shedding his wet jacket and Tessa stood patiently by the door, as if realizing he needed space. Cass stood in front of the window. "Has River told you why I broke up with him back in college?"

"Because you felt something was missing and realized you don't feel romantic attraction towards people, right?"

"Yeah, that was the reason," he replied, his heart thundering. "At the time. But… what if I was wrong?"

He followed a raindrop drizzling down the glass with his eyes as he waited for Tessa to answer, her silence deafening.

"Oh. You… you met someone?" Her voice cracked. "Is that what bothered you last night? You felt guilty for being with me when you… when you have feelings for someone?"

He turned slowly. Tessa's face was stark white, her freckles standing out against her pale skin, her shoulders hunched. She was hugging her arms to her chest and her eyes… Silver lined the gold.

He took a small step towards her. "Not someone, Tessa," he said slowly, every word feeling like simultaneous relief and risk. "*Someones.*"

Tessa's eyes widened, her arms falling to her sides. She opened her mouth, but Cass was too scared to hear what came out. "It's stupid, I know," he cut in and she snapped her mouth closed. He couldn't stay still. He turned away, pacing in the glowing moonlight. "I have no fucking right to even consider feeling like this after everything I put River through, and the two of you are finally happy. I don't want to come between that, I won't come between you, I don't even know why I'm telling you all of this because I don't want to just dump all my feelings on you, but last night—"

He spun around, going silent, as Tessa placed a hand on his arm. "Breathe, Cass. Come on, let's sit down and talk this out."

Cass would rather have dissolved into a puddle on the ground, but he was powerless to refuse her. She pulled him to the couch, and they sat down. Suddenly aware of how wet he still was, he peered down at the velvet and jumped up. Tessa snagged his arm, pulling him back down.

"Don't worry about the couch. It'll dry." She looked down, chewing her lip as if trying to decide what to say. "I can't speak for River, but you need to talk to him. From what I've seen, the two of you never really cleared the air and you've both just been ignoring everything that went down between you."

Cass nodded. "Yeah, we should've talked about it a long

time ago. It was just easier. For me," he added. He knew it had been harder for River.

"I can talk about me," Tessa continued, drumming her nails on her knee. "Cass, my feelings for you have been more than friendship for a long time now."

His head jerked up, shock rippling through him. "But River—"

"River knows. Don't worry. We've talked about it a lot. I've always felt the same for you and River, I just… well, I thought you could never feel that way, you know?"

"I didn't know I could either," he admitted, unable to make sense of what she was saying. "My feelings for River aren't any different from what they were a year ago. Hell, even a decade ago, I just… I don't know. It's almost like I needed the three of us to be together to recognize them for what they are."

She reached out and took his hand, and Cass thought his heart might jump right out of his chest. "It's a spectrum, Cass. Maybe you can feel romantic attraction for River and me and no one else. Maybe it'll come and go or feel different every day and that's okay. Just promise me you'll talk to him about it."

Cass nodded. He had no choice at this stage; he couldn't pretend any longer. Whatever River's reaction, he deserved to know. "I'll talk to him tomorrow, I promise." They were quiet for a moment, the sound of the rain and whistling wind lighting up the room. Tessa stroked her thumb across his hand, staring at their entwined fingers. "But, um… So you…" he stammered, and Tessa looked up at him, a glimmer of light shining in her amber eyes.

"Crazy about you, yeah."

He took a deep breath. He should be relieved, right? Happy, even? If anything, the knots in his chest felt more tangled. "I have no idea what to feel right now. This isn't how I expected tonight to go," he admitted, and Tessa laughed.

"Tell me about it. Talk to River, then the three of us will talk and we'll figure it out together, okay?"

The three of us. Together.

For the first time since Tessa had crashed into their lives and flipped their hearts upside down, Cass let himself hope for more.

CHAPTER THIRTY-FOUR

Tessa

Tessa must have dozed off in Cass's arms on the couch, because she woke in bed, alone, tucked in tightly. She checked her phone and she couldn't have slept for more than an hour or two. There were still a few hours until River was due home, and she assumed Cass was waiting for him. Whether he planned to talk to him right when he got home or not, he had to be drained after the night he'd had, and she was sure he needed space.

He liked them. Loved them? *Probably*, she thought, but he would need time for that. He'd spent most of his life so sure in the belief that he'd made the right decision ending things with River. So, naturally, Tessa had barreled in like a bull and smashed said belief to smithereens. She was good at that.

She'd thought her heart might break at first, thinking that he had met someone else. And now... her heart was happier than it had ever been.

And if it felt this good for her, how good would it feel for River to know that sometimes you could revisit the past without the world falling apart? She hadn't been the only one running from her past when the three of them had met, and both River and Cass were now confronting theirs head on.

Hers was still in a sealed envelope in her nightstand.

She glanced at the drawers and sighed before reaching down to pull out the letter. She ran her fingers across her name in Rhys's scrawl. It had been six and a half years since she'd seen her twin, but his handwriting hadn't changed; he had always written like his pen couldn't keep up with what he wanted to say.

She turned it over and blinked at the return address. She hadn't noticed when it arrived.

> *Rhys Reid*
> *4201 Cathedral Ave APT 604W*
> *Washington, DC 20016*

Her brother was back in DC? She hadn't been back since they'd moved to London. She bit her lip, dangling the letter over the open drawer, ready to drop it, as if it might bite.

"Fuck it," she said, tearing gently into it. If River could confront his parents and Cass could confront his feelings, she could read a damn letter.

Tessa,

I know I'm probably the last person you want to hear from, especially after so much time has passed. I haven't stopped thinking about you, though, all these years, and I don't want to leave it another six years before reaching out.

I'm so sorry for what happened between us. I'll never forgive myself for going to the press about you and Jay. I know how much that fucked up your life, not for the better, and nothing was worth that. Dad didn't give up gambling anyway. I'm not sorry you got away from them, though. They would never have stopped exploiting you, and seeing you go out into the world and do incredible things despite them, despite me and what I did, has been amazing.

I've grown up a lot since then. I realized as soon as everything went down that Mom and Dad weren't who I thought they were, so I left as soon as I could. I transferred to Edinburgh Uni to study music. I got the chance to move back to the states to study for my last couple of years, and I've been in DC ever since. I teach elementary school music at our old school, and it's pretty great. I'm only a few blocks from our old place. Would you believe that Mrs. Clarkson still lives there? I visit her every Sunday and she still makes those amazing lemon cookies. They always make me think of you begging for her recipe before we left.

I've thought about reaching out to you a hundred times since I left home, but I didn't know how to even start trying to clear the air. I miss you, Tessa. You were my best friend, the one person in the world I should have been there for. I'm so sorry I wasn't.

The reason I'm finally getting my head out of my ass and writing now... I saw what happened with you and Jay. Well, I saw the paper's version of it and know you well enough to put two and two together. Knew you, I guess. I'm so sorry, Tessa. I know he was there for you when I wasn't, and I can't imagine how hard it must have been to leave. I hope, wherever you are now, that you're okay. You were always the more independent of us, so I have no doubt you landed on your feet.

I know this is all completely out of the blue, and you were always better with words than me, so it might be an incoherent mess, but I wanted you to know that I still miss you. I still love you, Tessa, always will.

Love from,
Rhys

Tears slipped from Tessa's cheeks, splattering the paper, and she pushed it away to keep it safe. All this time, she had lived with anger boiling just below the surface, but she'd never been angry at Rhys. Betrayed, yes, but she'd been angry at her parents, not him. Now that she was older, Tessa looked back and saw a scared kid. That's all he had been; that's all she had been.

And now he was just a five-hour drive away.

There was a phone number at the bottom of the letter and Tessa's phone was in her hand before she could stop it. It wasn't exactly a civilized time to be calling, but it wasn't a school night, at least.

She dialed the number with shaking hands and held her breath as the phone rang. Just when she thought it would go to voicemail, it stopped ringing.

"Hello?"

Tessa's hand flew to her mouth, holding back a sob. He sounded just as he had when she'd locked him out on her doorsteps all those years ago. "Hi, Rhys," she said, her voice as unsteady as her hands.

There was a sharp intake of breath and a pause before he said, choked up, "Tessa?"

Tessa took a deep breath, wiping tears from her eyes. "Yeah, I... I read your letter. And I've missed you too."

River

River tapped his foot on the tiled floor of the elevator. Had it always been this slow? As happy as he was to be returning to New York with a book deal, he wanted nothing more than to climb into bed and thoroughly wrap himself around Tessa and Cass. Fuck, he'd missed them. He was sure neither of them would thank him for waking them in the wee hours of the morning, though, so he'd give them a couple of hours before descending on them.

He yawned as he forced the key into the lock, fighting grogginess from the nine-hour flight. He'd slept in fitful bursts, worried about what was happening with Cass and Tessa. When the flight had landed, he'd had a message from Tessa to say that Cass was home and everything was fine, but he knew he was missing the full story.

He pushed open the door and stilled at the sight of Cass sitting on the couch, his legs tucked beneath him and an unopened paperback on his lap. River closed the door behind him and dropped his bags. "Hey. It's not like you to be up so early when you don't have to be."

"I haven't slept yet," Cass admitted.

River strode across the room and searched his face. His skin was ashen, his eyes bloodshot and dilated. He sank onto the couch beside him. River reached out for his hand, but Cass held it back. River swallowed. "Do you want to talk about what's going on between you and Tessa? Is everything okay?"

Cass nodded, staring down at the plaid blanket, playing with the fringe. "Yeah. We talked and cleared the air."

"Good," River replied, though he could tell something was still off with Cass. He was curled in on himself, almost as if he was trying to hide.

"But I need to talk to you," Cass added.

River sat back and swallowed. "Okay, yeah. Whatever you need." He sounded much calmer than he felt. His heart was being viciously attacked by something sharp in his stomach.

Cass clenched his fists around the blanket, looking for all the world like he'd rather throw up. "I was wrong," he blurted, and River blinked in confusion.

"What?"

Cass closed his eyes. "When I broke up with you back in college, when I said I couldn't feel romantic attraction, I was wrong. I think I just didn't understand my feelings, and it scared me."

River thought his heart might have flatlined. It sure as fuck went still as he tried to process Cass's words. He sat perfectly still, as if any movement would shatter the already tense atmosphere in the room. "What are you saying?" he asked.

Cass looked up, his eyes brimming with tears. "I'm saying I love you. And I have loved you this whole time, I just… I didn't understand what my feelings meant until we met Tessa. Because I love her too. And fuck, I'm so sorry it's taken me so long to figure it out."

River just stared at him. He had waited for so long to hear those words, but had long ago accepted they were never coming. He could hardly make sense of it. Cass loved him, had loved him this whole time. And he loved Tessa too.

"I know it's probably too late now that you and Tessa have finally figured things out. You're happy now and I don't want—"

"Cass," he said softly, cutting off his rambling. His silence had caused panic to spread into Cass's eyes. "I've been waiting a long time for this. I'm just processing."

Cass nodded. "Yeah, sorry."

"Don't apologize. You've never had anything to apologize for." River frowned. "You're not just doing this, saying this, to make yourself fit into a box, are you? Or because you feel guilty? Because it's—"

"No, no," Cass said quickly, cutting in. "I've been putting my feelings together for a while now. Since the first night, when Tessa had that nightmare, I suppose. It was like… my feelings for you haven't changed. They just seem so much clearer with Tessa. Like they were all cast in shadows before and she just came in like blazing sunlight, you know?"

River knew—their missing piece; everything was brighter with Tessa in their lives. "You love me. Love us," he said, slowly, and Cass nodded.

"I do."

"Does Tessa know?"

"She knows I have feelings for you both, but I didn't tell

her I loved you. I… I wanted to tell you first. It's been so long, and—"

River could no longer fight the tears. They sprung to his eyes and spilled over onto his cheeks. *Cass loved them.* "It's not too late. It would never be too late," he choked out and folded Cass into his arms.

There would be a conversation to be had when Tessa woke up, sure, but River knew her heart was likely in the same happy state of disbelief he was.

"I love you," he whispered in Cass's ear. It had been almost two decades since he'd told him so, though, of course, he had never stopped. He never could. Loving Cass was as much a part of him as his own name.

Cass brushed his thumb across River's cheeks, wiping his tears away. "I'm sorry it took me so long to catch up."

River glanced towards the door, as if he could see through the walls to the bedroom where Tessa slept. Cass followed his gaze. "I think… I think it happened how it had to. I am who I am today because of all the shit that went down then, between us, the drugs, all of it. And we needed to go through that, to come out stronger, so we could be ready for her."

"Do you think we can do it? Make it work, somehow?"

"We'll talk to Tessa when she wakes up," River said, pressing a soft kiss to Cass's lips. "But yeah, I do. I think we were made to work together, the three of us."

The rule of three.

CHAPTER THIRTY-FIVE

Tessa

The first thing Tessa smelled when she woke was coffee. She hummed, burrowing her face into the scent. Why was it so hard? And... chuckling? She opened her eyes and her heart jumped in her chest as she took in River. She squealed, throwing her arms around his neck.

"Fuck, I missed you," she said, her heart finally feeling whole again.

"Likewise, princess." River closed the distance between them and claimed her mouth, kissing her like he hadn't touched her in months, not days.

"I'm so proud of you," she murmured when they pulled apart, running her fingers along the black ink on his face. "I can't wait to see your name on your books."

River glowed in the morning sunlight filtering through the drapes. "Thanks, baby. How was last night? Anyone you think you could work with?"

She nodded. "It was good, yeah. A bunch of people said they were going to email me on Monday."

"That's amazing. Proud of you."

She'd been in a daze when she stepped back into the venue. Walking around the room and networking was absolutely her idea of hell, but Aaron had stuck by her side. And as she talked to the producers and label executives, it struck her: she really was going to sign with someone who wanted her for her talent, not because she was Jay Hutchison's ex. And there had been plenty of people interested.

Including, much to her surprise, the head of Wicked Heart Records, the only label out there currently rivaling Empire. She'd done a double take when the woman had introduced herself, slipping her a card, and promising to call her on Monday. "I think we could make something pretty magical together, Tessa," she'd said before walking away with a smile.

For the first time in her career, Tessa really believed she might make it as a performer.

"Where's Cass?" she asked River, frowning at the space in their bed. The sheets were wrinkled enough that she knew Cass must have been in bed with them at some point, but cold to the touch.

"He ran out to get breakfast, thought we might all need extra coffee after such a late night."

Tessa searched his face for any sign that he and Cass had talked, but found nothing. "How was he? When you came home, I mean." She didn't want to hint at anything if Cass wasn't ready; that was his call to make.

A smile played on River's lips, and Tessa wanted to taste it. "Good, yeah. We talked about everything."

There was no tension in his shoulders, no worry etched in the lines of his face, but she asked anyway, "And how are you feeling about it all?"

River blew out a breath and pushed his dark hair back. "Honestly? I feel like my plane must have crashed and I'm stuck in some kind of limbo fantasy, because there's no way I've somehow convinced you to fall in love with me, gotten a book deal, and now this with Cass… It's way too good to be true, right?"

Tessa couldn't help laughing at the expression of disbelief on his face. "That's so fucking morbid, River. What the fuck?"

He chuckled, rolling on top of her and attacking her neck with kisses. Tessa squealed and squirmed under the ticklish kisses, before tilting his chin up and meeting his lips with her own.

"I'm really, *really* happy," he said when they broke apart, his voice breathy. Tessa committed those words, the moment, to memory; his sparkling eyes, tension free and full of hope, light dancing along his golden skin. "Are you? Happy, I mean."

Tessa didn't hesitate before nodding. "I'm so happy."

They both looked up as footsteps sounded and, a moment later, Cass walked in. He was laden down with a tote bag in one hand, a cup holder in the other, and a smile lit up his face as his gaze landed on them. "Good morning, princess."

"Morning." She reached out for him and he set the coffee down on the nightstand before climbing into bed.

He paused, his eye snagging on the letter. "You opened your brother's letter?"

"Yeah. I read it last night, and I called him. I think... I think I'd like to be a part of his life, and vice versa." She and Rhys had only talked for an hour, but it had been like no time had passed at all. He'd insisted she sleep after she yawned for a third time, but not before promising to call her the next day for a proper catch up. They'd even discussed perhaps meeting up.

"That's amazing, princess."

"So fucking proud of you."

Tessa snuggled into their arms. "I wouldn't have done it without you two. I would have probably held a grudge until I was old and grey." If she hadn't died of bitter stubbornness before she got the chance to turn old and grey. "After last night..." She smiled at Cass. "I realized that sometimes it's okay to revisit the past."

Cass pressed a kiss to her cheek. When she made to turn her face to catch his lips, he hesitated, worry clouding his eyes. Right, they should probably talk things out before she jumped on him.

As if he could see the impatience on her face, River chuckled and said, "Let's talk, shall we?"

Cass handed out the coffee and Tessa hadn't realized quite how sleepy she was until she took the first sip. She closed her eyes and hummed as she sipped at the smooth coffee courtesy of their favorite brunch spot.

When she opened her eyes, both River and Cass were

staring at her expectantly. She frowned. "Why are you both looking at me? I am absolutely the least qualified to start this conversation." Had they forgotten that she and River's first big conversation about their feelings had led to her literally fleeing the country?

River and Cass exchanged a glance and Cass twined his fingers with hers, holding her tightly. "Tessa."

"Yeah?"

"I need to tell you something, and I don't want you to freak out."

Nerves knotted in her stomach. She glanced at River, but he had a soft smile on his face that settled her. "Okay," she told Cass.

He squeezed her hand and when he met her eye, there was no uncertainty on his face. "I love you, princess."

They could have been in the middle of nowhere for the way the city sounds disappeared. Tears filled Tessa's eyes while something as close to peace as she'd ever known filled her heart. "I love you so much." The tears spilled, but Cass's lips were there to catch them. River rubbed her back. "How the fuck did I get this lucky?" she whispered.

Every crack in her heart had been worth it to get to the two men before her.

"What does this mean?" she asked, sniffing, still too scared to really hope that the three of them could be a... well, a trio, she supposed.

They all looked at each other, but it was River who spoke first. "Let it be known that, while I think labels are fucking stupid, I'm also a possessive asshole, and I would really like to call you both mine."

"I want that too," Cass said, smiling widely.

"Me too," Tessa agreed. It felt perfectly right; she was already theirs, heart and soul, and she didn't want to hide from the world how thoroughly she loved them. "So we're… a trio?"

"Some people call it a triad," Cass said, toying with the lid of his coffee. "Not that I googled it months ago or anything."

"You know that the press will probably figure this out eventually, right? People probably won't be nice about it," River pointed out.

"Yeah." Tessa sighed. "Fuck them, though. I don't care anymore." She'd lost years to her fear of the press and the public. The best revenge she could think of for how they'd treated her was to be happy, truly happy, with the people with whom she finally felt at home.

She said as much and Cass simply took the coffee cup from her hand, set it aside, and said, "I'm going to need to kiss you now."

And there was no lingering sense of sadness, of longing for something she'd never have when their lips met. There was no fear when they broke apart, Cass's lips moving down her neck, that he might change his mind. River leaned in to steal her lips, and all Tessa could think was that she would have this forever.

River pulled away for only a second before crashing into Cass, both of them still gripping her hands as they kissed. Without breaking contact, River's hands roamed, fingers trailing up Tessa's thighs. Her head fell back and suddenly

Cass's hands were on her too, tugging at the bottom of her t-shirt.

She pulled it over her head, and they both turned to her, licking their lips like they were hunters, and never had she wanted to be prey more. She lost track of whose hands were where, knowing only who she was kissing by their tastes.

Clothes were tossed aside, breakfast long forgotten. River lay back, tugging Tessa forward until she was straddling his hips. Cass guided her, gripping her waist hard and pushing her down slowly on River's cock. She panted, her head falling back against his chest while River cursed, fisting the blankets.

She heard the telltale click of Cass opening the lube and braced herself for the cold against her ass. But it didn't come. Instead, she felt the head of Cass's cock pushing against her pussy, brushing against River. "What do you reckon, princess? Can you take us both?" he whispered in her ear.

Tessa leaned back against him. "Yes," she gasped, and Cass chuckled. He pushed into her slowly and River's face went slack. They could feel each other more like this, she realized, the thought making her clench around them both.

"Fucking hell," Cass growled, the three of them stilling, adjusting.

Tessa had never felt so full, and nothing had ever felt so right. They were the perfect fit, perfect for her in every way. "I swear I was made for you," she moaned, rolling her hips. From this position, she had more control than she usually did.

But, of course, that wouldn't do. River's hands found their way to her hips, Cass's on top of his, and the two of them controlled her movements, fucking her slowly, intensely. There was nothing hurried or desperate about their movements, just deep, deliberate thrusts, striking a match against Tessa.

Tessa had been made of flames for as long as she could remember, and she had finally found the people who burned right alongside her. Pressure built in her blood, as if she might boil over at any minute, but Cass kissed her cheek and said, "Together."

She opened her eyes to see River looking up at the two of them with adoration and she put her hands on top of Cass's as the three of them tumbled over the edge together, blazing so hot she thought they might just set the room alight.

She didn't have to bite her tongue this time, to hold back the *I love you* desperate to slip from her tongue. She let it fall, and the echoes from River and Cass were all she'd ever need.

Panting, the three of them lay back on the bed, Tessa sandwiched between them.

"Do you remember the first time we laid like this?" River asked, brushing his fingers through Tessa's hair.

"When I had a nightmare. You warned me you were cuddlers."

"And you said you thought you could handle it," Cass remembered with a smile.

They'd come a long way from soft smiles in the back of the bookstore; from sneaking out in the early hours of the morning; from jumping out of her skin every time Cass touched her; from running away to find their feelings in frozen valleys and rainy New York streets.

Once upon a time, Tessa Reid would have laughed in the face of anyone who dared suggest she could find this kind of happiness. Falling into a triad, into River and Cass, was never what she had wanted. Even in her wildest daydreams, she never could have dreamed them up.

She'd spent her whole life reading fairytale romances, thinking that such things could never exist. But sometimes, the fairy tales paled in comparison to reality.

And perhaps Tessa liked her own stories most, after all.

TESSA REID SPOTTED KISSING
TWO MEN AFTER CONCERT

For Tessa Reid, it seems stealing the world's biggest rock-star from his wife wasn't enough. The Grammy-winner has taken things to a new level as she was spotted after her Wimbledon show this weekend wrapped around not one, but two men.

It looks like model-turned-photographer Cassian King is more than just the official photographer for Tessa's *Sinking Ships World Tour*. Bestselling romance author River Sage, whose latest release, *Gold Rush*, topped the Sunday Times Bestseller List, completed the trio as the three were photographed in a compromising position leaving the venue after Tessa's sold out show.

The three of them have previously been spotted together in New York, but this is the first confirmation that they might be more than friends. A source close to Tessa has confirmed to Brightside that they have been in a relation-ship for almost two years, indicating that Tessa wasted no time after her breakup with Jay Hutchison, who made headlines recently when he ended his twenty-year partner-ship with Empire Records after a stint in rehab.

Representatives for Tessa have declined to comment, though Tessa herself responded to our reporter's direct message with a comment that has been censored for publishing purposes:

@mikehillreporter: *Hi Tessa, I'm Mike Hill, a reporter with Brightside. We would love to talk to you about the recent pictures of you, Cassian King, and River Sage. Are you available to talk?*

@TessaReid: *Hi Mike, Brightside can go and **** itself. Have a nice night.*

THE END

Thank you for reading *The Rule of Three*!

I hope you enjoyed Cass, River, and Tessa's story. If you did, please consider leaving a review and sharing *The Rule of Three* wherever you like to talk about books!

If you're not quite ready to let the trio go, you can find a spicy bonus scene by visiting www.sophiesnowbooks.com/ bonus-scenes or by scanning this QR code:

The Spicy Stuff

If you should, for whatever reason, wish to revisit *just* the spicy moments... you'll find no judgment here! But you will find the spicy scenes here:

- Chapter Two - River and Tessa
- Chapter Seven - Cass and River
- Chapter Eleven - River and Tessa
- Chapter Fourteen - River and Tessa
- Chapter Twenty - River and Tessa
- Chapter Twenty-one - Cass, River, and Tessa
- Chapter Twenty-four - Cass, River, and Tessa
- Chapter Twenty-eight - Cass, River, and Tessa
- Chapter Thirty-one - Cass, River, and Tessa
- Chapter Thirty-five - Cass, River, and Tessa

Enjoy!

Acknowledgments

The Rule of Three was the fourth book I finished writing, but the first that really made me believe I could do this. I learned so much about writing while working on TROT, but, perhaps more importantly, I learned so much about myself. TROT forced me to face some pretty heavy self reflection. Watching my trio learn that they deserve love and respect taught me when it was time to walk away from situations where I wasn't getting that. For that, I will always be grateful.

I will be the first to admit that I'm an absolute nightmare of a human being when I'm writing something I'm really excited about, and nothing excited me more than Cass, River, and Tessa's story. I rambled and ranted, forgot to eat and sleep, and cried more times than is probably reasonable. I wouldn't have made it to *The End* of this book without the support of so many incredible people!

To my grandma, who never got to see me finish my first book—I will be eternally grateful to you for encouraging my imagination and being a place for me to call home when all I wanted to do was run away. I miss you more than words can say, and I wish you could be here for this.

To my husband, Kyle, who drove me to the forest on the day I first outlined The Rule of Three, sitting below my favorite tree, and then married me under that same tree a year later—thank you for always supporting my writing and not minding when I spend hours talking about story ideas I'll probably never write. I love you.

To my sweet baby boy, Pumpkin—you are an absolute nightmare and yet you're my favorite thing in the whole wide world. Thank you for keeping me company while I write, and walking all over my keyboard even when I asked you not to.

To Terry Holman, my first and favorite writing buddy— I would never have made it to the end of my very first first draft without you cheering me on and I'm so grateful to NaNoWriMo for bringing us together. Thank you.

To my sister, Gemma, who was the first person to read a messy draft of The Rule of Three—thank you for always reading whatever I hand you, even though I've never once taken your feedback on board when you've told me there's too much sex. I'm so glad to have a sister who loves romance as much as I do.

To Claire, my favorite reading/Taylor Swift/whatever hobby we're temporarily obsessed with buddy—thank you for never complaining when I send you twenty-minute voice notes just rambling about my story ideas, and for never judging me (much) whenever I read new kinds of spice and have another, "Oh shit, am I into that?" crisis. (I promise never ever to have that kind of crisis about THAT book series. You know the one I mean.)

To Leigh-Ann, Alaina, and Emily, who have cheered me on through my self-publishing journey—I'm so excited to watch your writing careers grow.

To my beta-readers, Cara Dion, Sam from Keir Editing

and Writing Services, and Jennica Roberts, and my incredible sensitivity reader, Kelsea Reeves—thank you for offering your time and feedback to help me make The Rule of Three the best I could make it.

To Jess, without whom I might never have figured my shit out—though I think we both know I use writing as an escape more than I probably should, everything I've learned from you has shaped my stories in a way I will always be grateful for (though not as much as it's shaped me.)

To Taylor Swift, who has changed me as a person more than anyone else—your music gave me a love of songwriting that has saved my life more times than I can count. Without you, this novel wouldn't exist.

And to you, Reader, for spending your time with Cass, River, and Tessa. For so long, they've been all mine and I'm so incredibly honored to share them with you. If you take anything from their story, I hope it's this: you deserve to be surrounded by people who lift you up; by people who will never tell you you're too much for talking about things you love; you deserve family, but blood doesn't make family—people do; you deserve the chance to fuck up and run away, and know there's always someone to run back to. And you deserve multiple orgasms, if you're into that. We all do.

Love,
Sophie

Sophie Snow lives in Scotland with her husband and cat, Pumpkin (who she loves dearly, even if he does bite.)

She writes spicy romance books with messy, queer characters and too many Taylor Swift references to count. She has been in love with love stories for as long as she can remember, and writing them as songs and novels since she was twelve.

A forest fairy in a past life, Sophie loves spending time in nature, drinking too much coffee, and trying out more hobbies than she can keep up with.

You can find more from Sophie by visiting her website at www.sophiesnowbooks.com, or scanning this QR code:

Bonus Content

- BONUS CHAPTER
- PLAYLIST
- *FINGERTIPS* LYRICS
- TESSA'S BANANA BREAD RECIPE

CORNELIA STREET

BONUS CHAPTER

Cass

Why the fuck was he so nervous?

Sure, he hadn't actually been on a date in almost twenty years, but this was River and Tessa. He'd been out with them more times than he could count. It felt different, though, walking into the restaurant hand in hand with them and tucking themselves away in a booth.

Tessa slid in first, then Cass, shielding her from view in case anyone spotted them and plastered pictures of her online. River sat across from them, then the three of them sat in a moment of silence that bordered on awkward until Tessa snorted and leaned back against the bench seat, laughing.

"I can't believe we said *I love you* before even going on a date. Why does this feel like the most awkward thing we've ever done?"

Her words broke the tension, and Cass felt his shoulders relax as River joined in with her, laughing.

"It's because we're already in love, so a first date feels so trivial," River said. "But first dates are always awkward, right?"

They ordered their food and drinks and Tessa snuggled into Cass's side, leaning her head on his shoulder. He breathed her in—lavender and sugar. "This isn't technically your first date. You were what, sixteen then?"

"Mhmm," he said, winding an arm around her waist and pulling her in close. "We shared a milkshake at our favorite diner and went to see a movie—"

"—which we didn't pay any attention to because the theater was empty and we spent the whole time making out," River finished, his dark eyes twinkling. When was the last time River had spoken about their history so calmly?

"So exactly how you watch movies now," Tessa said.

"Pretty much."

"I think it's fair to say we've refined our techniques over the years, though," River chimed in, running his foot over the inside of Cass's calf. Cass swallowed, the glint in River's eyes making him ravenous for more than dinner. River's lips lifted in a soft smirk, well aware of what he was doing to his best friend—*boyfriend*. That was going to be a tough habit to break.

Boyfriend. Even just thinking the word made Cass want to jump up and down, throwing confetti everywhere.

He jumped when a soft hand landed on his thigh. When he looked up, amusement lit Tessa's face.

"Can you let me out to use the restroom?"

Cass took a deep breath and slid out of the booth, sitting down again once Tessa was out. She leaned across the table, and Cass tried his hardest not to notice how low cut the top of her lilac dress was. Tried and failed.

"Behave," she admonished River, tapping him on the nose. "For now, anyway," she added over her shoulder as she walked toward the restrooms at the back of the restaurant.

Cass leaned his head against the back of the booth and chuckled. "I don't remember being this horny on our first date."

"Then you're misremembering. We were sixteen and desperate to get our hands on each other."

"That hasn't changed," Cass mused. "Everything else has, but not that."

"Everything else changed for the better," River agreed, reaching across the scratch tabletop and taking Cass's hand. Cass ran his thumb over the swirls of ink covering his skin. Unlike River, he'd never bothered with tattoos. He used the excuse that tattoos made models less desirable, but most of the models Cass had worked with over the past few years had some kind of ink. In truth, the thought of committing to something forever had always scared the shit out of him. Until River and Tessa, anyway. These days, he spent a lot of time wondering what their names would look like inked across his skin. Someday, maybe. For now, he was content to have dinner, knowing they were going home together and he could hold them in his arms all night.

He flicked his eyes over River's shoulder toward the restrooms and frowned. Tessa was leaning against the wall with a polite, almost practiced smile, a man standing in front of her talking animatedly. Noticing his frown, River turned to see what Cass had spotted.

"Looks like someone found a fan," he said, turning back around. A knot formed in the center of Cass's chest, the air in the room dropping several degrees. River chuckled, and Cass snapped his eyes to him, even though it felt criminal to look away from Tessa.

"What?"

"Nothing," River lied with a shit-eating grin. "It's just good to know what you look like jealous, is all."

"I'm not jealous," Cass protested, but he couldn't stop himself from looking back at Tessa. The man was leaning in closer. Tessa wasn't displaying any distress, but that didn't stop him from hating the sight of someone so close to her.

"You know you're going to have to get used to this, right? She has fans, and if everything goes well with her label, she's going to become even more popular." Tessa didn't care for the fame, but she wanted the chance to share her music and, now that people were warming up to her, this was only going to happen more frequently.

"They're just fans. They're harmless—you used to be one," River said. Cass was pretty sure he was trying to be reassuring, but he was right: Cass used to be one. He'd spent enough time around fans of Jay, some of whom actually liked Tessa, to know what kind of shit they were thinking about. Which was his only justification for standing up and walking straight across the restaurant, ignoring River's snort.

Tessa looked up when he was a few feet away, raising a

brow. The man, talking and gesturing in front of her, trailed off when Cass leaned on the wall beside her.

"All good, princess?"

"Fine," she replied, rolling her eyes. "Rick here was just telling me how much he and his husband loved *Fingertips*." She turned to Rick and nodded to Cass. "This is my partner, Cass."

Any shred of jealousy left his body as she introduced him as her partner for the first time. Cass committed the moment to memory so he could replay it over and over.

"Hey, I know you!" Rick said excitedly, killing the moment. Cass dragged his eyes from Tessa; something about Rick's face was familiar. "We met at the fan club listening party for Jay's last album a couple of years ago, remember?"

Shit. Unfortunately, Cass did remember. "Right. Good to see you again."

"You were in his *fan club*?" Tessa asked, and Cass was relieved to hear her laugh. Better amused than annoyed, he supposed.

"I wasn't in his fan club," he protested, holding his hands up. "I just went to some of the events they hosted. We all make mistakes."

She lifted a shoulder in a half-hearted shrug. "True. I almost married the assho—shit." Her eyes widened as she remembered Rick's presence.

"Don't worry, my husband and I took your side in the breakup," he said conspiratorially. "His music was mediocre until you and Aaron got involved, if you don't mind me saying."

"I don't," she said, looking equally surprised and pleased. She offered Rick and his husband tickets for her and Aaron's upcoming acoustic show, and Cass stayed quiet, watching with pride as they figured out the logistics.

She'd left everything behind in London with no idea what was waiting for her in New York: this. The start of the career she'd always wanted, and he and River were lucky enough to have front row seats watching her come into herself.

Rick was practically vibrating when he skipped away, giving them one last wave and grin over his shoulder. Tessa threaded her fingers through Cass's and tugged him away from the wall, back toward River. "You going to make a habit of this whole possessive interruption routine? That makes twice, now," she said, sitting down and sliding over. Cass took the spot beside her and frowned. Okay, technically, he'd done it twice. But last time didn't count; he'd been worried about her being around Jay.

He opened his mouth to protest, but closed it when he noticed her fighting a laugh. "I want to say it won't happen again, but I'd probably be lying. You're bringing out a new side of me, princess."

She considered him, sipping her milkshake. "I should hate it, but I think I might find it kind of hot. Is it hot?" She directed the question to River, who shrugged.

"I'm the wrong person to ask. Everything both of you do is hot to me."

They finished their food and got dessert to go; the restaurant was only getting busier and all three of them were ready to retreat to Tessa's apartment. The sidewalk was teeming with people until they turned onto a smaller side street, holding hands on the walk back to Cornelia Street.

As they passed a narrow alley, Tessa paused, tugging them both into the dark street.

"What are you—" Cass tried to ask, but she cut him off by pushing him against a wall and standing on her tiptoes to kiss him. They were partially hidden from the street by a dumpster, but still clearly visible if anyone stopped to look. The dark didn't hide Tessa's sparkling dress, but that didn't matter when she stepped back and dropped to her knees in front of him. He dropped their dessert bag.

"I've decided. The possessive thing is hot," was all she said before undoing his belt, pushing his pants and underwear down and wrapping her hand around his cock.

Cass cursed, slapping his hand against the wall as she drew her fist up and down his length, teasing his piercing with her thumb. "Jesus. We're like ten minutes from home, princess."

"Ten minutes too many," she said, bending her head and taking him between her lips.

Cass's knees threatened to buckle, but he held himself up, biting his cheek to stop himself from moaning aloud. River stepped forward, shielding Tessa from the street. If anyone looked at them, they'd just see River and Cass. It wouldn't be hard to figure out what was going on, but Tessa had at least waited until they were on a quieter street.

River stroked a gentle hand through her hair as she bobbed her head, taking Cass as deep as her throat allowed. She stared up at him, her eyes sparkling gold, practically begging him to possess her. He groaned, reaching for her hair. His hand brushed River's but, instead of pulling away, River twined their fingers together and they worked in tandem, building a rhythm that damn near made Cass lose his mind. Tessa's mouth was fucking heavenly. Every nerve in his body tightened, tingling with heat as she tightened her lips around him.

He was close, struggling to swallow down the gasps and moans desperate to escape his mouth. River stepped closer to him, their fingers still connected, and pressed his lips to Cass's. "Let go. Give it to us," he murmured against him. Cass gasped and River caught it in a kiss, sweeping his tongue over Cass's as he came in Tessa's mouth with a shuddering moan.

River pulled back and tapped Tessa under her chin. "You going to share, princess?"

Cass watched, half-lidded, as Tessa stood, his cum still in her mouth, red lipstick smudges all over her. River grabbed her face, pulling her into a kiss and taking Cass's cum from her mouth. Cum spilled messily over their faces as they shared him. Jesus. He watched them swallow and lick each other's faces, cleaning up the mess they'd made.

If he didn't get his hands on them soon…

They broke apart, and River swiped his thumb over a spot of red lipstick on Tessa's chin. "That was a good dessert appetizer," he said, reaching down to rescue the bag where Cass had dropped it. He paused upon realizing Cass's pants were still around his knees and pulled them up. His fingers brushed Cass's cock as he pulled up the zipper and fastened his belt. Tessa brushed off the skirt of her dress, and Cass grabbed for her, tugging her closer until he could hold both of them, his heart racing.

He pressed a soft kiss to River's forehead, then one to Tessa's cheek. "God, I love you."

"I love you," River murmured with a happy sigh.

"I love you too." Tessa stepped back, beckoning them toward the mouth of the alley. "Now let's get home so we can enjoy our second course."

Playlist

CORNELIA STREET - TAYLOR SWIFT

CALL IT WHAT YOU WANT - TAYLOR SWIFT

THE ARCHER - TAYLOR SWIFT

WHEREVER IS YOUR HEART - BRANDI CARLILE

AMERICA'S SWEETHEART - ELLE KING

STFU & HOLD ME - LIZ HUETT

HO HEY - THE LUMINEERS

FEELS LIKE THIS - MAISIE PETERS

SUGAR - MAREN MORRIS

BECAUSE I LIKED A BOY - SABRINA CARPENTER

FORGIVE MYSELF - GRIFF

fingertips

I was untethered until you put my roots in the ground
Told me I was safe and I found, I believed you, for once in my life
I didn't feel the need to prove myself right

They called me stubborn, aggressive, angry, abrasive, precocious in all the wrong ways
You told me "Fuck all the rest, 'cause we know you best, and we like how you always say
what you wanna say"

And we make it work, what we have, pretend we don't need more than that
Cause there's always something in the way

So please let this be enough for me
Stood at the precipice, right at my fingertips, always just a little bit out of reach
I swear I could scream
It's like the end of the world, and we're on a sinking ship
This can't end well, with you at my fingertips

But still I am willing to wait and see how it goes down
With you I gladly would drown
I would sink to the end of the world and despair
And I'd just happy to see you there

So please let this be enough for me
Stood at the precipice, right at my fingertips, always just a little bit out of reach
I swear I could scream
It's like the end of the world, and we're on a sinking ship
This can't end well, with you at my fingertips

And I followed a long line of minor keys
Wrong notes and make believe
And you broke the bars on the cages and hearts
And we all slipped off the edge at one point in time
Now you're right here and I still can't kiss you tonight

And we make it work
What we have
Pretend we don't need more than that
Just trying to get through the day

So please let this be enough for me
Stood at the precipice, right at my fingertips, always just a little bit out of reach
I swear I could scream
It's like the end of the world, and we're on a sinking ship
This can't end well, with you at my fingertips

TESSA'S STRESS-BAKING BANANA BREAD (VEGAN)

Dry Ingredients

2 cups flour
3 teaspoons baking powder
A pinch of salt

Wet Ingredients

2-3 ripe bananas
1/3 cup neutral oil
1/2 cup sugar
2/3 cup vegan yogurt (ideally vanilla)
(optional, but not really) a handful of chocolate chips

Method

1. Mash the bananas (into fucking oblivion)
2. Combine wet in one bowl, dry in another
3. Mix together
4. Put in lined bread pan
5. Bake at 200°c/400°c for 1 hour
6. Serve to your favorite sweet tooth and let them thank you
   with multiple orgasms

Printed in Great Britain
by Amazon